More praise for Lisa Tucker

"Ingenious."
—*The Boston Globe*

"Tucker turns an engaging premise into a fascinating novel."
—*The Denver Post*

"An achingly tender narrative about grief, love, madness, and crippling family secrets. This intoxicating debut may remind [readers] of . . . Pat Conroy's *The Prince of Tides,* but it's not lost in [its] shadow."
(starred review)

"[An] engagingly intricate debut . . . The characters become as real to the reader as they are to [the narrator] . . . Though brimful of sentiment, *The Song Reader* never spills over into sentimentality."
—*The Philadelphia Inquirer* (Editor's Choice)

"[An] intriguing and heartwarming tale of family and struggle."
—*Times Leader*

"Engaging and bittersweet . . . a wonderful first novel."
—*Booklist*

"Incisive and ultimately startling."
—*Library Journal*

"A brilliant, hard-to-put-down novel, Tucker teaches us a life lesson. . . ."
—*Memphis Flyer*

"[A] sparkling debut . . . delightful and engrossing."
—Margot Livesey, author of *Eva Moves the Furniture*

"Tucker takes the . . . idea of the connection between music and the mind [and] formulates it into something innovative and emotional . . . [and] compelling."
—*Santa Monica Mirror*

…ral levels . . . You['ll] root for Leeann and keep turning pages in hopes that she finds happiness."

—*St. Louis Post Dispatch*

"[A] page-turner which features several compelling plots working in tandem . . . Tucker's writing presents an enlightening notion of family."

—*Bookselling This Week*

"The plot is every bit as fascinating as the premise."

—*Standard-Examiner*

"[A] convincing musing on the importance of memory."

—*Santa Fe Reporter*

"[T]he book is an anthem to the power of music in individual lives. It's Tucker's way of gently encouraging all of us to take a minute and listen to the music of our lives."

—*Ventura County Star*

"A novel of remarkable wisdom and tenderness . . . Every splendid page inspires courage."

—Kevin McIlvoy, author of *Hyssop*

"It's the relationship between the two sisters that makes this a page-turner."

—*The News-Times*

"[M]y pick for best book so far in 2003. [A] spectacular novel . . . surprising, funny, sad, easy to get into, well-plotted, original, and rich in its characters."

—*Culture Dose*

"[A] beautiful and bittersweet debut . . . funny and touching, heartbreaking and wise."

—*Romantic Times,* top pick

shout
down
the
moon

a novel

lisa tucker

New York London Toronto Sydney

An *Original* Publication of POCKET BOOKS

 A Downtown Press Book published by
POCKET BOOKS, a division of Simon & Schuster, Inc.
1230 Avenue of the Americas, New York, NY 10020

ISBN: 0-7434-6446-X

First Downtown Press trade paperback edition April 2004

10 9 8 7 6 5 4 3 2 1

DOWNTOWN PRESS and colophon
are trademarks of Simon & Schuster, Inc.

Book design by Jaime Putorti

Manufactured in the United States of America

For information regarding special discounts for bulk purchases,
please contact Simon & Schuster Special Sales at 1-800-456-6798
or business@simonandschuster.com.

This book is for Scott and Miles.
A Love Supreme by way of the A Train,
My two beautiful guys,
You really were waiting in tomorrow.

one

I know he's coming. His sentence was seven years, but after less than three, he's made parole. Mama sends me the news on one of her yellow stickies: FYI, with the date he's being released— June 3, 1991—circled several times in thick black pen.

On the phone I remind her of the letter I sent him after Willie was born, explaining I wouldn't be writing anymore, it was over between us. I talk as though I believe the letter convinced him, and change the subject while she's still feeling relieved.

For weeks I expect him to show up at the club. Sometimes I peer out into the blackness of the audience, wondering if his eyes are on me, if he is listening. Once, I'm sure I hear him laughing right before the first set and I screw up one of the verses of our big opening number: a medley of oldies we call "Yesterday Once More." Our keyboard player, Jonathan, frowns and later, grumbles to the other guys that I'm an airhead. He doesn't like me, none of them really do. Before I came along a year ago, they were the Jonathan Brewer Quartet, no chick singer, strictly jazz. They didn't make any money as Fred Larsen, our manager, likes to point out. Fred likes money and he likes me just fine.

Fred renamed the band, making me the primary attraction, the name on the marquee and the face in the advertisements. At the time I felt flattered; now I realize this means it will be easy for Rick to find me. And he does, but he doesn't come to the club. We're doing a two-week stint in Paducah, Kentucky; it's the middle of the afternoon on a Saturday in July so hot the blacktop feels soft under my sandals. I've been down the road at the drugstore, picking up chewable vitamins for Willie, and as I round the corner, I feel my breath catch as I see him, slumping in a lawn chair outside of my motel room with his head against the green concrete wall. Asleep.

He looks paler, a little thinner, but otherwise the same. His hair is still long with a few curls; he still has a gold earring in his left ear, and he still has the stubble on his chin that's become the style for guys now but he's had ever since I've known him. Even the clothes he's wearing are familiar: black cap pushed back a little, tight, faded blue jeans, white T-shirt advertising Lewisville Motor Sports, a place he used to work years ago, before he met me. In a way, I'm relieved—I imagined terrible things happening to him in prison, things that would mark him, change him—but I'm also more nervous.

Asleep, he looks younger, almost innocent. And so much like Willie, that's what hits me the hardest.

He hasn't heard me coming, I could still back away, but I don't. Willie is with my friend Irene for the next few hours and this is as good a time as any. I say his name and he wakes up so suddenly that he bangs his head. And then he rubs his eyes and looks at me.

Instinctively, I cross my arms. When he last saw me, I was so skinny I could hide an ounce of weed in the waist of my junior size five jeans. Having Willie made me fill out every-where. Now I wear a misses size eight.

He stares at me for a minute, and then he's standing and mumbling, "Patty, Jesus," as he reaches for me so quickly that I drop my package.

His skin is hot and sweaty but I don't pull away. He's trem-bling and his voice is soft, telling me he's missed me so much, please don't make a scene, he's violating parole to be here, out of state. But he had to see me, just for a little while. He can't stay long; he has to see his parole officer back in Kansas City first thing Monday morning.

When I finally step back, I'm shaking too because it has occurred to me that I smell like Willie. And because I know we're standing two feet from the door to my room, and on the other side of the door is the evidence: diapers, Willie's clothes, stuffed animals, Ninja turtles, and Matchbox cars.

The thought that Irene and Willie may come back early

makes me decide what to do. I pick up my drugstore bag and shove it in my purse. "Let's go to the coffee shop across the street," I say, already moving in that direction.

I look back and see him still standing by the door. I know he wants to go to my room so we can be alone. "Patty," he mutters, but when I turn back around and begin walking, I hear him following me.

At the restaurant we order too much food to distract ourselves from the awkwardness. He sips his coffee and says he doesn't want to talk about prison; then he asks me questions about my job.

I tell him we're a cover band, playing pop and rock songs, old and new. I tell him about Jonathan's original pieces, how beautiful they are, no words, just the richest melodies and a deep, complicated interplay between the instruments, and how if the crowd is small, the group gets to play some of those songs in the last set.

I'm still describing one of the songs when Rick interrupts. "I've never heard you talk about music like this before."

He's leaning back, looking straight at me. I tell him I've been with the band for almost a year; I've picked up a lot of the language. I don't say that nearly everything I've learned I've had to overhear, since none of the guys will talk to me about music. Jonathan resents me even being on stage when he plays the instrumentals, even though he knows it's not my doing. It's Fred's biggest rule: "The Patty Taylor Band has Patty Taylor on all night." When I'm not singing, he wants me to shake a tambourine and smile, or dance a little in the tight gowns he has me wear. Once Jonathan complained that having a chick gyrating distracted the audience from his art, and Fred snapped, "You better get over your problem with her if you don't want to find your ass on the street."

"I can't wait to hear you," Rick says, tapping his fingers. "I always knew you'd be a star."

I don't bother telling him that the most I ever make—at the top clubs, the ones Fred has to sweat to get us in—is four hundred dollars a week. I'm hardly a star.

I ask him if he has a job yet and he shrugs. "I've only been out a few weeks." He smiles. "I've been busy . . . busy thinking about you."

Both of us are finished picking at our food when he lowers his voice and tells me he still has it. One of his friends kept it for him while he was in jail. And he can give me some. He can give me as much as I need.

I know he's talking about all the money he had: thousands of dollars he kept in a blue duffel bag in the bedroom closet, next to the other bag, the one that said Reebok, which he used to carry his guns. I'm surprised; I figured the cops confiscated all the cash when they tore our apartment to pieces the morning after he was arrested. I stare at the wall behind him and think about what that money could mean for Willie. But then I think what Rick might mean for Willie, and I don't respond.

"Come on," he says, and smiles a half smile. "What do I have to do? Stick the money in your hand?"

He's trying to remind me of the day we met. I look away, pretend to be interested in the old couple who've just sat down at the next table—but of course I'm thinking about that day now too.

It was late fall, my freshman year. Mama had gone on another of her drinking binges, and I was sitting on the bleachers of the deserted baseball field, trying to decide where to go. I didn't have any real friends; I couldn't bring anyone to my house, knowing how Mama was. I was tired of going to the Baptist church shelter, tired of having to tell them the same lie, that I'd run away, and then be forced to listen to the counselor telling me how worried my family had to be.

By the time Rick came along it was nearly dark. I might have been crying a little. I prided myself on my ability not to cry when Mama threw me out, but this time was different. This time she'd pushed me out the door before I could grab my Walkman. I had nothing to listen to but the sound of my own lonely breath.

He parked his car by first base and walked over and stood in front of me.

"I've driven by here three times tonight," he said. "You haven't moved. Are you all right?"

I mumbled, "Yeah," and tried not to look at him. I knew who he was, even though I didn't know his name. He and his friends had fancy cars and bad reputations; of course they stuck out in a town as small as Lewisville, Missouri. One of the girls at my school said they were a gang of big-time drug dealers, but I figured she was making it up. This wasn't New York or L.A. Our local paper covered Cub Scout food drives and car washes, not gangs and drug busts.

I heard him exhale. "You need a place to stay tonight." When I didn't answer, he opened his wallet and started pulling out twenties. "Go to Red Roof Inn. Debbie works there. Tell her Rick sent you."

I shook my head, but he stuck the money in my palm and told me to do it. Then he said, more quietly, "I'm not going to hurt you."

He left before I could give the money back, and I didn't see him until the next morning, after I woke up in the beautiful Red Roof. I was never sure the hotel was a good idea, but I got cold. It was a few blocks away. I wanted the clean sheets and the TV.

He was waiting in the lobby. When he asked if I wanted some breakfast, I was floored. I hadn't had anybody offer me breakfast since I was seven years old.

Later, Rick admitted it was partly charity but not just that. He thought my hair was absolutely gorgeous. From the road, when he was driving by, he could see it was blond and very long, way past my waist. And when he saw the rest of me, he thought I was like a girl in a dream he had, a girl he'd always been looking for. To me, he was like the big brother and uncle and boyfriend I'd never had, all rolled into one. Meeting him, I'd finally found my luck.

I wait for the waitress to pour more coffee and take our plates before I change the subject, away from money and our past, back to the band. Rick listens to me talk about the places our band has been. I tell him we're based in Kansas City, but we're on the road most of the time, playing hotels and little clubs. I'm in the middle of a story about a wedding we played in Fayetteville, Arkansas, when he tells me he has to know.

I give him a startled glance.

"What did you name him?" He clears his throat. "Or is it her?"

I feel like I've just been punched. I was so careful not to be in Lewisville the whole time I was pregnant. I lived in a home for pregnant girls down in Kansas City. I never saw anyone who knew us, or so I thought.

I force a confused look, insist I have no idea what he's talking about.

"Just tell me the baby's name, Patty," he says, his voice urgent, his hands flat on the table. "Please."

"He's not a baby. He's almost two and a half." I pause before whispering, "William."

"William Malone," he says, but I correct him. Willie has my last name. Mine.

"Right," he says. Then softly, amazed, "I have a son . . . Does he know about me?"

I feel tears in my throat as all at once I'm remembering when Willie was born. I was alone in the county hospital. My counselor from the home didn't show up and there was no one else to call; Mama hadn't even spoken to me since I'd thrown away the pamphlets from the clinic and refused to get an abortion. When the pain got bad, I started screaming for him. Rick, help me. Rick, it hurts. Rick, I need you, please come. The nurse gave me a shot of Demerol and I got confused and thought he was on his way. I asked her, "Is he here yet?" over and over. When the doctor came in, he looked at me as though I was pathetic, slightly nuts. I'd already told them the father was dead; I didn't want to say he was in prison.

Remembering this is too hard; I can't sit in this restaurant anymore. I tell him good-bye, and then I'm running between the booths and outside, across the street, back to the place Willie and I call home for now.

"Patty," he says, touching my elbow. He has caught up with me outside of my room door, and he's so close I can feel his breath on my hair.

"Go away," I stammer.

"You don't want that." He turns me around to face him; his hands are on my shoulders. "You don't want that," he says again, looking in my eyes as though he's willing it to be true.

I don't pull away when he gathers me in his arms and whispers, "I love you." I know he means it. For so many years, his love was the one thing I could count on, the one thing I knew would never change. And he let me get closer to him than anybody ever had; he let me see him be weak. Only I knew that he sobbed for fifteen minutes when his best friend got his throat cut in a bar fight. Only I knew that he fell on his knees and screamed to God for help when I was standing on the rail of the Lewisville River Bridge, about to jump, because I couldn't live without him and I couldn't stand our life.

After a while a businessman drives up in a dusty Plymouth. He's fiddling with his bags, trying not to stare at us. Rick lowers his voice and says, "Let's go in your room. Just for a few minutes," and I put in the key as an answer. But before I open the door, I look at him, remind him this is just for a few minutes, and he nods.

The hotel room is small and cramped with ugly, square furniture, but the mess of Willie's toys and clothes make it seem softer, more colorful. His little blanket is lying in a heap on the floor between the bed and the dresser. Rick picks it up, quickly passes it over his face, inhales, before setting it on the dresser. Mama bought the blanket and Willie's favorite stuffed animal, the green beagle with the blue-and-white cap he sleeps with while I'm at work—even though she didn't want me to have Willie. She was holding the presents when she showed up at the hospital when Willie was two days old. She'd joined AA; she said she was there to take us home.

"He's beautiful," Rick says, as he fingers a picture of Willie and me that sits by the bolted-down television. "He looks like you."

I know that isn't true but I don't say it. I'm sitting on the edge of the bed, watching him. He's moving towards me and I know he will touch me if I don't stop him.

Mama used to say that Rick and I were nothing but a physical attraction—this was whenever she was sober enough to remember who he was. She was wrong, but the physical attraction was undeniable. Even after three years of living together, we still fell on each other pretty much every time we were alone.

He's kneeling in front of me; his hands are resting on my hair. He's mumbling, "You look so good," and he's leaning forward, but I'm telling myself I'll stop him before it goes much further. But I don't stop him as he puts his lips on my neck and down to my shoulders and then down lower, giving soft kisses through my shirt to my breasts. After a while his hands are moving on my thighs; he whispers, "This is my dream," and I realize I'm losing the will to stop him. Then I hear Willie's laughter and I go rigid. He and Irene are at the door.

"Shit," I mutter, and jump up. My hands are straightening out my shirt and shorts; Rick is standing too.

"Well, hey, it took you long enough," Irene says, when I throw open the door. "It sure is gloomy in here," she adds, walking to the blinds and pulling them open with a screech. She spins around and sees him but he doesn't look at her. He's too busy watching Willie, who has run over and is hanging on my leg.

I pick him up and he feels heavy, sleepy. I ask Irene if he had a nap and she shakes her head. "I drove him all over town, but he never conked."

"Mama," he says, and buries his face in my shoulder as he points his little finger at Rick. They have the same eyes, eyes so big and brown and soft they seem to absorb you when you look at them.

After a minute, I snap on the TV and set him in front of it. When I introduce Rick to Irene, she walks over and sticks out her hand. "So you're Willie's father," she blurts out, and I want to kick her, but Willie doesn't notice.

Rick nods and shakes her hand but he doesn't say anything. He stands with his arms crossed while Irene smiles and talks and tries to figure him out.

11

"Well, I guess I better go wake up Harry," Irene finally says. Harry is her boyfriend, our bass player. It's three o'clock in the afternoon; as usual, the guys in the band stayed up all night jamming. Irene calls herself a day person and she likes me because I am too—now that I have Willie.

When we get to the door, I thank her for taking care of Willie, but she grabs my arm and pulls me outside. "Wow, Patty," she says. "He's really something."

While she's telling me how cute Rick is, I'm looking through the door, trying to see what he's doing with Willie. I don't feel annoyed with Irene though. She's a good friend; six nights a week, she sits in my room and watches Willie while the band plays. She tells me she doesn't want to come to the club anyway, she's sick of music. She also says she's tired of being on the road with Harry, that she's going back to Kansas City soon and get herself a nice place, settle down, find a real job rather than making jewelry for peanuts like she does now. I listen but I know she isn't serious. Irene adores Harry. She says he's the only man who can make her laugh even when she's furious.

"I guess this is a lot for you to deal with, honey." She's squinting now, worried. She knows Rick was in jail but she doesn't know why. At some point, she thinks to ask if I need her to send Harry over to throw him out. Harry is six-three and weighs at least 250 pounds. Irene calls him her gangster boy because he's black and he's from New York.

"You know Harry won't really hit him," she whispers, "but he can look the part."

I tell her no, I don't need that, and she pats my arm. She says to give a yell if I need anything at all.

Before she walks across the parking lot, she turns back and gives me another worried look. I shrug like this is no big deal. I can handle it. I can handle anything.

When I get back into the room, Willie is lying flat on his back, sound asleep. The TV is off and the air conditioner has shut down; it's so quiet I can hear Willie breathing. Rick is sitting next to him, lightly stroking Willie's fine blond hair. Blond hair is the only thing Willie got from me, and Mama says it's bound to darken before he's much older. Willie's eyebrows are dark already, like Rick's.

"He's so little," Rick whispers, and smiles. "It's hard to believe he's two."

I tell Rick his birthday was back in February, but I don't talk about what it was like that day: miserable and raining and nothing like what I'd hoped for him. We had to make five hundred miles by six o'clock in order to have time to set up for the gig; Willie had to eat his birthday cake in the van. I told Willie we'd go to McDonald's for dinner as soon as we got into town but then there wasn't a McDonald's, at least not on the main drag. Harry tried to cheer him up, told him Burger King was better.

"This is no ordinary hamburger shack, Willie," Harry said. "It's a palace. We're in the presence of the Supreme Lord. The Burger Duke? No. The Burger Prince? No. The Burger Master himself. The Burger Emperor. The most holy, Burger King."

Willie looked confused but he laughed because Harry was grinning and wearing a cardboard Burger King crown. When he opened his toy though, he started crying again. It wasn't a Hot Wheels like they had at McDonald's, it wasn't even a toy to his way of thinking, it was just a coloring book.

Poor guy, I thought, as I pulled him on my lap. The only things he wanted for his birthday were a Happy Meal from McDonald's and a tricycle. He got the tricycle, but he hadn't been able to ride it yet; it was packed in the back of the van between Dennis's drums.

Later that night after the gig, I sat in our hotel room, drinking a beer, making a list of my accomplishments on the back of a napkin. I was desperate to convince myself that I was doing all right. That I was making a life for Willie and me, even if it wasn't perfect. Even if it wasn't close to perfect.

One: I hadn't touched any drugs, not even weed, since the day I found out I was pregnant. Two: I'd worked hard and completed my GED before Willie was born, so he'd never have to feel like his mother wasn't good enough. Three: I'd been there for him day in, day out for two years. Four: I'd supported the two of us.

I wrote down the number five but I was stuck; no matter how hard I tried, I couldn't think of anything else. I was near tears; I'd planned on a list of at least ten accomplishments. As I drank another beer, I stared at number four—supporting the two of us—wondering if it was the reason I was drawing a blank, if it was messing up my list the same way it had messed up Willie's birthday.

Rick is still running his fingers through Willie's hair. "You like all this traveling?" he says, looking around the room and then at me. "You always said you wanted to stay in one place. A home."

I did say that, Rick is right. I didn't even want to leave our first apartment, run-down though it was. He made me move to the new complex outside of Lewisville, so we could have a dishwasher and air-conditioning. I cried when his friends came to load up the furniture.

Of course he remembers that, but now I tell him the traveling isn't that bad. Then I shrug. "I don't have a choice."

It feels true. No question, it was worse the first year of Willie's life. Even though Mama had stayed sober and turned into a surprisingly good granny, it was still hard. I worked nights as a dishwasher while Mama stayed with Willie. My feet ached all the time, my breasts leaked milk, and my take-home pay wasn't even a hundred and twenty a week. But then I saw Fred's ad in the *Kansas City Star,* and I got up my nerve and went to the audition. By the time I told him about Willie, we'd been rehearsing for two months and were ready to hit the road. He frowned and shook his head but he didn't complain. I decided not to tell him that I wouldn't turn twenty-one for another month. According to the press release he sends out to the clubs, I've been singing professionally for five years, I studied vocals at the University of Missouri, and I won a singing contest in Kansas City while I was still a teenager.

Only the last thing is true. I did win that contest. Rick drove me to the auditorium and he sat in the front row. I'd

15

been nervous all morning, but as soon as the piano started, I forgot everything but the music they'd given me to sing. It was a wonderful Gershwin song, "I Loves You Porgy"; I just wanted to do it justice, get it right. And I did get it right, I knew that when I hit the last note perfectly and the applause started, loud and furious, like a thunderstorm waking me from a dream. I was smiling, bowing. I felt alive.

All the contestants were supposed to wait in the hall while the committee decided the winner. I was standing down a little bit from everybody else when Rick came up. He hugged me and said how proud he was, but then he took my hand and pulled me around the corner and down another hall.

"I have to go back." There was no one around but still I whispered. "Rick—"

"Watching you . . . I can't wait." He pushed my hand on the crotch of his jeans. "Feel that?"

Before I could object, he pulled me inside a janitor's closet and shut the door. I was still sweating but I shivered when I felt the cold steel bucket with the dirty mop against my leg.

I could hear the loud laughter of one of the other contestants, an older girl named Elizabeth. They all seemed to know each other—most of them were friends, taking music classes at the college. When one of the guys had asked where I studied, I told him the name of my old high school. Then he asked me the name of the music teacher, and I found myself stammering like an idiot. I'd dropped out in the middle of freshman year, before I could try out for chorus.

"I don't belong here anyway," I said softly, more to myself than to Rick. He was kissing my neck. His response was a groan.

By the time I heard them announce my name over the loudspeaker, I'd forgotten that I cared. Rick heard it too and put his hand over my mouth. "Keep it down," he said, and laughed. "What will they think if they hear their little contest winner doing this?"

Afterwards, Rick went with me to pick up the certificate and the five hundred dollars I won. I was leaning against him when one of the judges asked what I was going to do with the money, if I would use it to further my singing career.

"She'll probably buy crap for the apartment," Rick said. He was smiling. "That's what she does with the money I give her."

I didn't say anything. I felt ridiculous, but it was true. Whenever I got any money, I ended up spending it on our place. It seemed like there was always something else we needed: spaghetti strainer, soap dish, laundry basket, welcome mat. Always one more thing and then our place would be a regular home.

It was less than a week after the concert when Rick and his friends were arrested during a heroin deal. And then, at the end of the month, my period didn't come. For a long time, I winced whenever I thought about the possibility that Willie had been conceived in a janitor's closet. Later I felt like maybe that Gershwin tune had something to do with it. Like one of my eggs came down, ready and happy, because it heard that gorgeous music.

"I can't believe he's real," Rick is saying, touching Willie's pink, dimpled knee. "Our kid."

Rick leans down and lightly kisses his forehead. After a minute, he sits up straighter, reaches for my hand, brings it to his lips. Whispers that he loves me. That he has to have me with him again. Me and Willie too.

I stand up and motion for him to follow me into the bathroom. When I shut the door behind us, I tell him it's time to leave now. He starts to reach for me but I back up against the wall. As he comes closer, I tell him I can't be with him anymore. I've changed. And when he grabs me anyway, pressing his body against mine, licking my ear, I pull away and tell him a lie. I say there's somebody else now, I'm sorry. Then I whisper that if he doesn't leave, I'll have to call the cops.

He drops his arms; the anger passes across his face so quickly that most people wouldn't see it. Then he slumps down on the toilet and puts his face in his hands. He stays there for a while, and I'm trying not to look at him, trying not to notice the slight movement of his shoulders that means he's crying.

Finally, he stands up and leaves without saying a word. I lock the door and collapse in the chair by the window, barely able to breathe. It isn't until later that I realize he took it with him. The picture of me and Willie.

two

Rick & Patty Forever. When he spray painted that on an abandoned barn, he was twenty-three; I had just turned sixteen. He wanted it to be a surprise; he wouldn't tell me where we were going as he drove up Highway 29, towards St. Joseph, all he said was to keep my eyes open. It would have been hard to miss. The letters were ten feet tall, two feet wide, black on dusty white, and the barn was on top of a hill, right next to a billboard advertising a Howard Johnson's.

He parked his car on the shoulder of the highway and we took off running straight up the hill, him pulling me to go faster, faster, like he thought if we got enough speed, we would leave the earth, go right to the clouds. He was panting and out of breath as he grabbed me in his arms in the doorway of the musty barn. "If I could, I'd write it everywhere. On the sky, on the leaves, on the side of Mount Everest."

I've heard that every couple believes they're the first to discover love. Irene says it's part of the magic, the feeling that you two have something no other lovers have ever experienced. I know what she means, but I don't think it applies to Rick and me. Rick didn't think we discovered love. Words like discovered and thinking had nothing to do with it. The two of us were like waves slapping against a beach or death from a gunshot wound to the head: inevitable, unchangeable, just so. "We have to be together," he would insist if we fought, and especially if I hinted at leaving him. "We need each other like normal people need air."

No matter how angry I was, I always found this strangely comforting. This was what a family was supposed to be, I thought. People you were stuck with. People who couldn't get rid of you because you left a bowl in the sink or forgot to do the ironing or "gave an ugly look" or "dressed like a stupid little slut."

Mama had thrown me out for the last time back in March. Rick wanted me to move in with him and there was no reason not to. I was over at his place all the time anyway. And she didn't really care. I was a fool to keep calling her and telling her I was fine.

We'd been living together for eight months when we got "married" that day in the barn. We'd been drinking all morning; when he first told me he'd decided it was time for us to exchange vows, I laughed and said, "To have and to hold, for richer, for poorer, something, something, the end."

"No. Do it right."

"Okay," I said, still giggling. "From the beginning. I, Patty, do take you, Rick, to be my not-really-wedded husband."

He grabbed my wrist. "You think this is a joke?" We were sitting on the ground; he brought his face close to mine. "You think I'm kidding?"

"No. I didn't mean—"

"Because to me, there is nothing funny here. This is deadly serious. You understand?"

I sat up straighter and told him yes, I understood. After he let go of my wrist, I rubbed it against my jeans, but casually, as though I had an itch. It felt raw and sore, bruised already, but I didn't want him to know. Whenever Rick hurt me, even if it was only an accident, he insisted on hurting himself too, only worse. Often he would punch his chest and thighs, over and over, hard enough to leave marks the next day, as I pulled on his arms and pleaded with him to quit. Finally he would, but only when we were both shaking and sniffing, licking salty tears from our lips, ready to collapse into each other and take comfort for what had just happened to us.

It seems strange now that it always felt like something that happened to us—like a car accident or a tornado or any other act of fate—rather than something he caused.

Rick meant it when he said he was serious. He wanted the traditional vows from start to finish. The only change he made was ending with "forever" rather than "till death do us part."

21

"Death will never come between us," he said, tracing the outline of my face with his fingertips. "If one of us dies, the other will too."

He knew how important this was to me. I'd told him many times how worried I was that he would die and leave me alone, the same way Daddy did.

After we said everything, he reached into his jeans pocket and pulled out a beautiful diamond ring. I was choking back tears as he slipped it on my finger because I finally understood that he'd planned all this: the ring, the wedding in the barn with the last word of the vow, the most important word to us both, spray-painted on the outside wall.

"I'll never stop loving you," I whispered. "Forever."

"Forever," he repeated, as he lifted my hair and eased me backwards to the floor. It was filthy and uncomfortable but I didn't complain. His hands were pulling off my clothes, beginning to explore my body, which he knew so well. Better than I did.

After a while he closed his eyes, but I didn't. I wanted to see him; I wanted to burn this into my memory. It wasn't a real wedding; still, I thought it was the high point of my life, that I would never be happier.

Highway 29 is the quickest way to Omaha, where we're booked for the next three weeks. Today we'll have to drive past that barn and I'm nervous, though I know it's silly. It's been weeks since I saw Rick in Kentucky, and he certainly won't be at the barn. Even the graffiti is probably painted over, or at least faded in the weather and wind.

The club is a prime location, Fred says. Much better than the little supper clubs we've been doing for the last few months. It's a new room for Fred, and he picked us over all his other bands because he has so much faith we won't screw up. That's what he told me; he told Jonathan we better not screw up if we planned to keep eating.

We left Quincy, Illinois, this morning. We've been on the road for hours, but when I ask Jonathan if we can pull in at the next exit, he frowns. It's only three o'clock, not time for dinner, but Willie is hot and cranky; I know he won't nap unless he eats something. He only took two bites of the grilled cheese sandwich I ordered him for lunch. He wrinkled up his nose and said, "Yuck," and then he got distracted by Irene and Harry, who were laughing and pointing at their food as if they agreed.

Irene and Harry don't have to deal with Willie's whining if he's hungry. They always ride by themselves in Irene's Honda. Dennis and Carl ride in Carl's Camaro, and Jonathan leads in the van. He lets Willie and me ride with him because he doesn't have a choice; I don't have a car. It's the one thing in the world I want, bad. I almost had enough cash saved for a down payment, but then Willie got an ear infection last spring that took three doctor's visits and three different expensive antibiotics to kick.

Jonathan rarely speaks to me, but sometimes he'll talk to Willie, mostly grunting acknowledgments of Willie's attempts to babble to him. It's easy for him to ignore us. We sit in the back of the van; the equipment is crammed behind us so tight

I can feel the PA system pushing on the seat whenever
Jonathan hits the brakes. He usually has the radio on: classical,
or jazz whenever he can tune it in. A talk show if all else fails.
Anything but the pop stations.

Jonathan hates even the word popular. Popular means sellout, and of course he sees me that way too, since I only sing
pop songs. I want to tell him you can't sell out if you've never
been in, but I doubt he'd understand. He's twenty-seven, but
he's already been playing professionally for ten years. He con-
siders himself a real musician, an artist. He thinks his compo-
sitions deserve to be recorded by a big-name jazz label and
played all over the country.

His music is beautiful. Even Fred recognizes how talented Jonathan is. He's admitted that he became the quartet's manager two years ago because he didn't have a choice;
Jonathan blew him away at the audition, and he couldn't say
no. And he tried hard for them for a while: he got them into
clubs, even got them a spot at a big-name jazz festival in
Kansas City. But there was never enough money and finally
Fred gave them his standard speech: I'm not in this for charity, I have a house to pay for, a family to feed, and then the
punch line—he'd hired a singer. Everybody grumbled a little but Fred said he was sure they were mainly relieved. They
were damn near starving; they'd taken to sleeping in their
cars, in the van; Harry had to borrow from Fred once to
replace a string on his bass. At least they would have food
now, a place to stay, cash in their pockets. Later, Fred would
get the quartet into a top-notch recording studio, he

promised, and send out demo tapes to his many connections out west.

Whether or not Fred really has big-time West Coast connections, he does know everybody who is anybody in music around here. If you get on Fred's bad side, so the rumor goes, you'll have to move a thousand miles to work. Carl and Dennis didn't want to move. Harry and Irene didn't either. They figured a gig was a gig. They were happy with the idea of a demo; they were ready for some success.

Only Jonathan objected. He quit, after saying he'd rather flip burgers than do cover tunes. Somehow Carl and Harry talked him into coming to the first rehearsal, but for the next week, there was a lot of whispering, secret meetings, frantic calls to Fred. Often I ended up sitting on my stool for an hour or more, waiting for them to come back or for Fred to tell me I could go home, the rehearsal was canceled. I never asked any questions; I was afraid of causing trouble and having to go back to the restaurant and beg for my dishwashing gig.

It took me a while to accept that my big opportunity was someone else's big disappointment. In Jonathan's mouth, my name was like a curse word—Patty Taylor, the chick singer who came along and ruined everything. Fred said I had a lot of guts because I didn't break down with all this hostility, but he was wrong; I did break down. Sure, I held it together at work and even at home. Willie still had to be cared for, and Mama was griping at me constantly about what this job would mean, taking a baby on the road; I didn't want to give her anything else to complain about. But every day, driving back from rehearsal in Mama's Ford, I would turn up the radio and scream and cry and carry on like I was a candidate for the nuthouse. I was so damn lonely. I felt like all of me ached for someone to touch me, love me. Or like me, at least. Smile when I walked in. Say a friendly hello. Anything.

If I had a car now, I couldn't scream because of Willie, but I could cry a little if I felt like it. And maybe I wouldn't feel like it, maybe I'd be fine if I could accomplish this one simple thing—stopping to get my son food—without having to deal with Jonathan's disapproval.

"It won't take long," I say, looking at the back of his head. He has black hair, already flecked with gray. It's thick, long, and always messy. Irene says he's trying to look like Beethoven— not the composer, the dog.

When he doesn't respond or move, I say, "All right, I'll get something to go."

"I wanna go in," Willie stammers.

"That's fine," Jonathan says, glancing in the rearview mirror. He shrugs as if to say, there's no rush, what's the big deal?

Now I'm glaring at the back of his head. I'm absolutely positive he frowned, but I'm just as positive he'll never admit it. He doesn't want anyone to think he's uptight about getting to Omaha in time to set up and do a sound check tonight, in case there's any problem. He's a perfectionist about work, but he has to act cool. Musicians are always cool; it's an unwritten but absolute law.

"Let's go, buddy," I say, as I unhook the strap on Willie's car seat. Jonathan has pulled into the first truck stop off the exit. As usual, he doesn't think to come around and open the sliding door of the van, even though it's awkward and difficult to push from the inside.

He still hasn't moved from his seat, and I ask him if he's going in.

"I'll wait for them," he says, meaning Carl and Dennis. They were right behind us on the highway, but they haven't pulled up yet. Irene and Harry have; I look over at the Honda and notice Harry lying back in the passenger seat, sound asleep. Irene smiles and waves, but she doesn't open the door. She never risks waking Harry; she wants him to sleep as much as possible so he'll be rested for the gigs.

About ten minutes later, Willie and I are sitting at a booth, waiting for our food. He's in a booster seat and talking a mile a minute. His feet are thumping against the bottom of the table; already he's managed to dump all the silverware onto the floor.

Jonathan slumps down facing us, and shrugs when I ask what happened to Dennis and Carl. "I guess they decided to go on," he says, opening the slick plastic menu. "Carl knows Omaha. They'll find us eventually."

For some reason, Willie decides to stop talking now. The silence between Jonathan and me feels awkward, though it's only a continuation of the last five hours in the van.

Jonathan crosses his arms and looks out the window. I open my purse and pull out the Chloraseptic. My throat is bothering me a little and I want it to be okay before we open tomorrow night.

After he orders, Jonathan opens his book and starts read-

27

ing. He never goes anywhere without a book. I've heard him telling the other guys they have to read such and such; it's so deep, cool, fascinating.

I have a book to read myself, but I don't want Jonathan to know about it; he might laugh at me. It's called *Jazz for Beginners*, and I've been carrying it around for the last few months. It helps me figure out what he and the guys are talking about.

Sometimes it shocks me how little I know—and not just about music. Jonathan can name a bird that flies by, he can compare one tree to another, he can talk about history and religion and politics and the news. A few weeks ago, I overheard him say that he's teaching himself Spanish, just for the heck of it. He carries around books on the solar system, on math, on sculptors and painters. Pretty much every minute that he's not playing or composing, he's learning something.

Of course Jonathan would never think of talking to me about the book he's reading. I don't feel bad until the waitress comes with our food and smiles, asks if I need another soda, if I need anything. Her eyes are full of pity, and I realize she thinks Jonathan is my husband, Willie's father, and that he's clearly ignoring both of us. Before I say no thanks, we're fine, I make a point of smiling and opening my diaper bag, grabbing a magazine. I don't want her to think I'm pathetic. I'm not pathetic.

I have no interest in the magazine though. Also, it seems rude to read while I'm eating with Willie, even though he isn't talking; he's watching Jonathan and looking around at the other people in the truck stop. And eating his hamburger, thank God. He hasn't even objected to the mayonnaise slathered all over the bun, though he usually calls it "ick" and won't take a bite until I scrape it off.

I'm halfway through my salad, still thumbing through the magazine, when I realize Jonathan has put down his book and is looking at me. Then he says, "Thinking about cutting your hair?"

The question comes as such a surprise, I give Jonathan a sideways glance, wondering what he's up to. But he nods at the magazine, open to the hairstyle page, and the look on his face is neutral, like anybody making polite conversation. Maybe even a little interested.

"I might," I say slowly.

When he asks why, I notice he still has the same mild, polite expression on his face. So I tell him that I've had it long since I was fourteen and I think I'm ready for a change. "Plus, it's so heavy," I say, pulling it up with my hand. "It's too hot for summer."

Willie whines that he's hot too and I pick up a napkin to wipe him off. He's been dipping his french fries in ketchup and it's smeared all over his fingers and running down his mouth to his chin.

"But if you do cut it," Jonathan says, "you might regret it as soon as it gets cold."

I say, "True," and glance out the window but my lips have moved into a smile against my will. It seems like a miracle: Jonathan is being nice to me.

After he takes a bite of his sandwich, he points to the magazine and says, "It's good to see you studying the problem." He's smirking now, barely able to contain his laughter. "I'm sure a decision as important as this requires extensive research."

I want to kick him, but mainly I want to kick myself. I'm such a fool.

When I don't reply, he says, "All right, we don't have to talk about hair," leaning his head to the side, still smirking. "What would you rather discuss?" He reads from the magazine cover. "Glamour makeup in ten minutes? Or maybe the hot new fashions for fall?"

What I want to say, what I have to bite my top lip to keep from saying, is "No, let's talk about why you're an asshole." But I can't let myself fight with Jonathan. I tell myself it's immature, but I know there's another reason. I've never mentioned it to anyone and I try not to dwell on it too much—it messes up my confidence.

The truth is, I only sound good because of Jonathan. With him backing me up, I can cut this gig. But if he quit or, God forbid, if Fred fired him, I'd be exposed as what I really am. Competent, yes, but weak in certain areas. Definitely not the power singer I'm supposed to be.

Fred hired me because he was impressed with my range and depth, my ability to belt out whatever music he put before me. My problem, as I found out when we started playing six nights a week, was that my voice was inconsistent. By the third night, my lungs were hurting and sometimes I got into trouble. I had too much vibrato when the tune was supposed to be

30

clean, or worse, I couldn't hold the high note without taking a noticeable breath, leaving a nasty silence in the middle of what should have been the climax.

But Jonathan would cover for me. He'd use his keyboards as a distraction, an enhancement, whatever it took. And he made it look like it was supposed to be that way, like I was singing perfectly. After almost a year of playing together, we're so in sync that sometimes he seems to know what I need before I do. I'm always careful not to look at him then; I'm afraid I'll get confused, think it means more than it does. He's just being a professional, doing what's best for the band.

"We don't have to talk at all," I say, after I tell Willie to eat up. My cheeks are burning; I want to get back in the van, on the road.

"I was just joking, Patty," he says, leaning back, replacing his smirk with a small smile, lowering his eyes so they're half-open, clearly bored. He's back to being cool.

I can't resist blurting, "No, you weren't. You think my magazine is stupid and so am I. But that's fine. I don't care what you think."

"Of course you don't," he says, and he sounds mad suddenly, although I can't imagine what I've done.

"Well, why should I?"

"Exactly. You've just started out and you already have your own band. Why should you care what I think?"

I put the magazine back in the diaper bag, out of sight. "It's not my band. You run the rehearsals, Jonathan, you decide the sets. You decide everything."

"But you're the attraction. The product. You're the one Fred is grooming for bigger things. And in the end, you'll get the prize." He stands up and grabs his check off the table, hissing, "Most likely to succeed in an anti-intellectual, art-hating world."

Even Willie is surprised at how mad Jonathan seems. He points with a french fry at the register where Jonathan is handing money to the waitress, and asks if Jonathan is leaving without us.

I'm wondering the same thing, but I tell Willie no. And I force myself not to worry as he drinks the rest of his milk and we head to the bathroom. I have to pee, that's all there is to it. Even if we do get left at a truck stop in God-knows-where, Missouri.

As we walk up to the van, Jonathan is sitting motionless in the driver's seat, staring out the window. When we get in, he doesn't say a word, he just starts the engine, turns on the radio. Willie is asleep less than five minutes after we hit the highway. I stare out the window, read the billboards, and try not to think about what just happened.

When we finally pass the barn about an hour later, it takes me by surprise; I'd forgotten all about it. It has been painted over, white, and it still looks fresh, like it hasn't seen one hard winter yet. But as we get closer, I think I see the graffiti peeking through the paint, like a shadow. Maybe it's real, maybe the barn needs another coat, but I doubt it.

It's only in my mind, I think, and my eyes start stinging. My stupid mind, which wanted to respond to what Jonathan said about me being a product but couldn't think of anything to say other than "I am not."

What I wanted was to defend myself. To scream that I know what he thinks and he's wrong: I do care about music; I've wanted to be a singer my entire life. When I was in the seventh grade, my teacher called Mama and told her I had talent, I should get lessons. Mama never even considered it. "Keep it down in there," she would yell if I was singing in my bedroom and she had a hangover. When she was drunk, she would laugh at me. "Who do you think you are, Judy Garland?"

Seeing the barn is the last straw; I feel hot and so depressed I can't imagine making it through the next hour, much less the rest of the drive. The classical piece on the radio isn't helping: the cello sounds lost, lonely, heartbroken. I tell myself I'm just having a bad day, but it doesn't change my mood. I force myself to look at Willie, to think, I'm Willie's mother, that's important. And I have a job, a good job I worked hard for. We're making it, the two of us. That's enough for now. It has to be.

We're still forty miles from Omaha when Willie wakes up, but I don't mind amusing him; I need the distraction. I tell him we're going to a new place. A new hotel. Maybe they'll have cable so he can watch the Pooh show on the Disney channel.

"I don't wike the van," he says, after a while. He reaches around like he's trying to adjust his diaper. "It makes big needles in my butt."

He's picked this up from Harry, who always jokes that his butt is the only part of him that gets any sleep on the road.

I laugh, even Jonathan laughs a little, so Willie says it again. He loves to see everybody around him laughing, happy. And he wants all the guys in the band to like him. Of course he does; they're the men in his life. My poor baby. They're the closest thing he has to a father.

three

Willie is the only one who keeps his good mood when we get to the club and discover we aren't getting hotel rooms. Free lodging is part of our contract, but some club owners have found a way to cut costs: they put the band in a house, or worse, a trailer.

Irene is nodding while Willie is telling her how fun it will be to wake up in the morning at the trailer and watch cartoons together. But then she turns to me and says, "A prime location? This dump? What is Fred smoking?"

The three of us are slumped on stools at the bar, watching the guys unload the equipment. The stage is in the corner on the far side of the room, and it's so small the amplifiers won't fit. Jonathan says to put them on the floor; we'll have to run the wires tomorrow. Carl complains there are only two spotlights and one of them is burnt out. Dennis is fussing about the setup for his hi-hat. Harry is shaking his head.

The trailer is a few miles from the club; all we've been told is that it has three bedrooms, each with two twin beds. The club owner, Mr. Peterson, said it will easily accommodate a five-person band. But we have seven people; Irene and Harry usually get their own room, so do Willie and I. Even when we get four rooms, we have occasional grumbling from Carl and Dennis, who don't see why they have to share while Harry gets the extra private room simply because he has a chick. Sometimes Jonathan ignores them, sometimes he offers to give one of them his room, but they never take it. They say he deserves the space because he's the leader.

"I wish I had enough cash for Harry and I to stay somewhere else," Irene says, after pouring herself a soda from the bar. Mr. Peterson told us to help ourselves to anything except liquor. For liquor, we have to start a tab. Willie has helped himself to a package of crackers and three glasses of Sprite. He's not that thirsty, but he likes to watch me pull out the nozzle of the soda sprayer.

By the time we get to the trailer, it's after ten and all I want is to get Willie to bed. "What room do I take?" I ask Dennis, since he's right next to me. He doesn't answer, so I look at Jonathan and say, "I really don't care. I'll take the smallest one. Whatever."

He doesn't answer either. Fine. I go down the hall, dragging our suitcases and Willie's toy bag, pick the first room I come to and snap on the light. It's beyond ugly; it looks both nondescript and glaring, the way things look when you're fighting off nausea. The twin beds are Early American and the spreads are pale green with nubs; the floor is covered with cheap indoor/outdoor carpet. Two of the drawers on the small chest against the wall are missing their handles. Of course there's a painting over the bed. Every place we stay has a painting. Ocean scenery is popular, so are tropical forests. But never the sights we can see from our windows: a flat field filled with corn, or a muddy lake, or a truck stop on a slab of concrete plopped down in the middle of nowhere.

When I look at the painting here, I have to laugh. It's a landscape, cotton fields in the South, and in the background, a stately plantation with pillars like in *Gone with the Wind*.

I go back into the living room to get Willie, and he's cranky; he says he doesn't want to miss the party. Jonathan is slumped on the brown plaid couch, staring at nothing; Dennis is on the floor, rolling a joint with Carl, and Irene and Harry are standing out on the front porch, whispering, probably still trying to figure out the room business. I tell Willie he's not missing anything and drag him away.

He complains while I change his diaper and put his pajamas on, but almost as soon as the light's off, he falls asleep. Since he was a little baby, he's always been a good sleeper.

All I want to do is join him, but late or not, I have to go to the kitchen and use the trailer phone to call Mama. She gets mad if I don't give her the phone number of each new place as soon as we get in. She says Willie could be dead on the side of the road, and how would she know.

I want to keep it short, but unfortunately, I've barely said hello when she starts a rant about Rick's Lincoln "lurking" across the street from her house.

I know this is unlikely. Why would Rick go to her place when he can obviously find me easily enough? And Mama doesn't even live in Lewisville anymore. It was part of her new start when she got sober: she packed up everything and moved to Evans, a small town east of Kansas City, a quiet, peaceful place, she said. The only house she could afford on her file clerk salary was a run-down shack with peeling paint and a leaky roof and a backyard that barely fit a wading pool, but she felt it was worth it. She wanted me to bring Willie and live with her. And she didn't want me ever to run into Rick again. She made sure our phone was unlisted; she left no forwarding address.

Even though she started drinking when I was seven—and throwing me out of the house when I was twelve—she has somehow convinced herself that Rick is the source of everything bad that has ever happened. Rick and my father dying, that is. I don't know how she got through AA, since I've never heard her admit that she herself did anything wrong. But she adores Willie, and that's what matters to me now. He calls her Granny, and she laughs and kisses him and fusses over him, and it's like we're a normal family for the first time in years.

I take a breath and ask why she thinks the Lincoln is Rick's. After all, I remind her, he probably has a new car now. It strikes me as I say this that there was no car outside my hotel room the day Rick showed up. It was as if he appeared out of nowhere and disappeared the same way.

"Well, it sure looked like his." I hear her take a deep drag from a cigarette. "But okay, maybe it wasn't. I am a little jumpy since that man got out."

"Jumpy?" I force a laugh. "You're a nervous wreck."

She pauses for a moment. "Patty, tell me the truth. You ain't tried to get in touch with him, have you?"

"What?"

"I know how you are, that's all I'm saying. You could never resist them boys who look like two-bit movie stars."

I let this slide, even though it's completely ridiculous. Them boys? I've never been with anybody but Rick, as Mama knows full well. I tell her of course I haven't tried to contact Rick, and then I listen as she extracts promises that I will call her and the police if I lay eyes on one hair of his head.

I feel a little bad that I'm not keeping this promise, but the truth is, she doesn't really want to know that I've seen Rick. She just wants to hear that everything will be fine. Ever since she got sober, my job has been to reassure her. When Willie had terrible colic: "Don't worry, Mama. It's normal for babies, but it won't last long." When he fell and smacked his head on the sidewalk last year: "He's not bleeding; he didn't lose consciousness. I'll just get him checked out at the ER, but you don't have to come. Don't worry."

Whenever I call her from the road, there's something she's nervous about. She heard there might be a tornado coming to our area; where will we go for shelter? It's going to be really hot

39

next week; what if Willie doesn't drink enough? There's a man on the loose in Illinois; she heard all about it on *America's Most Wanted*. Oh Lord, isn't that close to where we are? What if this man on the loose steals her little grandson?

"Don't worry, Mama," I always say. "It will be all right. I can handle it." Whatever it is.

She hates being nervous. Being nervous makes her chain-smoke. Being nervous makes her want to take a drink—and that's a lot scarier to me than a tornado or a TV-show bad guy.

I try to change the subject to Willie's complete lack of interest in the potty chair I've been dragging around for the last three months. Another thing she's worried about. But she doesn't bite. "You know what bothers me the most, Patty Ann? The idea of that man seeing Willie, putting his hands on him. It turns my blood cold."

I find myself thinking back about how gentle Rick was with Willie, patting his knee, playing with his hair, kissing his forehead, stroking his little knuckleless fingers. Finally I exhale and tell her not to worry. "I will never let Rick hurt my son."

She's still going on about this when I interrupt and tell her I really have to get some rest. I rattle off the trailer number and hang up before she can object.

The whole time I was talking to Mama, I could hear bits and pieces of the band's continuing argument about the room problem. When I walk into the living room, I decide to ask Irene if she wants to stay with Willie and me. I plan to sleep with him anyway; one side of his bed is against the wall, but the other is exposed and even though I've put pillows against him, I'm afraid he'll fall out. Before I can ask her though, Jonathan says the couch is comfortable enough and he's sleeping there, end of discussion.

I tell them all good night and head down the hall. It's so dark in the bedroom that I hit my shin on the frame of the bed, but I'm too exhausted to curse. The air conditioner is on full blast; after I put on my sleep shorts and T-shirt, I lie down in bed, snuggle into Willie.

A few minutes later, Willie rolls over and throws his little arm around my neck. "You are my heart," I say, but softly so he won't wake.

For the first few days, Omaha isn't too bad. The trailer is tough, but at least the club is better than we thought. It's small, but it's in an upscale neighborhood, and it does a healthy business from the very first night. Mr. Peterson, the owner, seems pleased with us, although he refuses to let Jonathan do any instrumentals. He tells Jonathan he personally likes jazz, but it won't go over with his audience. But he offers to let the guys do a special concert a week from Sunday, in the afternoon, and he tells them he'll put out a newspaper ad and charge a five-dollar admission, split it with them. They've made it clear that I'll have no part in the concert, but still, I'm glad about it. It puts everyone in a good mood.

We don't have to rehearse much; so far our sets are working with this crowd, mostly people in their thirties and forties, old enough to remember sixties and seventies songs, young enough not to mind a little newer rock. We've only had a few requests and they've all been the usual ones, slow songs like "Without You" and "Endless Love." Jonathan has a briefcase full of fake books; he can play almost anything straight through, no practice. As long as the song is slow, it's not hard to get it together: Dennis brushes the beat on the snare; Harry does a simple bass line, and Carl does a riff in the key. Usually, I know the words already. Fred brags that I know every song ever written and it's pretty much true. I used to listen to the radio for hours when I was stuck in the car outside some run-down house, waiting for Rick to finish a drug deal.

Weird as it sounds, that time with the radio was one of the happiest parts of my life back then. I would start with rock, my favorite, and then move to Top 40 and country and even mellow old stuff like Perry Como and Frank Sinatra. And I sang along with all of it, at the top of my lungs. The windows were closed and it was dark; nobody could see me. I felt like I could sing twenty-four hours a day. I felt like I could sing through anything: a nuclear blast, a car accident, cancer—a drug deal.

Of course now that I'm singing professionally, I can't sing along with the radio as loud as I want. I always have to protect my voice. I have to be ready for a night like tonight, when a crowd has gathered to hear us at our best.

It's Friday around ten o'clock, and everyone is a little nervous. The room is full, and Fred is here too. He drove up from Kansas City without his wife, which means he doesn't want any distraction. Already, after the first set, he has a lot of suggestions. Dennis and Jonathan need to smile more. Harry needs to turn down his amp; the bass is drowning out the sax.

I need to make more eye contact with the audience, especially the men, who pay for the drinks. Carl needs to pay attention; Fred says he heard him screw up the melody on "Let's Stay Together."

We're on break, having a little meeting in the back by the bar. I was hoping to call the trailer, ask Irene if Willie is asleep yet. He was complaining of a stomachache when I left, but he had two greasy hot dogs for dinner; I hope it's just that and he's not coming down with something.

After a few more minutes of Fred's lecture, Mr. Peterson comes over and asks if we can start early. The jukebox isn't cutting it and two tables of customers have just left.

Fred smiles. "Of course." Then he tells us to get up and make it hot, make it kick. As the guys start to walk away, he grabs my hand. "You sound beautiful, my dear. Better than Darla."

Darla was Fred's discovery twenty years ago. She was a local celebrity before she hit it big. She put out three records, all sold well, but then she died in a plane crash while on tour in Japan. Fred told me the whole story. When he says I'm better than her, it's his ultimate compliment.

I smile at him, though I wish he hadn't said this right now. Dennis heard it for sure, maybe they all did. And they're right: it isn't fair the way Fred always compliments me and not them, but there's nothing I can do.

Before we can start, we have to wait for Carl. He's talking to a woman, as usual. All of us get propositioned occasionally, but Carl has groupies everywhere. It's not just because he has the glamour job as saxophone player. He has white-blond hair and icy blue eyes; Irene says he looks like a young David Bowie. Sometimes he goes home with a woman after the gig but he never brings her around the next day.

We're halfway through the second set and everything is going fine. It's a warm August night; Peterson has the front door propped open to let the music draw in people walking by, and it's working. Every table is full and there's a crowd standing in the back. Both waitresses are busy all the time, taking orders, bringing refills. No one is drunk yet, or at least they're not yelling or making catcalls.

We've done four up-tempo things and now we're slowing it down, doing a song that just came out on the radio a few weeks ago. It's called "More Than Words" and it's very lush the way Jonathan has arranged it. I'm on the second verse. The dance floor is packed with couples holding each other, smiling. I'm doing what Fred told me to, making eye contact with the men. When I look to the left, I look directly into his eyes for a second before I comprehend that this is real, he's really standing by the edge of the stage, staring at me.

It isn't Rick. I quickly glance around, thinking Rick must be here too, but no, he's all alone. He towers over all the customers. He's six foot four at least, with a neck as big as my waist. He calls himself Zeb; I've never heard his real name. He's a dealer friend of Rick's, and he was arrested the same night Rick was. Obviously he was paroled too.

I've always been afraid of Zeb. The rumor was they used him to mess with people, threaten to beat them bloody if they didn't pay what they owed, threaten to kill them if the beating didn't work.

Zeb's arms are crossed, his mouth looks tight, mean; his eyes don't move from my face. I freeze right in the middle of the verse. I freeze, and I don't even know I've stopped singing because I've stopped thinking too.

Jonathan improvises, goes to the bridge, adds a solo. Harry and Dennis are right with him, but Carl is off a bit, trying to catch up. I hear all this but I can't think what it means; Zeb still has me caught in his gaze. The band has gone on to the end; the applause is weak, but there. And then Carl talks to the audience, jokes about how hot it is in Omaha, asks if they're ready to party, and so on.

Finally, Jonathan whispers my name and the spell is broken. I smile at the audience as I slowly walk back to him, and I'm still smiling as I lean over, put my ear by his mouth.

"What happened?"

"I'm sorry." My hands are shaking; I hold them together, twist them, trying to calm down.

"Do we need to take a break?"

"No," I say, too loudly, and Jonathan hushes me. I can't take a break now. I have to stay on this stage all night. I have to stay right here until Zeb leaves.

Jonathan asks what's wrong, but I'm moving back to my mic. I have to sing; I have to fix this. I have to, or I'm going to pass out.

Fred is talking to Peterson by the bar, probably calming him down. Carl is running out of amusing stuff to say to the crowd. Jonathan tells Dennis to count it off. And then we're playing again, a loud rock song. I'm all right.

It isn't until the set is over that I realize Zeb's not standing there anymore. I was afraid to look; I even moved my mic stand as far as possible the other way, crowding Harry.

But I still don't want to leave the stage. I'm sure he's in the club, somewhere. Unfortunately, I don't have a choice. Fred has his hand up, motioning for us to follow him. This time, we meet in a hot, stuffy back room not much bigger than a closet, with metal shelves stocked with large cans of olives and boxes of cocktail napkins. Fred needs privacy.

First, he says in a low voice that he's very disappointed in me. I wince a little; he's never said anything like this before. Then he turns to the guys and asks if this happens often.

"No," I say quickly. "It's the first time and I—"

Fred puts his hand up. "I don't want your opinion." He looks at Jonathan. "Tell me the truth."

Jonathan says, "No," and throws in, nodding in my direction, "Something must be wrong."

"Well, Patty," Fred asks, "is there something wrong? Is that why you just stood there and killed the set? Killed this room for me?"

Harry says, "The set was good, Fred. We only had one—"

"No." Fred is shouting. "The set wasn't good. You looked like a bunch of clowns. And you—" He spins around to face me. "You looked like an amateur."

"I'm sorry," I stammer. "It won't happen again."

"You're damn right it won't. If it does, you're out of this group."

I feel like I'm going to throw up; I have to lean against the shelves for support. And it just gets worse. First, Fred rants and raves about how important this club is, how Peterson has connections throughout the Midwest. Then he gives us a little speech, explaining that Peterson has agreed to give us the rest of the night, but if we screw up again, that's it, our gig is canceled and Fred is bringing in another band.

Finally, he turns to face me, and his voice is deceptively gentle. "Are you following all this, my dear? Or is it too complicated for you?"

I can't speak; I can't find my breath. I thought Fred respected me. I counted him as the one person in this storage room who thought I was capable, even smart.

"At least nod or shake your head, Patty." His mouth is a sneer. "Show some sign you can process simple English."

I nod but Fred doesn't stop sneering until Jonathan says, "Give it a rest, Fred. I'm sure she understands."

Before I leave the storage closet, Fred puts his hand on my arm and hisses, "You better get your act together, my dear. Even an ass as lovely as yours can be thrown out. Comprendo?"

"Yes," I whisper, and Fred smiles, but it's an icy, cruel smile. My legs feel like noodles but I manage to walk away, make it to the stage.

If Zeb is there for the next two sets, I don't see him. I'm concentrating like I never have in my life, trying not to fail.

And I don't, thank God, none of us do. We sound great, I know it, and so does the audience. Even after the last call, they beg for another song, and then another, until finally Mr. Peterson comes up on stage and says he's sorry, they'll have to come back tomorrow or any time during the next two weeks.

"Let's give a big round of applause for the Patty Taylor Band," Peterson says, and he's beaming. Fred is too, when he comes up to congratulate us and say good-bye before he heads back to Kansas City.

He flatters me, says I'm better than Darla, even says he has high hopes for my future. But it's not the same. After he leaves, I realize I finally understand why Irene and the guys say you can't ever trust Fred: he's mean and he's two-faced.

Peterson and the waitresses are cleaning up; everybody's still on stage discussing what they're going to do now. Jonathan and Harry want to stay in the club and jam for a while. Carl and Dennis want to go to Denny's and eat first. I just want to get home to Willie, who may be sick, I don't know, because I never had a chance to call.

Jonathan will give me the van keys if I ask, but I don't want to leave by myself. The club is empty, but what if Zeb is still out there, waiting for me?

I turn to Carl. "If you're going to Denny's, could you drop me at the trailer?"

"You want to ride with me?" Carl grins as he lowers his sax into his case. "Does this mean what I think it does?"

"Don't be stupid," I say, but I force a smile. "It's right on your way."

48

He walks close and puts his hand on my back. "But what's in it for me?" he says, lowering his voice. "What do I get out of the deal?"

Carl has a running bet with the other guys that he can get me to sleep with him. I overheard them talking about it during the first month of rehearsals, when they thought I was in the bathroom. I also overheard a lot of dirty remarks. For weeks after, I felt so self-conscious standing in front of them. It was stupid, but it had never occurred to me that they'd be scrutinizing my body. I figured they were busy enough judging my attitude (she's stuck-up, she thinks she's hot shit), my dealings with Jonathan (she doesn't understand who's in charge, she's a prima donna), my relationship to Fred (she's got her nose so far up his ass, no wonder he gave her the band).

Normally, I shrug off Carl's come-ons, but tonight is different. I want to see Willie so bad and I need to be alone. "Carl, stop," I whisper, stepping back. "Please."

"Please," he says, and grins. "Is this an invitation? Does this mean you've come to your senses and decided it's time for us to do the deed?"

"No," I say firmly, but there are tears standing in my eyes and I'm blinking furiously, hoping nobody notices.

"What are you doing, man?" Jonathan suddenly says, looking at Carl. "This is getting ridiculous."

"I'm just kidding around."

"But you're going too far." Jonathan shakes his head. "She's about to cry."

I feel like a big wimp, but I tell myself it doesn't matter, all I care about is getting home. Carl's cheeks have gone pink; he's crossing and uncrossing his arms; he won't meet my eyes. He didn't mean to hurt me, I know.

"No problem," Carl finally says. "I'll drop you off."

"Okay," I say, trying not to look at Jonathan. I want to thank him for standing up for me, but I know I can't. Whenever I've thanked him for anything, he acts even cooler than usual, like I'm making a big deal of nothing or even like he's not sure what I'm talking about.

Carl and Dennis are moving to the back door; I'm following, when I hear Harry say, "Hang in, Patty. Fred goes off, then he chills. We've all been there. Don't take it too seriously."

"Thanks," I yell, but I'm not sure he heard. Jonathan is already playing the first few chords of one of his original pieces, "Susan's Eyes." Irene told me Susan was his girlfriend until about a year ago. "They were super tight. They used to read poetry and play chess and go everywhere together. I don't know what happened, even Harry doesn't know. My guess is she dumped him." Irene snickered. "Probably she realized he couldn't love anybody like he loves his keyboards."

I heard him talking to his parents once about Susan. Jonathan doesn't call his parents that often, but when he does, usually from pay phones on the road, he always sounds happy to talk to them. I can tell from his answers that his parents are both on the line, and they're asking about the band and the gigs, what he's composing, what he's thinking about. They all seem very close, which must be why I remember the Susan conversation—because it was the only time I've heard him sound annoyed with them. He said three times that he didn't want to talk about Susan. Of course then I was dying to know what there was to say.

Dennis and Carl are outside now, and the instant I'm out there with them, I remember Zeb. I'm so nervous walking to the Camaro that I stumble on the curb. I keep looking around as we drive, trying to see if anybody is following us. After a few blocks, I finally turn around and breathe normally again.

Carl and Dennis are sitting in the front seat, bitching about Fred. I don't join in, but I laugh when they mention his five-hundred-dollar suits and fake leather shoes, his jet-black hair, obviously dyed since he's pushing sixty, and his ridiculous habit of calling every woman "my dear."

"You sound better than Darla, my dear," Dennis says, as I get out of the Camaro. He has Fred's la-di-da voice down perfectly, so I laugh again. Carl still won't look at me, but he nods good-bye.

When I open the trailer door, Irene and Willie are curled up on the couch, sound asleep in front of the TV. I pick him up and she opens her eyes, mumbles, "He's good. Never got sick." She sits up and yawns. "Everything go all right?"

"Just fine," I whisper, because it feels true now that I have Willie in my arms, his sweet sleeping breath on my neck. He's only wearing a diaper, but I don't want to risk waking him; extra blankets will do for tonight. Tomorrow, I'll have to remind Irene that it's way too cold in here for Willie to sleep undressed. She should know; she's the one who turned the air-conditioner knob to sixty as soon as we walked in the trailer. "Peterson pays the utilities," she said. "Might as well turn this dump into an igloo."

Irene stumbles into her room as soon as I take Willie to bed. She's tired, she doesn't want to talk. I feel the same way, but an hour later I find myself still awake, reviewing everything that happened tonight. It seems like maybe the guys are beginning to accept me, see me as part of the group. And who knows? Fred's hostility might turn out to be a blessing in disguise—as long as I don't get fired.

Of course the main thing I'm worrying about is Zeb. I want to believe his showing up has nothing to do with Rick, but I'm finding it hard. Why would he send Zeb here, though, instead of coming himself? It doesn't make sense.

I'm telling myself that it might be just a coincidence. Maybe Zeb was in Omaha to visit family or do some job, and he wandered into the club like any other customer. Maybe he was just staring at me because he was surprised how different I look. After all, it's been more than three years since he's seen me; I've changed a lot.

In any case, there's no point in dwelling on it right now. I say that in my head over and over, as the digital clock next to the bed announces three o'clock, three thirty, four. At 4:10, the guys come in. I hear them talking, but I don't hear them banging around in the kitchen and I don't hear the CD player. They're doing what Irene and I asked, being quieter so we can sleep. Another good sign, I think. Things just might be looking up.

four

It's a little over a week later, Sunday, and the guys are leaving for their afternoon concert. Peterson kept his word and advertised the event in the local paper and on the jazz radio station; he expects a good turnout. They all seem excited and a little tense, even Harry, the coolest of the cool. Willie is waving bye to them all and I say, "Good luck." It's the best I can do; if anything, I feel I'm being too generous. The last week has been horrible. I can barely remember why I thought things might be getting better.

It started when Fred sent me flowers the day after I froze on stage. It was a huge, expensive arrangement: red roses, white carnations, yellow chrysanthemums inside a large cut-glass vase. He had them delivered at the gig, before the set, while the guys were tuning up. Unfortunately, my hands were shaking a little—I thought they might be from Rick—and I dropped the card. Dennis picked it up and read it aloud to everyone, doing his perfect imitation. "Your talent continues to amaze me, my dear. Keep up the good work and I'll have you in a studio when you return. All the best, Fred."

I tried to contain the damage. I stuck the vase in the corner, out of sight; I rattled off something about how ridiculous Fred can be. But it was too late. The grumbling had started about all the promises Fred had broken to them, how stupid he is, how incapable of recognizing real talent. I was a little offended, but I already knew they felt this way, so I went along, complaining that it's like Fred is schizophrenic, going back and forth about everything. Carl frowned and said, "What do you have to worry about?" and the rest of the guys just stared. So I shut up and made a point of ignoring them for the rest of the night. Unfortunately, the point was lost on them; they were too busy ignoring me.

It got worse after that. Irene said it was Fred's studio comment that really got to them—and Fred's response when Jonathan called him a few days later to ask if he still planned to record the quartet and send out demos, like he promised, and if so, when. Fred hemmed and hawed but the upshot was he wanted Jonathan to write some new songs first. They could be jazz, fine, but they had to have crossover potential. Most important, they had to have lyrics. They had to be written and arranged specifically for me.

When Irene confided this, she was very upset for Harry, for all of them. I mouthed the appropriate response, something about Fred being a big liar, but it wasn't easy. It had never occurred to me that Jonathan would write a piece I could sing, and I loved the idea. It would be beautiful, unusual; maybe it would get picked up by some record company; maybe it would make us all stars. At least maybe we'd see some real money for a change. I'd finally be able to open a savings account.

Of course Jonathan had no intention of doing this. In fact, he was threatening to quit again. All week, the guys spent every afternoon in Carl and Dennis's room with the door shut, discussing their options. Irene told me Jonathan felt like Fred had no commitment to them or their music, and they were wasting their time working for him. But the rest of the guys felt like the opportunity to play at good clubs like Peterson's made up for it. And what about the concert they were doing this Sunday? It was more exposure than they could hope to get on their own, playing at dinky, no-name colleges.

"And she won't be there," Dennis reminded Jonathan. "It'll be the real shit, us and the music. She's a meal ticket for now. That's the way we have to look at it."

Irene didn't tell me this part. I overheard it when Willie ran over and opened the door and I went in to bring him back out and apologize.

I didn't apologize, but I didn't confront them. I was as worried as anybody that Jonathan would quit this time. The meal ticket business was depressing but better than the alternative.

The week was hard on Willie too—that's what I'm thinking as I watch him waving good-bye to the guys. "They're talking grown-up stuff, buddy," I had to keep telling him, as an
explanation for why they were all closed up in the room. And
even after he understood that you don't open a door without
knocking, I had to tell him he shouldn't knock, it would just
bother them. He was so proud, holding his little fist in the air,
showing me he'd remembered the rule. It broke my heart to
say no.

Today I'm taking him swimming. There's a public pool on
the way to the club and it's a hot August afternoon; it'll be good
for him to get outside. I asked Irene if I could borrow her
Honda but she said she'd go with us, she needs the exercise.

The wading pool is packed with other kids, and Willie's so
happy he can't quit smiling. He loves other kids, especially the
bigger ones, the four- and five-year-olds who include him in
their pretend games. They boss him around, tell him he's a
dragon, not a dinosaur, tell him to sit there, don't move, okay
now move, now attack, but he doesn't mind at all. He even lets
them splash him in the face, and when I ask him, "Are you
okay, buddy?" he's giggling so hard he can't answer. I think for
the hundredth time that he'd love preschool. He needs more
children in his life, not to mention more family.

As I watch the other kids at the pool, I catch myself wishing that Willie had some of the normal, everyday things they
do. A decent house, or even an apartment, just a place where
he could keep his toys, spread out, and stay for more than a
few weeks. A mom who works, fine, but not such freaky

hours, who's home at night and can read to him before he goes to bed.

My favorite thing to daydream about is the house Willie and I will have if the band ever makes it. The house wouldn't have to be big or fancy, but it would be way out in the country. All around would be yellow fields and purple wildflowers, maybe a winding brook for Willie to wade in on a hot day. On the front would be a porch big enough for a swing, a beautiful white one like our next-door neighbors had when I was growing up. The neighbors who looked at me with pity so often I couldn't stand them—but I loved their swing.

Inside the house, the entire floor would be covered in the softest, thickest carpet. I would be able to get right out of bed without worrying about the cold boards. My kitchen would have a microwave that's built in and a refrigerator that makes ice. The bathroom would have a big old claw-footed tub, like the ones you see in the movies, and after Willie was in bed each night, I'd get in and soak as long as I want. Then I'd go crawl into my bed with the three pillows and the thick pale blue quilt. I'd have a really good lamp and a table next to the bed, and on my table would be all kinds of books, not just the one music book I own now.

We haven't been at the pool long when I find myself thinking about Rick, but that's not strange; I've been thinking about him a lot this week. I still don't know why Zeb was at the club. When I told Irene what happened—and about Zeb's reputation—she seemed nervous too. "It's kind of eerie," she said. "Like he sent this creep to spy on you."

"But we were just doing a gig. What's the point?"

"I don't know, but I'm telling you, there must have been something he thought he'd find out. Something he wanted to know."

Her comment has stayed with me; I'm still pondering it as I sit on the side of the wading pool, soaking up the sun, watching Willie. Irene is doing laps, or trying to. The regular pool is crowded with teenagers horsing around, dunking each other. They're at most five or six years younger than me but they seem like babies. It's not just because I have a job and Willie; I felt this way when I was their age. I was with Rick, and Rick never horsed around.

There is one couple who reminds me of the way Rick and I were. They don't look anything like us—he's too short and skinny, she has a deep tan I couldn't get if I stayed outside for months—but they act like we did. They're lying on a blanket and they're making out, seriously: her hand is caressing the back of his thigh; he's licking the hollow of her neck, pressing his bare stomach against hers, then his pelvis against hers, now his whole body. They're not doing this because they want an audience though. It's clear they don't realize they have one. They've forgotten they're surrounded by strangers; they've forgotten they're at a pool. They're so taken with each other and what they're feeling that no one else exists.

When he slides his hand around her breast, cupping it with his fingers, I realize I shouldn't be staring at them like some peeping Tom. I force myself to turn away, feel my face burn that I watched so long. Willie is holding a plastic ball, trying to float, and I smile to encourage him. He's still happy, that's something, even if for me coming here suddenly seems like a mistake. I'd forgotten what a pool is like, the shimmering water, half-naked bodies, kissing couples. It makes me feel things I don't want to feel.

After Irene sits down beside me, I try to turn it into a joke. I laugh and tell her I feel like a horny old lady, surrounded by all these hormone-driven teenage kids. She laughs too, then points to a man over by the snack bar, says he's cute and offers to introduce me to him.

I squint at her. "You know that guy?"

She laughs again. "No, but I'll just walk over and tell him my friend needs it. Now."

Her voice is loud; I elbow her in the ribs, tell her to keep it down. She laughs harder and shapes her hands into a megaphone. "I'll tell him my friend hasn't had it for an entire year. Twelve long, desperate months. I'll say if he doesn't help out my friend this minute, she may go postal in the pool."

She's threatening to do it, standing up, pointing to him; it's getting ridiculous. I tell her to quit. I grab her ankle and threaten to drown her if she keeps on saying this. I tell her he isn't my type anyway, and I'm not even slightly interested.

After a minute, she sighs and sits back down. "Okay. But damn, I'd think any guy with the right equipment would be your type after a year. It has been a year, right? Who on earth are you waiting for? Johnny Depp?"

I say, "Tom Cruise," because I know Irene hates Tom Cruise and she'll go on and on about why he's completely overrated. I want to distract her; I don't want her to ask me that question again—the one in the middle. She knows I haven't had a serious relationship since Rick, but she always assumes I had dates before I joined the band, while I was working at the restaurant. So far, I haven't been able to bring myself to correct her.

Irene has taken Willie into the big pool when it hits me that this might be the one thing Mama and I have in common. After all, she has never been with anyone except my father. She's never even had a date in all the years since he died.

Mama adored Daddy. She must have told me a thousand times how happy they were. He was the love of her life. He treated her like a queen. When he died it was the worst thing she could imagine. It took away all her hope.

It wasn't the kind of tragedy that makes the newspapers. One Sunday, Daddy was on the roof, patching up a leak, when he just fell. I was standing outside jumping rope, but I can't say I saw it happen. First I heard a noise, more like a yelp than a scream, and then I discovered him sprawled out on his back on the driveway. I walked over and he looked normal enough for me to ask if he was all right. Even though I noticed the small river of blood coming from his head, I still didn't understand why he wasn't answering me. As I ran in to get Mama, I realized the radio was still on the third rung of the ladder, and still playing.

I used to think Mama blamed me. For the longest time, whenever she got drunk, she would pressure me to tell her what I had been doing that must have distracted him. I was in second grade; even though I couldn't think of anything to tell her, I was never really sure I was innocent.

I can't remember how much she drank before he died, but I'll never forget how hard she hit the bottle afterwards. At night, whenever I got up to get some water or go to the bathroom, I'd find her sprawled out on the couch, mumbling that she couldn't bear to sleep in their bed. In the morning, she would cradle her head in her hands and yell at me for everything: for dressing too slowly, for letting my spoon clank against the cereal bowl, for leaving a spot of toothpaste foam on my lip. I guess she was happy sometimes, but only for fleeting moments and never when I needed her to be. I remember when I told her I got the lead in the sixth-grade play, she shrugged. I convinced myself she didn't hear me, but I was careful not to say it again. I didn't want to know if I was wrong.

She didn't start throwing me out until I was twelve. The first time she told me to leave, I thought it was a joke. It was a strange night. I had just started my period, and Mama decided that she would drink to my "becoming a woman." Every evening she had a reason for drinking, but this one was friendlier than most. I sat with her, I let her toast me. We ate saltines dipped in ranch dressing and talked about (but never cooked) supper. I remember how happy I was when she mentioned that I would have my first kiss before long.

I was chattering about boys at school, which ones might like me, which ones I thought were cute, when her mood started to change. She told me she didn't want to hear any more about my social life, and poured herself another shot of whiskey.

After a while, she started talking about how she met Daddy. This was one of her favorite topics when she was drinking. I knew the whole story by heart. Daddy was with another girl when Mama met him at the warehouse where she was working then. Evelyn was the other girl's name. This Evelyn was well liked and pretty; she had a good job as a supervisor. "But he didn't end up with her, now did he?" Mama would say, and laugh. "I'm the one he married."

I never really understood why Mama was so interested in Evelyn, but I always nodded along. One time, when I asked her where Evelyn was now, she said, "Working in a ditch, for all I care. Ten kids and no teeth. On welfare. Wrinkled up and ugly as a prune."

Mama called herself ugly sometimes. I tried to tell her she was pretty, but she insisted that she was too short and too heavy to be pretty; her face was too square. She was twenty-nine when she married Daddy, an "old maid," as she put it once. He was twenty-four, blond, and very handsome, everybody said so, according to Mama. They also said she was robbing the cradle, but she told them to get lost.

"I wasn't robbing no cradle. That Evelyn was a slut, but hell, I was still a virgin when your daddy came along."

I nodded, thinking that I would be a virgin until I was at least twenty-nine, hopefully longer. The whole sex business seemed more frightening than fun, especially on that day, when I was having my first period, and bad cramps to boot.

I could have listened to Mama discuss Daddy for hours. But after seven or eight drinks, she changed course and started in on her other favorite topic—all the sacrifices she'd had to make for me.

She'd worked full-time to put food on the table and clothes on my back. She'd taken care of me for twelve years almost by herself, because even when Daddy was alive he was gone six nights out of seven with his truck-driving job. She'd listened to my constant humming and whistling and singing and blabbing about my childish ideas. She'd put up with all my selfishness and ingratitude.

I always felt bad when she said these things, though I figured it was probably true. She had taken care of me. I was selfish sometimes, and loud, although I was trying so hard to be quieter. I thought if I could only be quiet, like she asked, then she wouldn't get mad at me.

"Today you're a woman though," she said. "You can go out on your own. Then you'll see what it's like. You'll see it isn't easy as you think."

She'd said today, but I had no idea that she meant this very minute until she stuffed the Tampax box in my backpack, "for the road," she said. I had nowhere to go, and I told her so, repeatedly, but she ignored me.

"Everything is about you, you, you," she said. "You're the princess. Well, things have got to change."

She threw the unzipped backpack outside, and when I ran out to get it, because I was worried about my homework blowing away, she locked and bolted the door.

A child with some pride would have walked away, but I wasn't that child—yet. I banged on the door, begging and pleading and crying for her to let me in. When I saw one of the neighbors looking at me, I went around to the back door and started banging there. I must have done this for at least two hours before she finally relented. She was really plastered by that point. She thought it was funny, except when she was yelling at me for disturbing the Fowlers, who lived next door and had called her to complain.

Until I told Rick this story, I was sure what I'd done wrong would be obvious to anyone as soon as they heard what had happened. I felt this way about all my fights with Mama, actually. This is why I never told anybody about them. There had to be something I was doing, or why else did this keep happening?

To say Rick saw it differently is putting it mildly. He'd had his own experience living with an alcoholic; it was something we had in common. His mother was alone, too—his dad had disappeared when his youngest brother was a baby—and she'd been a drinker as long as he could remember. He was the oldest of five, and he had plenty of practice protecting his brothers and sisters from his mom's rages. He wanted to protect me, too, but it was tough because I kept going back to Mama. I kept thinking I could fix things with her if only I tried a little harder.

Of course it's all different now. Now she's sober, and even though she and I have our problems from time to time, she's always good to Willie. Sometimes I'm still surprised by how kind she is to my baby. It feels like a gift or even a miracle.

Willie and Irene are back from the pool; I'm helping him spoon out his slushy, when I glance back over at the couple on the blanket. They're still so engrossed in each other that they don't even look up when the lifeguard blows his whistle to empty out the pool for a safety check. They're not going at it as heavily now, but somehow it's even sexier, the way he's tenderly touching her cheek, staring into her eyes, straightening out the strap of her purple bikini.

Rick bought me my first bikini. It was blue, my favorite color. The first time he saw me in it, he whistled until I blushed.

About a half hour later, when Irene suggests we leave so we have time to hit the store and still make it home before the guys, I say fine. She's impatient to see Harry and find out how the concert went. I'm not eager to see any of them, but at least the stress in the trailer will distract me from my own mind.

I don't miss Rick, but I miss being loved. This is what I've been telling myself at the pool each time I think about him. And this is what I always tell myself to explain why, after three years, I still dream about him.

None of the dreams are close to X-rated. Sometimes they're headed in that direction—we're kissing, taking our clothes off, touching each other—but something always happens to interrupt, as if my dreaming mind is determined to protect me from making a mistake and being with him.

I guess it's not surprising that Willie is almost never in those dreams I have about Rick. Usually he doesn't exist, but even when he does he's off somewhere, and safe; I don't have to think about him. The only time I dreamed about both of them was right after Rick came to Kentucky. It was a stupid dream—the three of us were in the Lewisville mall, shopping for training pants for Willie—but I still woke up in tears.

Foolish tears, I reminded myself. True, I grew up without a father and so did Rick, and true, it's sad that Willie is growing up the same way. But there's no alternative that I can see. Only a fool cries over what can't be changed.

five

The store is crowded, and Irene needs all kinds of odd spices and fresh mushrooms, onions, tomatoes—she's planning to make her special spaghetti for Harry and for the rest of us, too, she jokes, if we're nice. When we make it to the trailer, the van isn't there, but the Camaro is in the driveway, and parked in the street, a brand-new-looking truck. Probably a woman for Carl, I suggest, but Irene says no, the truck's too expensive; it has to be a dealer. For the last few days, Carl and Dennis have been complaining that they need a hookup, they're nearly out of weed.

Willie and Irene are still at the trunk of the Honda; he insisted on helping carry in the groceries. When I walk in the door and spot him, I blink a few times, like my eyes are the problem, not what they're seeing. It is a deal, that part is true. The weed is spread out on a newspaper on the table, and there's a scale and bags. The guys are coughing, smiling; obviously they've had a sample.

Dennis laughs. "Haven't you ever seen a buy, Patty? God, you're so sheltered."

Irene is inside too now, standing at the door next to me, quickly trying to take this all in. She turns to Dennis. "Patty knows him, idiot. He used to be her boyfriend."

"You've gone out with druggies?" Carl's voice is sleepy, stoned. "This is a new side to you."

Willie has put down his grocery bag, and now he's looking at Rick. I wonder if he remembers seeing him in Kentucky. A minute later, I decide he must: why else would he go over and stand right in front of Rick?

"Hi," he says, and his voice is shy, but he's smiling his biggest, sloppiest smile. He's still in his green swimming trunks; he didn't want to change because the big kids told him dragons always wear green. He looks adorable with his little chest and his chubby stomach sticking out, his cheeks and nose sprinkled with new freckles.

Rick smiles too, reaches in his pocket, gets out his keys. "You want to look at this?"

The key ring is shaped like a lion's head and glittering like gold. Of course Willie marches closer, sticks his hand out. Rick hands the keys to him, and at the same time, pulls Willie up on his lap.

I force myself to take deep breaths, stay calm. I flash to what Mama said about calling the cops if I see Rick and I almost laugh. Considering what Rick's doing here, it's impossible.

Jonathan always sits in the recliner where Willie and Rick are sitting; it looks strange to see them there instead. When I remember the van wasn't in the driveway, I turn to Harry and ask where Jonathan is. Harry says he's hanging with a local jazz reporter who came to the concert; he won't be back for a while. This makes me more nervous, although I can't imagine how Jonathan could solve this problem.

Irene says she has to put the groceries away. She asks if I want to help; I say no. I don't want to leave the room, leave Willie. "Just for a minute," she whispers.

I follow her into the kitchen but I keep looking back, glancing at Rick and Willie. Rick's hand looks so big resting on Willie's pink shoulders, but Willie seems happy, still absorbed in the key chain. Rick is talking to Carl about the possibility of getting them another ounce next week. He sounds like he does this kind of thing all the time, but I know he's acting. What I haven't figured out is why.

Rick used to call weed "baby load" and guys like Carl "pee-wee chippers." He dealt drugs, true, but he wouldn't consider peddling anything for under five hundred dollars; it was too small-time. This transaction can't be more than a hundred, and yet here Rick is, sitting in a trailer in Omaha, putting on like the band is his most important customer, like all he wants is to please.

"What?" I ask Irene, as soon as we're in the kitchen.

Her voice is low. "I don't like this."

"Neither do I. But what can we do?"

She leans against the counter. "I'm going to tell Harry he's up to something."

Before I can say I doubt that will help, Harry appears. He gives Irene a hug, tells her the concert went great. She asks him how they hooked up with Rick, and Harry says he came to the club; he's a big jazz fan. I know this is crap. Rick rarely listened to any music. He said it broke his concentration.

While Irene is telling Harry that Rick could be dangerous—he's Willie's father, he's got to be here for some reason—I'm peeking into the living room. Willie's off Rick's lap, but he's still standing close to him. They're arm wrestling, or at least Rick has his hand out, but Willie's using his whole body trying to knock it down. Rick is smiling, saying, "Come on, show me what you're made of." He looks up, notices me watching. He stares into my eyes like he's asked a question and he's waiting for my answer. I quickly look away, move back into the kitchen.

Harry is laughing softly. He says he wasn't born yesterday, he's been around, he'd know if any shit was happening. Irene puts her hands on her hips and asks if he doesn't think it's odd Rick never mentioned he knew me. Harry shrugs. "I think he did say something about Patty. I don't remember. We didn't talk chicks, we talked music."

I'm not surprised Harry is reacting this way. I've hung around the guys enough to know that they like dealers; they even like the idea of crime. To hear them talk, crime is like

70

jazz: outside the mainstream, against society, cool, hip. They don't have a clue what it's really like.

Irene asks Harry to tell Rick to leave. He says he can't do that, but Rick will leave soon anyway. "We just have to settle the finances." He pulls her close, rubs her neck. "You're so uptight, girl. Want a hit?"

Irene says no, somebody needs to keep their head together here. When she says she's going to start dinner, I walk back into the living room, hoping Harry's right, Rick's about to go.

He isn't, he's still talking to Carl. Willie is over by the television now, running his fire truck by the baseboard. He doesn't seem to be paying attention, but still, I don't like him being any part of this.

I walk over to him, whisper, "Why don't you go in our room, buddy? Set up all your cars on the bed, make a big traffic jam."

"No," he says loudly. "I stay with the big guys."

"Please, baby. I'll help you."

He stands up reluctantly and drags his feet in there. As soon as I sit on the bed and start lining up the cars though, he gives me his whole-face smile and says he loves me "bigger than an elephant." I reach out and pull him to my chest, hug him until he's squirming to get away.

"Cars," he reminds me.

For the next forty-five minutes, we play cars. The bedroom door is shut; I tell myself we're fine, we'll just stay in here until Rick leaves. I look out the window every few minutes, hoping I missed the sound and the truck has disappeared.

Finally, there's a knock on the door. I assume it's Irene giving me an update, but it isn't.

"Your friend has dinner ready," he says. Willie says "Yum," and escapes before I can stop him.

Rick steps into my room, glances around. We look at each other for a minute before I whisper, "What are you doing here?"

He stares at me. "Helping out your band."

"For real." There's a note of pleading I can't keep out of my voice. "I don't understand what's going on. First Zeb shows up at the club and now this. What do you want?"

He comes so close I can see the little scar above his lip, a patch of stubble on his cheek he missed during his morning shave—but he doesn't touch me. After a moment, he says, "I'll do whatever it takes to get you back, Patty. You know that, right?"

"But there's nothing you can do," I say, looking at the wall behind him. "I told you it was over; I told you—"

"I haven't forgotten," he says. "I remember exactly what you told me."

Before I can say another word, he's turned around, walking to the door.

I stand for a minute, thinking or trying to, until an alarm goes off. Willie. I have to go out and see what he's doing.

He's already climbed into his booster seat. He tells Irene he's hungry, then he says, "Feed me, Eeyore," and grins. He's heard Harry tell Irene, "Feed me, Seymour"—a line from one of their favorite movies. Willie grins because he knows Irene will crack up; she always does when he says this.

When Irene gives him a plate of spaghetti, I sit down next to him and start cutting it up. She's the only one in the kitchen; she says Carl and Dennis are outside, and Harry is waiting for her in their room. They're going to eat on the floor, alone, to share this special meal. Irene even bought plastic wineglasses for the occasion.

I mouth the word Rick and she points to the living room. "I gave him spaghetti," she whispers, and shrugs. "He said it smelled good. What could I do?"

She doesn't ask if I want some, she just fills my plate. I'm way too tense to eat, but I thank her and take a bite, tell her it's delicious. Then she's off to eat with Harry, and Willie and I are alone, but not for long. Rick comes in and, without saying anything, sits down on Willie's other side. Willie says hi and tells Rick about the pool where he got to be a dragon and all the other kids were scared of him because he roared so loud.

"Let me hear you roar," Rick says.

Willie does, and spits a chunk of chewed-up spaghetti on the floor. Rick laughs, surprises me by leaning over and wiping it up with his napkin.

I'm still holding my fork, but it's useless. There's no way I can eat now.

For the rest of the meal, I watch Rick talk to Willie. Rick is used to kids, I'd forgotten that. He even took care of his sister's baby one weekend when she was trying to chase down the baby's dad. He asks Willie questions, but not in the forced friendly way a lot of grown-ups do, and when he tells Willie something, he takes his time and emphasizes the part most likely to be interesting to a kid. Willie is in heaven when Rick describes his brand-new red truck that goes 140 miles an hour. When Rick says he'd like to see some of Willie's toy trucks, Willie gets up so fast he knocks his booster seat to the floor.

"You haven't finished, buddy," I say, but he's gone down the hall.

Rick pushes his cap back, looks at me. "He's a sweet kid."

I pick up our plates and set them in the sink. When I turn around, he's still looking straight at me. His eyes look so dark, they're almost black, and they're narrowed a little, as if he's concentrating hard, struggling to understand.

I quickly turn away, but I can feel his eyes on me as I dump Willie's juice in the sink, throw away the napkins, and wash the table. Even when Willie returns with a fistful of trucks, Rick's still staring. I pretend an interest in the trucks, hope I'm not blushing. When I find my thoughts wandering to the cut-off shorts and old tank top I'm wearing, I'm disgusted with myself. It doesn't matter what he thinks of me anymore. It doesn't. It can't.

By ten thirty, I'm starting to feel numb. Rick seems to have no intention of ever leaving, and nobody has asked him to—as usual. A few months back, when a guitar player Jonathan knew came to sit in one night at the club, the guy ended up crashing with the band for two weeks. Irene says it's part of being cool: welcoming people to your house for as long as they want to stay. Of course the people you welcome have to be cool, too, and Rick certainly seems to be. He doesn't get in anybody's face, doesn't cause any trouble. Best of all, he still hasn't asked for any money although the guys have been smoking his good weed for the last four hours, and drinking his vodka too, since about nine.

I could tell him to leave, but I can't imagine it would work. The whole point of this seems to be to get into my life, hang out in my space, whether I like it or not.

I don't like it, and yet he's been so amazingly nice to Willie—that's another reason I'm going numb. He let him sit on his lap in the driver's seat of the truck and pretend to drive for almost an hour; he let him turn the directional on and off, honk the horn, blast the radio. I stood in the driveway, speechless, but forcing a smile whenever Willie glanced at me.

After I got Willie into his pajamas, he wanted to go back to the living room and say good night to the "new guy."

When Rick gave him a quick hug, whispered, "Good night, buddy," Willie stepped back and announced, "Buddy is only for Mama!" But he giggled all the way down the hall.

After I'd tucked him in bed with his beagle and kissed him good night three times, he asked why the new guy called him buddy.

"He must have heard me call you that."

"No," Willie said. "Tell me why!"

"That is why," I said, but my voice was shaking a little as it struck me that Willie might know a lot more than he seemed to.

Now that Willie is asleep, I have nothing to distract me from my nerves. Rick is still listening to CDs with Carl and Dennis. Irene and Harry have come out of their room and are doing the dishes. I offered to help, but Irene said no because if I did, Harry wouldn't. So I'm watching them and pacing back and forth in the tiny kitchen, glancing into the living room every few minutes.

By this point, even Irene has decided that Rick might be okay. "Maybe he's just desperate to see you and Willie," she whispered, handing Harry a dripping plate. "It's kind of cute, him going to all this trouble."

Carl and Dennis are sprawled out on the floor, thoroughly wasted. They're discussing the CD, primarily bragging about how much better musicians they are and laughing for no reason. I don't hear Rick at all, though I know he's been drinking too; I saw him pouring himself a glass about a half hour ago. I haven't seen him touch the weed.

By the time the CD ends, Carl is so drunk his voice sounds slurred. I've been down the hall, checking on Willie; when I come back, I hear him telling Dennis to wait before he puts on more music; he has something important to tell Rick. I assume it's some drug thing, but I stop to listen.

Carl looks at Dennis, then at Rick. "I want to have sex with your old girlfriend." He raises his eyebrows. "I hope you don't mind."

Dennis cracks up, but I feel as if I've been punched in the stomach. I can barely catch my breath as I force myself to walk into the living room, get closer to Rick. His voice sounds even as he says, "Is that so?"—his face seems calm. But when I'm about five feet away, I see it: the twitching of the skin around his left eye. It's a tic he's had since he was a kid; it happens whenever he's angry, but it's no big deal; no one even sees it unless he points it out. Or unless they've known him forever, like I have.

"Yeah," Carl says. He tries to get up but he stumbles and sits back down. "And she wants me too, I can tell. It's just a matter of time."

"Never," I say, but my voice is a squeak. I've just realized that the black canvas behind Rick's chair isn't Jonathan's synthesizer cover. It's the side of a gym bag. It's Rick's, and I know what's inside.

I look at Rick. "He doesn't mean it. He's drunk; he's just joking around."

Carl crawls over to me, lifts himself up on his elbows, and reaches for my calf. "Never say never, Patty."

Rick's voice doesn't rise or change as he tells Carl to get his hands off me. Carl and Dennis both laugh, and I whisper, "Don't," and jerk my leg away. They're being complete idiots, but they don't have any idea who they're dealing with. How could they, when I haven't told them?

As soon as I walked in the door and saw Rick, I should have done something. Warned them, at least. This is all my fault.

When Carl grabs the rubber edge of my shoe, I pull my foot loose and move to the other side of the room. But it's too late. Rick lifts the black bag and pulls out his gun in one smooth motion. He stands up and points it directly at the back of Carl's head.

"I told you to keep your hands off her."

Carl rolls over, sees the gun, and his mouth falls into a surprised O. Dennis scoots back a little, closer to the wall. His face still looks like he's laughing, but the sound is gone.

I look at Rick, tell him to cut this out, put the gun away. After a moment, he lowers his arm. He sounds surprised. "You think I was going to kill this little turd?"

"No." I take a breath. "Of course not."

"He deserves it. He talks like you're nothing but shit." Rick points at Dennis with the gun. "So does this piece of crap."

He pauses, glances at Harry, who has come in to see what's going on and is standing very still in the doorway of the kitchen. "But the homeboy, these two assholes, they aren't the problem, are they, Patty?"

Harry takes a step into the room. "We're peaceful, man. We're not messing with you."

"Shut the hell up. I know damn well who's messing with me." Rick blinks, wipes his mouth with the back of his hand. "I've been waiting four hours to see his ass. I'll wait all night if I have to."

It takes me a minute to realize what he's saying, and when I do, I can't believe it. "You're talking about Jonathan?"

Rick laughs. "You think I'm stupid? Zeb told me the way you smiled when that prick was whispering to you on stage. And even in Kentucky, you sat there with me and talked about how much you loved that asshole's music."

I shake my head. "Rick, you're way off—"

"Am I? I thought maybe I was, until today. You walked in and saw me and didn't say hi or shit. You turned to the homeboy, said, 'Where's Jonathan?' like you were worried I'd done him already."

Irene is in the room too now; she mumbles, "No," and Harry takes another step forward, puts his hands out palms up. "You got it wrong, man. Brewer isn't hitting on your woman."

I force a laugh. "This is silly, Rick. Any of these guys can tell you. Jonathan and I don't even talk."

"Right, baby. Right. And I'm the king of England."

Rick repeats what I said in Kentucky about Jonathan's music. It's just like he said; he remembers every word. He says he had a feeling I meant Jonathan as soon as I told him there was somebody else.

"But there isn't somebody else; it's not even true." I'm getting desperate to end this; I keep thinking I hear something, Willie opening the bedroom door, or God forbid, the van pulling up. "I just said that so you'd leave."

He misses the point, says I wouldn't want him to leave if there wasn't another guy. We argue for a while, but it doesn't convince him, even though Harry and Irene keep stammering out things to back me up.

Dennis and Carl are still on the floor; they haven't moved or spoken since Rick got out the gun. Every time I look at them, I see how scared they are. Dennis is only twenty-two; he'd just left college when he got with the band. Carl is twenty-four, but Irene calls him a pretty boy, and that's what he looks like, lying there, watching Rick. A boy, not a man.

I ask Rick if everybody else can go to bed, let us work this out ourselves. He laughs and says he's not an idiot, he knows if he doesn't keep his eye on them, they'll go call Jonathan and warn him.

Irene's voice is a whisper when she asks Harry if he thinks Rick really will hurt Jonathan. But Rick hears her and fingers the gun, smiles a mean smile. "You never know. It depends on what he says. Whether he pisses me off."

I see in Irene's and Harry's eyes that this has the same effect on them as it does on me. Jonathan pisses a lot of people off. It's his personality. Even with a gun pointed in his face, he might say something obnoxious.

"Come on, Rick. You don't want to go back to jail. You just got out."

"I'd rather go to jail than let that motherfucker have you."

As soon as the words are out of Rick's mouth, the van pulls into the driveway. I hear it and I know Rick does too; he doesn't move to the door, but he stands up straighter, tightens his hand on the gun, tucks in his bottom lip.

I go to him, put my hands on his shoulders. "Rick, this is totally ridiculous. There is no other guy." I lower my voice, wishing so badly I didn't have to admit this. "I've never even kissed anybody but you."

He pulls away, looks into my eyes. He's surprised, but he wants to believe me, I can tell.

"We need to have a talk," I say. I'm straining to hear the van door close as I rush ahead. "Let's go in the truck so we can be alone. Please."

After a moment, he exhales. "All right." He reaches for his bag. "Come on."

Rick is holding the bag and the gun in one hand, my arm in the other, as we walk down the driveway, past Carl's Camaro and Irene's Honda and finally the van. I can see Jonathan in the front seat, hear the radio playing a jazz tune. It's too dark to see his expression but I know what he's doing. He's waiting until the song is over. He always does this if he likes a piece, even when it's extremely inconvenient, when we're rushing to get gas or food and get back on the road to make a gig.

Thank God he's so stubborn. I glance at Rick, but he's looking straight ahead, as if Jonathan doesn't exist, as if the whole scene never happened now that we're together again.

As soon as we get in the truck though, Irene comes to the front window and peers out. She's squinting. I'm sure she can't see us, but Rick slams his fist on the steering wheel.

"We have to get away from these assholes," he yells, and starts the truck. He takes off so quickly that I lunge forward and hit my knee on the glove compartment.

"Where are you going?"

"I don't know." His voice is angry, but he takes a deep breath. "It's up to you."

"But I can't go anywhere. I can't leave Willie."

"Willie will be fine. Your friend will take care of him."

I consider jumping out, but Rick floors it as soon as he turns the next corner. By the time he reaches the stop sign at the end of the trailer court, his speedometer is pushing sixty.

For several blocks, I don't move or speak as I try to think of a way out of this mess. But then he starts to slow down. He

81

drives down a long gravel road, past a farmhouse. He stops the truck in front of a field. When he cuts the engine, it's so dark I can barely see him. I have no idea where we are.

He leans back against the seat, but he doesn't say anything. It's so quiet. All I can hear are crickets and an owl hooting in the distance and the sound of his breathing. I'm trying to figure out what to do now, what to tell him so he'll take me back. I know he isn't worried about Jonathan anymore. Rick isn't stupid; he had to realize I'm not involved with Jonathan when Jonathan didn't move as we walked by.

"You know what it was like?" he finally says.

His voice is quiet but it startles me. "What?"

"Boonville."

"No."

"The lockdown was eighteen hours a day. Eighteen hours a day, for three years, I was in the same cell . . . The only way I stood it was thinking about you. Telling myself it was bullshit, what you said in your letter about us being over. That you were waiting for me. You would always love me."

I gulp, but I don't respond. My eyes have adjusted to the darkness. I can tell he's looking straight at me.

"I know you still care, Patty. You say you don't, but it's not true." He pauses for a minute, then puts his hand in my hair. "I could feel it when I touched you in Kentucky."

I lean my head away. "I only agreed to talk." I take a breath. "I really want to go back to the trailer."

"But that makes no sense. I love you. Those guys don't even like you."

It depresses me to realize it's so obvious how they feel, but I repeat that I have to get back. He shakes his head; then he sighs deeply and leans his forehead against the steering wheel.

I watch him for a couple of minutes. Finally I try, "Rick, there's really nothing to talk about. I told you, it's—"

"But we belong together. You and me and Willie. Those assholes in your band don't give a damn about you or our kid. They don't even see how smart he is."

I'm so surprised I can't help blurting out, "You think Willie's smart?"

"He's two years old and he already knows the words for everything. Shit, he knows the make of every toy truck he has. And he can count up to twenty. I heard him; he only left out sixteen." Rick sits up and faces me. "Hell yes, he's smart. He's like a little genius."

I feel my eyes well up. I can't believe he noticed this. No one ever does except me.

I try to turn away from him, but he leans over and cups my face in his hands. "I'm his father." His voice becomes soft. "I just want us to be together, the three of us. Be a family."

The tears are coming now. I don't want them to, but they are. I keep thinking how sweet Willie looked when he said hi to Rick. And later, how he kept babbling about the "new guy" as I buttoned up his pajama top, how shy he sounded when he asked, "I tell him good night?"

When Rick pulls me against his chest, it just gets worse. It feels so familiar. For all those years, he was the only one I could turn to. Of course I moved in with him, even though I hated his friends and I hated what he did. He was the one person in the world who cared about me.

I still remember the night I decided to stay with him for good. Mama and I'd had another fight, a really bad one. It started when I made her angry by rolling my eyes while she was telling me why she had to quit her latest job: because the other secretaries were jealous of her work. She was always getting fired back then and falling back on what was left of Daddy's life insurance.

I had my Walkman stuck in my ears, but it wasn't on, I was pretending to ignore her. She stumbled back from her bedroom, holding a stack of letters in one hand and her glass of whiskey in the other. She said the letters were from Daddy, from one of his truck-driving trips, before I was born.

I couldn't help it; I turned around and looked at her.

"He told me to get rid of it," she said, shaking the letters in my face.

I already had a hunch what she meant, but I stared at her like she was crazy.

"He was talking about you, Missy. He said he wasn't ready for some squalling baby."

When I still didn't respond, she screamed that I was an ungrateful brat and slammed her empty glass against the wall. "Do you know what I went through for you? Your daddy was so mad, he almost went off with that slut Evelyn. You owe me, Patty Ann. You owe me your life!"

She wanted me to thank her, but I wouldn't do it. I was looking at all the pictures of Daddy on the coffee table. In her favorite picture, he was standing in front of the garden of daffodils he planted in our front yard. He had blond hair, thick like mine, and he wore it long too, like a hippie. A hippie truck driver. I could see why Mama fell so hard for him. His face looked so open and friendly, like he would welcome anybody.

I told Mama if I could, I'd give her back my life, since it wasn't worth anything anyway.

We went on like this for a while, yelling words so ugly I don't remember most of them anymore. And then she threw me out of the house. That's how the fights always ended. And I would run to the pay phone down the block and call Rick.

It was pouring rain that night. When he drove up ten minutes later, I was slumped down on the curb, soaking wet and shaking with sobs. He pulled me to my feet and held me in his arms. He told me my mom had to be lying; of course my dad wanted me. Then he said she was a drunken bitch and I shouldn't go home anymore. I should stay with him.

His arms around me now feel just like they did that night: strong and protective, but gentle too. He even smells the way I remember, like Lava soap and sweat and something slightly sweet that always reminded me of peaches. And the words he's saying seem familiar. Telling me he's here, it's going to be all right. That Willie and I don't need to be with all those assholes anymore; we can be with him.

When he leans down and kisses me, it's just like that night, after we got to his apartment and he wrapped me in a blanket and dried my hair with a towel and tried to make me soup, but he couldn't, I don't remember why. We sat on his couch, and he kissed me on the forehead, on the tip of my nose, on my lips, over and over again. Exactly like he is now.

We kissed for at least an hour that night before he took me into the bedroom. But it's only been a few minutes and he's lifting up the back of my shirt. This confuses me. I'm still crying. I thought he was trying to comfort me.

"Hey, wait," I tell him. I try to pull back, but he holds me tighter, smothers my mouth with his. His hands are suddenly urgent as he fumbles with the snap on my bra.

I twist my face away and squirm out of his grasp, scoot until I'm up against the passenger door.

"It's time to go back to the trailer," I say, sniffing. "I didn't—"

"Not now," he says, as he lunges for me again. He presses his body against mine. His breath is fast in my ear.

I tell him to cut this out, stop, but he doesn't respond. His hands are all over me now. When I feel him, hard, against my thigh, I yell, "Rick, I'm serious!" and try to push him off. He knocks my arms out of the way.

"Not now," he repeats. He kneads my breasts in his hands, whispers, "You feel so good."

My only thought as I reach back for the door handle is that I made a mistake. I shouldn't have cried. I shouldn't have wanted him to comfort me.

The door opens so quickly I can't get my balance, and I fall out backwards onto the gravel. My elbows are bleeding; by the time I stand up and begin running, he's out of the truck too, following me.

The field seems flat, bare, and enormous. As I run, I hear my heart pounding in my ears. And I hear him. He's coming closer. It's so dark I can't see where I'm going. I can't think about what's happening, why I'm running in this field. It's only Rick. I know him. He loves me.

Right before he catches up with me, I find myself remembering the stupidest thing. He couldn't find a can opener. That's why he couldn't make the soup.

He grabs the belt loops of my shorts and spins me around. I'm out of breath, but I manage to scream, "Let me go!"

He's panting too but he doesn't say anything; he just pushes on my shoulders and forces me to the grass. Before I can get up, he kneels beside me and grabs both of my wrists in one hand and pins my arms over my head. Then he raises my shirt.

"No, Rick!" I'm trying to catch his eye, but he's looking at my chest. He doesn't see me. He doesn't seem to hear me, even though I'm shouting, "Rick, please! I can't do this!"

I twist my arms to free my wrists, I try to fight him, but it's useless. He's so much stronger; he manages to yank down my shorts and my underpants with his one free hand. And then he unzips his jeans and crawls on top of me.

I haven't done this since I gave birth. The pain is sharp, sudden, surprising. I let out a cry, tell him it hurts. "Please, Rick," I whisper. "Please don't."

"Just relax," he says, and kisses my cheek. "There," he says, and lets out a deep groan. "Oh yeah."

When I plead with him to stop, he mumbles, "Ssh." When I say it again, he kisses my nose and puts his hand over my mouth.

After a while, the pain is lessening, but there's a sharp rock poking into my back, his forearm is pulling my hair, and he's holding my wrists so tightly together my fingertips are going numb. But the worst of it is that he still has his other hand covering my mouth. I'm telling him about the rock, about my hair, but he can't hear me. I say I'm afraid, but all he does is breathe and moan, "Jesus. Baby."

By the time it's over, I've stopped trying. When he releases my arms and rolls off me, I pull up my shorts and begin stumbling to the road. After a few minutes, he's up too and following me, throwing words at my back. "Wait up. Come on, Patty, don't be pissed. I know I should have gone slower. I'm sorry."

I don't turn around. I can tell he's tired; I'm moving much faster than he is now. As I get farther away, he begins screaming my name, begging me to wait, listen. I still don't turn around. And when I spot the farmhouse, I take off running.

Within minutes, he's running too; I hear the dry grass rustling behind me. But before he gets to me, I'm up the front steps and banging on the door. The old man is engrossed in a TV program; he just points to the kitchen when I say my car broke down a mile back and I need to use his phone.

For a while, I stand in the hot, dusty kitchen, waiting to see if Rick will try to drag me out of here. I can't call Irene until I'm sure he's gone; I don't want her in the middle of this.

Finally, I hear an engine. I run to the window just in time to see his taillights disappear.

The old man's mail is stacked on the radiator next to the refrigerator; when I read the address to Irene, she says she and Harry will figure out the way and be right over. She lowers her voice. "Are you all right, kiddo?"

"Bring my baby to me."

"Honey, he's asleep."

"I need Willie! I need you to bring him to me!"

"Okay, Patty. Okay."

After I hang up the phone, I thank the old man and go out on the porch to wait. I sit down on the steps and put my head on my knees, look down at my shoes. I'm still wearing the water sandals I had on at the pool, which seems unbelievable to me. This is all the same day.

six

Irene is really good at figuring out how people feel. She always says she could see her parents' divorce coming from a mile away, even though she was only eleven at the time. Her jewelry business is just a hobby, something she can do on the road, but even the bracelets she makes are designed to help people with their feelings. They're made of small glass beads—emotional beads, Irene calls them—and with every sale she gives out a key to the colors. It's not what you'd expect: hope is purple, not yellow; anger isn't red, it's a weird swirl of pink and green; blue doesn't mean blue, it means happiness, at least according to Irene.

You're supposed to twirl the bracelet around on your wrist

until you know how you're feeling by the color that attracts you most, the one you stop and stare at. When she gave me a bracelet, back when I first joined the band, I twirled it so much it broke. Irene said this meant I was confused about how I feel. Naturally, this made her even more determined to help me.

I know all this, but tonight I don't want her help. When I walk down the porch steps and over to the Honda, I'm already annoyed that she didn't bring Willie like I asked. She didn't bring Harry either. She says she came alone because she was worried and she wanted to talk. She says she could tell from the way I sounded on the phone that Rick had hurt me.

Then, without even lowering her voice, she says she was afraid he raped me.

When I hear that word, I yell at Irene for the first time in the year I've known her. "He did not!"

"Honey, I'm on your side," she says, more quietly. "But okay, okay." She picks some dry grass out of the back of my hair, squints at the dark stain on my shirt. "Something happened though, right?"

I tell her the stain is blood, but it's from a scrape on my elbow. No big deal. Then I say, "I don't want to talk about this," and snap on the radio. I turn the dial until I find something meaningless but upbeat. When she's still looking at me, I tell her to go on, drive.

It isn't until we get to the trailer that I realize I can't go in; I can't face the guys. I imagine them sitting around talking about me and Rick, snickering about what happened. Of course the blond bimbo has a bad-guy ex. Stupid chicks like her always do.

"I wasn't the one who brought Rick here," I whisper, as I look through the living-room window. I can see the back of Carl's head and Jonathan's profile. "It isn't my fault."

Irene's door is open, but she stops and turns to me. "No, it isn't."

"But they always think it is. Everything is my fault to them."

"Come on, kiddo. They're really not that bad."

"You have no idea." I slump back against the seat and nod at the trailer doorway where Harry is standing, barefoot, waiting for her.

"Hold on," she says. "I'm just going to tell him we're all right."

She said "we," but I know she means herself. Of course Harry would be worried about her. She was driving to pick me up, and I was with a criminal with a gun.

I watch them talking for several minutes. Obviously, she's telling him more than she's all right. The porch light is on; I can see him nodding slowly. And then he glances in my direction and I feel like I'm going to be sick. I figure she's probably telling him what she thinks Rick did to me. Something new for them to talk about.

That does it. I can't take it anymore. I jump out of the Honda and rush to the porch.

"Move over."

"Hey," Irene says, frowning, but Harry gets out of my way.

I walk inside and straight up to Jonathan, sitting in the reclining chair, looking at a sheet of music.

"I quit."

He blinks. "What?"

"I quit. I'm out of the band. Not that I was ever in it. But it doesn't matter anymore. I'm leaving."

Carl had been blowing softly on his horn, but now he's quiet. I can feel him staring at me. I know I look like hell: in addition to the grass tangled in my hair and the blood on my shirt, there's dried blood on my elbows and dirt all over my ankles. And the zipper on my shorts isn't zipped up all the way. It won't close. Rick must have broken it.

I frown at Carl. "Take a picture, it lasts longer."

Dennis laughs nervously, and I spin around and glare at him.

"Go ahead, laugh. I don't care anymore. Everything about me is funny or stupid, right? The only thing I'm good for is a meal ticket. And entertainment. Sarcastic cracks about me and Fred, how I really got this job. Bets about whether I'll sleep with Carl. And you all think I will. Because I'm such a nothing. A whore."

Jonathan clears his throat. "None of us have ever called you a whore, Patty."

I rock back on my heels. "What word do you use? Slut?"

Irene is at my elbow. "Come on, honey. You don't want to talk about this right now."

"Yes, I do. I want them to spit it out. I want them to say what they think to my face for a change, instead of behind my back."

For a moment or so, the room is totally quiet. I'm still standing with my arms crossed, glaring at them all, but it's becoming difficult. I feel dizzy, unsteady on my feet. When I hear Harry start talking, I can tell from his tone he's saying something apologetic, but I can't make out the words. Irene says I look weird and I should sit down. When I don't move, she takes my arm, tells me to come to the couch. I shake my head. I have to get to the bathroom. I'm going to throw up.

I race down the hall and shut the door behind me, kneel on the cold tile, retch, but nothing comes. My stomach is too empty; I haven't eaten since this morning. When I stand up, I'm swaying again. I grab the sink for support, lower my head, and take deep breaths. After a few minutes, I feel a little better, but then I catch a glimpse of myself in the mirror. There are four reddish-purple marks on my cheek and one right under my chin. It's so easy to tell what caused it; even a child could see it's the outline of someone's hand across my mouth.

I slump down on the floor and lean my face against the wall. I whisper Rick's name and the betrayal is so overwhelming it feels like my heart is breaking, but I don't cry. I want to, but I can't. It's as if I've gone past the part of my life where crying is an option.

Irene is knocking on the door. I want to take a shower, but I never take a shower at night; she'll make a big deal out of it. When I come out of the bathroom, she wants me to come to her room, lie down and talk. But I don't want to. I want to be with Willie. Willie who is innocent of all of this, of everything.

She puts her hand on my arm. "Listen, kiddo, maybe we should call somebody." Her voice is a whisper. "You know, one of those hotlines."

I jerk my arm away. "Are you still on that? I told you, he didn't rape me!"

"Patty, please—"

"No! Don't say another word!" Harry is standing in the hall now. Jonathan is right behind him. I'm sure they heard me yelling, but I don't care what they think. I'm past that too.

I turn away from them all and go into my room.

Willie is snoring softly. I remember how tired he was: he'd missed his nap because we were at the pool. He's lying on his side, clutching his beagle; both pillows are still against his back. I stare at him for a minute before I push some toys off the other bed and flop down on it. I wish I could sleep with him but I can't. I'm too dirty.

Tomorrow I will call Fred. As soon as he can find a replacement, I'll take Willie and leave. I'm not sure where we'll go, but I'll think about that later. Right now, all I know is I have to get away from here.

The next morning, Willie wakes up at eight. It's late for him but much too early for me. I go through the motions of the morning: fix him a bowl of cereal, force myself to choke down some toast, drag him into the bathroom with a pile of toys to play with on the floor while I finally take a long shower, set him in front of *Sesame Street*. I have to keep the TV volume low; Jonathan's asleep on the couch.

I go into the kitchen, figuring now is as good a time as any to make the call. Marge, Fred's secretary, says he won't be in the office until this afternoon. "It's important," I tell her. "Make sure he calls me back."

"You're really serious about this?" Irene asks, as she comes into the kitchen to start her coffee.

I say yes and escape into the living room. Willie wants to make Play-Doh people; when I get that cleaned up, he wants to go to our room and pretend the bed is a bus for the hundredth time. I don't mind; I'm glad to get away from Irene. She keeps coming into the living room, presumably to say something to Willie but really to give me another penetrating, worried look.

The guys start waking up around two thirty; they're all up and slumped at the small kitchen table, munching donuts and drinking coffee, when the phone rings. Willie and I are behind the rocking chair, building a blanket fort, and I hear Jonathan answer. He talks to Fred for a minute, tells him Saturday went fine, mentions a problem we had with the PA that appears to be fixed. And then he says, "She isn't here right now, but I'll tell her you called." I run in there, but it's too late. He's already hung up.

"Why the hell did you do that?"

He shrugs. "I thought you might want to think about it more before you talk to Fred."

"It's none of your business what I want."

I pick up the receiver and dial Fred's office. Marge says she's sorry; he just tried to call me, but unfortunately he got called to a meeting as soon as he put down the phone.

"Dammit." I turn around and frown at Jonathan, at them all. Dennis is tapping out a beat on the donut box, Carl is reading the liner notes on a Pat Metheny CD, and Harry is getting a shoulder rub from Irene. They look like they always do: calm and of course, cool.

It's infuriating.

When Dennis says, "You want a donut?" I say, "Screw you." Nobody laughs. Even when I go back in the living room, nobody laughs.

This is progress, I think. Before they thought I was an airhead, now they think I'm a bitch. Big improvement.

I try Fred again at five but Marge says he never returned from the meeting. She says I can call him at home if it's an emergency, but I say no, it can wait until tomorrow.

Willie has finished his macaroni and cheese dinner and now he wants to go outside. I've been avoiding this all afternoon. The backyard of the trailer is fenced in, nothing but grass and flowers, but still I don't want to go out there today. I imagine rusty nails buried in the grass, swarms of bees hidden in the flowers. I imagine quicksand or an open well, even a hole all the way to China.

I go out with Willie, but I'm too nervous to be any fun. Every car that turns down our street makes me jump. Even the sound of the neighbors arguing next door makes me so tense I want to grab Willie and run until we find somewhere safe.

I'm putting on makeup for the gig when Irene comes into my room. She plops down on the bed next to Willie and tickles him; then she asks if I realize that when I quit, the guys will be out of work too.

"Fred won't book them without a singer. And he won't put another singer with them. He'll think they can't work with singers because you left."

I'm kneeling in front of the dresser applying cover-up stick to the bruises on my face. I hadn't thought about what would happen to the band, but I look at Irene's reflection in the mirror and say flatly, "They can't work with singers. No one should have to put up with what I have."

"Don't you think you're being a little unfair?"

"No, I think I'm being totally fair. Before I was stupid, now I'm finally being fair."

"Okay, okay. Let's not talk about this anymore." She sighs. "I don't think it's what's really bothering you anyway."

I ignore her hint and look at Willie. He's "reading" his book about baby farm animals: he points to each animal's picture and then points to the words underneath and makes something up. When he gets to the cow, he says, "The cow goes moo 'cause it wants more grass." I smile and tell him he's doing a great job.

Irene smiles too; then she turns to me and her voice grows hesitant. "Listen, honey. Are you worried he's going to come back for you? Is that what's going on here?"

I'm putting on my eyeliner. My hand doesn't slip. "No."

"That's why you want to leave, isn't it?" She looks at me in the mirror. Her eyes are full of concern. "Because of what he did to—"

"No, I told you. I want to leave because I hate this band."

Willie looks up. "You hate the big guys?"

"Not really, buddy." I force a laugh. "I'm just teasing with Irene."

It's late; I have to get dressed. As I stand up to get my dress out of the closet, I tell her I'm sorry it worked out this way. "I don't want to hurt you and Harry, but I have to do what's right for me."

"Sure you do, honey," she says quietly. "I just hope you know what that is."

Obviously, the guys are also thinking about the consequences if I quit. That's the only explanation I can come up with for the way they're acting tonight. They're being positively friendly—for them. Of course, they don't invite me to go out in the alley and get high between sets, but they do ask if I need a drink whenever they get one, and they make what can only be called nice remarks. Dennis claps after I finish "Street Life." Harry says I really belted out "Heart of Glass." Even Carl mumbles something about how well I'm doing, given how tired I must be.

Only Jonathan doesn't participate. I assume he shares their attitude, which is why he hung up the phone before I could talk to Fred, but he can't cut being friendly to me, not even to keep from losing the gig.

Sometimes he stands up for me; sometimes he seems to hate my guts. I'm sick of wondering what's going on with him.

My eyes feel like burning slits; I don't care about Jonathan;

I don't care about being praised; I just want to finish the night and go home. At twelve fifteen, Peterson says we can end early. It's a typical light Monday. There are only two couples left in the club, and he says there's no point in finishing the set. As soon as I put my mic back in the stand, I grab my purse and ask Jonathan for the van keys.

Jonathan says he'll give me a ride; he left some sheet music at the trailer and he wants it for tonight's jam. The rest of them say, "Good night, Patty," almost in unison, as we walk out. I shake my head. It's as if they have no idea how obvious they are.

As we pull out of the parking lot, Jonathan turns on the radio and I lean my elbow on the window. There's a cool breeze blowing, even though it's still three weeks from Labor Day. This feels like the longest summer of my life.

When we stop at the traffic light, Jonathan glances over and asks why I'm quitting.

I frown. "What's it to you? You want to quit anyway. You almost did a few days ago."

"That was a matter of principle. I thought Fred needed to know he can't play games like he has with us. I wanted it to be the case, at least once in his life, that a musician stood up to him and said no. I don't need your money, Fred; I don't need your contacts. What I care about you'll never appreciate and never understand."

"Well, mine's a principle too. The principle is, I'm tired of being treated like dirt."

He goes through the light and turns left. After a while, he says, "You have options."

"Like?"

"You could tell Fred you want another group. I'm sure he could put together a new band for you in a week. Every musician I know is desperate for steady work."

I pause for a minute. "Why are you saying this?"

"I promised the guys I would have a talk with you before you call Fred. They're worried about what will happen to the quartet when you leave."

I look out the window. The night is clear and the stars are so bright, they seem close enough to reach out and hold in your hand. "But aren't you supposed to talk me into staying? Isn't that the point?"

"I told them I'd see what I could do. But I've come to the conclusion you'd be better off with another band."

When I ask him why, he pauses for so long it occurs to me that he's forgotten the question. But then he turns down the radio and says in a low voice, "I realized last night we'd been cruel to you. It wasn't intentional; we justified it in the name of our art. But art is about finding beauty, finding truth. It shouldn't coexist with cruelty. That's not the kind of musician I want to be."

Now I'm surprised. "This is because of what I said?"

"No, because I saw you."

"What?"

"Before, you were just a symbol of what I hate. Commercial culture, anti-intellectualism, Fred. But last night, I really saw you for the first time." He rubs his eyes as he drives into the trailer court. "It blew me away."

I'm not sure what he means, but I don't want him to be more specific. I don't want to discuss anything about last night.

"Well, maybe you're right. But I can't work with another band."

"It would be easy to make the transition. Fred would hire experienced people. The new group could be up and running within a month."

"I just don't think it would work."

We're in the driveway now. I can see the TV reflecting blue on the windows. I hope Irene didn't let Willie fall asleep in front of it again.

Jonathan doesn't get out. He pushes his shaggy hair back, turns to face me. "You should at least consider it."

I think about how often he covers for my weaknesses and mistakes. Obviously, he knows about this too. Does he think I'm such an idiot I don't even realize I'm not that good?

That decides it. I want him to know that I know too. But when I tell him I'm fully aware of my weaknesses as a singer, he bursts out laughing.

I give him the finger and jump out of the van. I don't need this tonight.

I storm into the trailer, and see Irene. Willie's in bed, thank God. She says hi, but I walk right past her into the kitchen. I need a beer.

Jonathan is still laughing when he comes in. When I shut the refrigerator, I turn around and he's standing right there. With my heels on, we're the same height. I can see the amusement in his eyes perfectly. It makes me want to spit on him.

"Where did you get the idea you're a weak singer? I never said that."

"You didn't need to." I twist the cap off. "You're always covering up my screwups."

"But any keyboard player would."

"Oh yeah, right."

He shakes his head. "Patty, the point of a backup band is to make the singer sound good. You're not weak. I'm supposed to accompany you . . . If anything, I don't do enough to support you. I get bored playing the same simpleminded tunes night after night . . . unlike you."

I was feeling enormously relieved until he got to that last part. I was almost grateful. That's why I'm even more furious.

"You always have to throw in some dig about me, don't you, Jonathan? Make sure I know just how stupid you think I am. Well, guess what? You have no clue. You think you're bored now? Try working as a dishwasher. Try stuffing your hair in an ugly hairnet. Try standing on your feet for twelve hours scraping dried food off plates. Try being yelled at because you can't keep enough glasses clean to satisfy the waitresses." I take a big gulp of my beer. "You think I'm stupid because I'm not bored singing the same songs? Up yours. Compared to the other stuff I've done, this job is a dream come true!"

He's leaning against the wall. I've been glaring at him, but he hasn't been glaring back. And now he half smiles. So does Irene, who appeared in the doorway while I was yelling.

"What?" I ask, as I look back and forth at them.

She raises her eyebrows. "What you just said."

I stand there for a moment before I flop down at the kitchen table with my beer. Now I get it.

No one says anything then. I'm lost in thought, remembering how I felt when Fred first told me I had the job. I blabbed the news to a total stranger in the parking lot outside Fred's office. On the way home, I took my last ten dollars and bought a bunch of red and yellow helium-filled balloons that said Congratulations. When the clerk asked who they were for, I grinned and said me. I remember Willie started giggling when he saw the balloons—and when I told him what happened, he clapped his hands together like he understood, though, of course, he couldn't have. He was barely eighteen months old then.

This is what I wanted. Even tonight, there were moments when it was perfect, moments when I felt that odd sensation of losing myself in the music and, at the same time, feeling so aware, so alive. It really is my dream come true. How could I have forgotten this?

After another minute, Jonathan turns to Irene and says he's going back to the club now. He takes his keys out of his pocket, but he doesn't get any sheet music.

I follow him to the door. I have to thank him for what he's done for me. But I barely have the words out when he says it's no big deal. And right before he walks out, he throws in, "I still think you should consider changing bands."

When I turn around, Irene is frowning, shaking her head. "Why in the hell did he say that?"

"You're asking me?" I say, and force a laugh.

"Brewer is strange, that's all there is to it." She rolls her eyes.

I nod, but I'm thinking about what he said. Maybe I should change bands, especially if Fred could put me with a band in another city. Supposedly, Fred has contacts for a thousand miles. He could put me in a band in Utah or Tennessee or Ohio. Maybe he could even put me on a tour of Japan, like Darla. Somewhere far away, so I wouldn't have to keep glancing out the trailer window every time a car goes by, or the breeze shifts, or a harmless squirrel races up the branches of the harmless front-yard tree.

seven

It's Saturday morning, and we're in the middle of a bad thunderstorm. The rain is pelting against the roof of the trailer; the wind is throwing trash can lids and lawn chairs and bending down trees, but the gusts are steady, almost 4/4 time; I can tell by the slapping of the branch of the willow against the back window. Willie is still asleep, but I've been awake since it started, around four thirty. It must be about six now, I'm not sure. The power went out after a bright white flash of lightning and a clap of thunder that sounded like the sky exploding. Incredibly, Willie barely stirred. The phrase "sleeping like a baby" was made for him.

I know I need to sleep, too; tonight is our last night in

Omaha, and Peterson expects the club to be packed. But I can't, and it isn't just the storm. I've been walking around in a daze since Tuesday when Mama called. I haven't even been able to think about the band, my future, what Jonathan said to me. When I talked to Fred, I told him it wasn't urgent after all; it could wait until the end of the month, when we get back to Kansas City. Irene said I was doing the right thing. "You don't want to make any decisions while you're upset."

Irene thinks I'm still upset about what Rick did to me—and I am. But she doesn't know what Mama said.

She called at seven thirty in the morning. She knows I work nights; normally, she never calls that early. The phone rang and rang before I woke up and rushed out of my room to get it.

I didn't have a chance to worry something was wrong: she blurted out the news as soon as I said hello.

"They put him back in. It's in this morning's paper. They found a gun and it seems that's enough. Listen to this."

Then she read me some of the article, her voice growing excited when she got to the part about how Rick may have violated parole by being in possession of a weapon. That he'd had a car accident seemed irrelevant to her, although I caught some disappointment in her tone when she said he wasn't seriously injured. He could have been, according to the papers. He'd been speeding and he'd plowed right into the side of a building. The only thing that saved him was the airbag in his truck.

The truck sustained thousands of dollars' worth of damage.

The paper mentioned that it only had nine hundred miles on it, nearly brand new.

"Is he in the hospital?" I whispered, as I poured Willie his juice. He was up too now, sitting in his booster seat, eating Cheerios out of the box. His eyes looked bigger and softer than usual. Rick's eyes.

"Weren't you listening? He only got a concussion and a few scratches. He was released from Liberty Hospital yesterday afternoon and they took him straight to jail."

"For how long?"

"It doesn't say. Not long enough, I'm sure. Unless they get him for something else. Whatever he was doing before he ran into that wall."

"When did it happen?"

"Sunday night. I already told you that."

She also told me it happened in Lewisville, but she didn't say where. When I asked her, she said, "Let me see." She took a drink of something, probably her usual coffee. "Oh, here it is. You remember that old schoolhouse over on the west side? Right past the park? That's what he hit, the side of that old schoolhouse. It's a wonder it didn't collapse. It's got to be fifty years old."

My mouth had gone dry; it was difficult to talk. I mumbled that I'd call later and hung up the phone.

Sunday night. The same night he came here. He must have gone straight back from Omaha. Maybe he stopped at his apartment first, or maybe he drove right to it.

The old abandoned schoolhouse. Of course I remembered

that place. Rick used to go there when he was a kid to escape his mom's drinking. He told me that as we were driving there one night, a few weeks after we met. He also told me it was special to him.

"I forgot what a dump it is," he said, when we were standing inside what had been the first-grade classroom. "I haven't been here for years."

He was holding a flashlight, shining it around the room. The dusty alphabet banner was still tacked above the chalkboard. There were a few broken desks scattered on the right side. And on the left, by the windows, there was a mattress covered with a tattered blanket, and next to it, a pile of empty beer cans. "I found that mattress in the trash," he said. "The beer I used to steal from Mom's boyfriends."

It was a dump, no question, and yet it seemed romantic to me. It reminded me of the bombed-out places where couples hide out together in war movies. I could imagine fixing it up and the two of us staying here forever. We'd put flowers in every room. We'd write sweet notes to each other on the chalkboard every morning.

When I told Rick I liked this place, he squeezed my hand. "I've never brought anybody here before. I knew you'd understand."

After a while, he went over to the corner by the mattress and pulled out two candle ends. He lit them and put them on the windowsill. Then he sat down on the mattress and motioned for me to sit next to him.

I walked over slowly and sat on the edge of the mattress,

hugging my knees to my chest. I had on my heavy jacket, but it was still freezing. It was the end of November; it had been snowing on and off all day.

Rick planned to have sex here, tonight. He hadn't said so, but I knew. The last time we were together, he'd said he couldn't wait much longer. This was why he'd brought me to this place that was so special to him.

He knew I was a virgin. He could tell I was nervous. He scooted closer, put his arm around me, and kissed my cheek. "I'll be gentle," he said quietly, as he unzipped my jacket. It was so cold I could see his breath. "I won't hurt you, Patty, I promise."

It wasn't as passionate as it would be later, but it was nice. He tried to be gentle; he took his time, and the pain was short-lived and no worse than a pinch. And most important, he wasn't disappointed with my body, my inexperience, or anything about me. That was what I'd really been nervous about.

Afterwards, when we were lying under the ratty blanket, our legs and arms twisted together to keep warm, he explained why he'd wanted to do it in the schoolhouse rather than in his apartment.

"When I was a stupid kid, I used to flop on this mattress and dream I had a girl beside me. She was older, fourteen, fifteen. She had long blond hair and gray eyes. And she had a gorgeous body. I could tell just by looking at her that she would feel so soft. I didn't want to have sex with her, I just wanted to touch her. I thought if I could just touch her once, she'd become real."

He paused and placed his little finger on the mole next to my eyebrow. When he spoke again, his voice sounded small. "It's true. You're real."

I lifted myself up on my elbow and smiled. In the candlelight, I thought I could see in his face how he would have looked as a kid.

All the rumors about him seemed ridiculous to me now. We'd been together every day since we met at the baseball field, and he never had any drugs, not even weed. And a bad guy wouldn't take me to this schoolhouse. A bad guy wouldn't look as vulnerable as Rick did lying on the mattress, telling me that he'd dreamed of this moment when he was a kid.

For weeks after that night, Rick called me his "real girl." And later, he still said it sometimes—usually when he'd done something wrong and wanted me to forgive him.

The last time was only a few weeks before he was arrested. It was a Sunday in May, but it was unusually hot and so sticky the air itself felt dirty. For over two hours, I'd sat outside Zeb's ugly shack, melting into the vinyl seat of the Lincoln, waiting for Rick to finish an important "meeting," only to walk in and discover Zeb asleep on the floor and Rick sitting on a metal kitchen chair, snorting lines of coke off a TV guide with Karen, a stripper friend of theirs, on his lap. And the window air conditioner was on full blast. It was so cold I felt goose bumps poking out on my damp, sweaty legs.

By the time he caught up with me I was already out of Zeb's neighborhood, walking through town. He drove along slowly, disrupting traffic, yelling for me to get in the car.

Finally he parked the Lincoln in front of the dry cleaner and jumped out and blocked the sidewalk.

"Get out of the way."

"Come on, Patty. You know how I feel about the slut. I was just—"

"Get out of the way!"

He did, and I walked on. But before I got far, I heard him. "Real girl, I need you. Real girl, don't leave me."

He was loud; it sounded ridiculous; people were staring at him. I used this as an excuse to turn back and tell him to be quiet. But when he put his arms around me, I didn't pull away. He muttered an apology and whispered, "Don't make me go back there. Don't make me be like I was, alone in that school-room, only dreaming of having this. Of having you."

After a moment, I walked to the car and got in. And a little while later, I told him I forgave him.

All those years with Mama had turned me into someone who could forgive almost anything. It wasn't about being good or kind; it was about survival. Forgiveness allowed me to put the past aside and tell myself each night that things would be different tomorrow. Forgiveness let me separate out the bad thing that happened from the person who'd made it happen— and this way, the person could remain in my heart and mind, and in my life.

I always forgave Rick; I didn't even have to try. Even when I was standing on the railing of the Lewisville River Bridge, the night I almost killed myself, I forgave him.

I haven't thought about that night in years. But this week is different. This week, it's just one of the memories I've had. It's as if Mama's phone call, and what Rick did, have broken down all my defenses, erased all the distance I've tried so hard to put between my life now and my life then.

I don't want to think about the schoolhouse. I don't want to think about that afternoon outside Zeb's. And most of all, I don't want to think about what I felt, who I was, that night on the bridge.

It was the worst night of my life. Even thinking about it now makes me feel like I'm becoming nothing again.

I was up on the railing. Rick was below me, holding out his hand. "Goddammit, Patty, cut this out! You know I didn't mean all that shit!"

The night was so quiet. I could hear the water rushing below me. All I wanted was to let myself fall and be sur- rounded by that water. I thought it would feel soft, like the blanket one of the neighbors quilted for me after Daddy died. I thought it would cover me up, let me hide in it forever. I didn't want to hide from Rick; I wanted to hide from my own mind. My mind was screaming at me. My mind was calling me names: slut, whore, nothing.

We'd just come from a party. It was all older people, his friends. Until after midnight, he talked to guys and flirted with other women while I sat in a chair in the corner, next to the blasting stereo, and pretended I didn't care. But then he came over and knelt down beside me and mouthed the words, "Are you all right?"

His eyes looked so tender. I nodded, and he put his hand

on my face. I turned my lips to his palm and kissed it. He reached up and traced the outline of my eyes with his other hand. Then he smiled and kissed me.

We were shielded by the music. Neither one of us knew the CD was about to end. Neither one of us knew that when it did, the room would grow silent and everybody would glance in the direction of the stereo. Everybody would see him on his knees in front of his little teenage girlfriend.

Rick usually didn't bring me to these parties. He said they were bullshit; he said I'd be bored. Maybe he meant it, but I knew there was another reason. He didn't want them to see how he was with me. He thought it would make him look weak.

When he realized everyone was looking at him, his face grew confused, but only for a second or two. He stood up and laughed. "What is it?" His voice was loud. "Are you horny?" He grabbed his crotch. "Do you need some of this?"

I felt tears spring to my eyes.

I know Rick saw those tears. But he'd been speeding for hours. And he was with his friends. He couldn't deal with a blubbering girl.

Three guys were leaning against the wall not five feet away. They laughed too, and the whole room laughed after one of them said, "If she needs it, man, better give it to her."

He jerked me to a standing position. My arms and legs felt weak and floppy, like I'd turned into a rag doll. And then he pulled my body against his, and started feeling me up right in front of everybody.

I was more embarrassed than I'd ever been in my life. I

could feel their stares, hear their snickers. "Go for it." "She wants it, man."

After a while, I closed my eyes. I had to stop the tears and I couldn't bear to look at him. I was too stunned to object when he lifted up my blouse. He turned me around so no one could see my breasts as he put his mouth on them, but everyone knew what he was doing. He was smacking his lips.

When he let me go suddenly, I stumbled and fell against him. He threw his arm around my shoulders. "You want me to take you in the bedroom now?"

I had to get away from all those eyes. I mumbled yes, and everybody laughed.

"She loves it," he said, grinning, as he led me to the hall. "Jesus, she wears me out."

As soon as he shut the door behind us, he slumped down on the bed and let out a curse. He was sorry, I knew he was. But it was too late; he'd cut my heart to pieces.

I yanked off my blouse and pulled my pants down to my knees.

"Patty, what are you—"

"Let's go." I fell backwards on the bed next to him. My voice was a spit. "This is what you want, right?"

"Baby, come on."

"You told all those people I was horny. You told all those people I need this." I put my hand on his crotch. "What's the matter, Rick? Don't you want to give me what I need?"

His objections grew weaker and weaker as I pressed my breasts against his cheeks, stroked him with my fingers.

"This is what you want," I said, no longer a question. His breathing had become punctuated by groans. As I climbed on top of him, I felt a cold emptiness that seemed like power. I could be this girl. It wasn't that bad.

But when it was over, I wanted to die. And on the drive home, when Rick paused at the stop sign right before the bridge, I jumped out of the Lincoln and climbed up the metal rail. I couldn't stand the screaming anymore. The words were the same ones Mama yelled at me. Slut. Whore. Won't amount to nothing.

"Patty, for chrissakes, come here! This is dangerous!"

He was still holding out his hand, inching towards me. I climbed up higher, onto a flat concrete post, and looked down. It was so dark I couldn't see the water, but I could see shapes of rocks protruding along the banks.

I lifted my arms and told myself it would be like diving off the high dive but better. It was probably three hundred feet down. I would go so fast it would be like flying. And then the water would hold me in its arms, make me clean. The water wouldn't let go, ever.

Rick was moving to climb up too. I warned him not to come near or I'd have to do it now. I was almost ready, but I wanted to stay up here for another moment, listen to the music of the water moving below me.

He fell down on his knees and started punching his chest with his fists. And screaming. Over and over, the same words. "Oh God, please help me. Patty, please, please, forgive me."

After a while, I realized his screams were drowning out the ones in my mind. I could feel the wind blowing against my face, opening my eyes. I looked around, wondering why I couldn't find the moon. It had been there earlier. I remembered seeing it, full and brighter than I'd ever remembered, when Rick and I were on the way to the party.

I lost track of where I was. I took a step, still looking up, trying to find the moon, and I slipped off the concrete post. I felt a sharp pain as my leg hit the railing below but I was too stunned to cry out. I was dangling over the water; my hands were grasping for something to hold on to but there was nothing but air. My leg was twisted in the railing but it was slipping; the skin on my kneecap was ripping across the metal inch by inch.

I was seconds away from plunging into the river, but then Rick's hands were on my legs, dragging me back. My knee was gushing blood; I could feel the warm wetness running down my leg and into my shoe. But I didn't feel the pain. He had me in his lap; he was crying and rocking me. He was kissing my hair, murmuring, "I could have lost you. Christ, Patty. You could have died."

I had to have fifteen stitches. Rick told the emergency room doctor he was my brother so he could sign the consent form. They told me not to put weight on the leg for twenty-four hours. I clung to Rick's neck as he carried me to the car. He promised he wouldn't leave me alone until I was better.

For the past few months, Rick had been gone more than he was home—and I was so lonely. I'd left high school years ago,

I didn't have any friends, I didn't even know anybody my own age. I called Mama every few days, trying to catch her sober. Sometimes I tried to talk to her about curtains and rugs and recipes, but she knew next to nothing about any of this, nor did she seem to care. One time she said it was laughable for me to act like I was making a normal house when I was living with a drug dealer. I stopped calling for a while then. I could feel stupid and ridiculous all by myself; I didn't need her for that.

Rick did stay with me the entire week after that night I fell. He fed me and rented me movies and gave me pain pills—not the ones the doctor prescribed but other ones, better ones, he said. The wound on my knee got infected though. Neither Rick nor I remembered to put on the antibiotic cream and change the bandage every day. I went by myself to the emergency room the next time. The doctor who treated me seemed annoyed. He said the price of my carelessness would be a nasty scar.

The scar is as long as my kneecap, but it isn't that bad. It looks like a half-moon, that's what Irene said. I remember Willie used to pat it with his chubby hand when he was a baby. When he could say Mama (his second word; his first was choo-choo), he would pat the scar and babble Mama, Mama, Mama. It cracked me up. I wondered if he thought the scar was Mama.

I was lucky. I came so close to falling in the river. So close to dying and never having Willie.

Of course it wasn't Rick's fault that I climbed up on the bridge or that I fell. It wasn't his fault that I needed him so much. He loved me, I was sure of it. I needed that love. And it wasn't all bad. The good parts more than made up for the bad.

Even this week, most of the memories I've had have been good. When I was getting dressed for the gig on Wednesday night, I flashed to the afternoon when Rick gave me my first present: eighteen pairs of socks, all in different, bright colors, some crew, some knee-high. It was only a few days after we met, but he'd already noticed how often I was stooped over, tugging on the worn-out elastic of my old ones. He said that if my mother wouldn't give me money for clothes, he would. And last night between sets, when a table of customers insisted on buying me a beer and telling me how talented I was, I found myself thinking about when Rick first said the same thing. I was singing in the shower at our apartment; I thought he was watching television. When I turned the water off and pulled back the curtain, I saw him leaning against the sink. I felt stupid, until he said, "You know what? You have a beautiful voice." He handed me a towel and smiled. "You sound like an angel."

And just now, listening to the storm, I've remembered something else. I can't believe I'd forgotten this. I used to think it was the nicest thing anybody ever did for me.

We'd only been living together for a few weeks. We were still in the crummy apartment, the one with no dishwasher and no air-conditioning, but I loved it there. I knew he was dealing, but there was no bag of guns in the closet yet, no weird phone calls at all hours, no constant visits from his scary friends. We woke up every morning holding each other. We got to eat whenever we wanted, breakfast, lunch, and dinner, mostly at Denny's. We went there so often I had their menu memorized.

One Friday night, we were lying in bed, talking about our families. Rick told me that when his dad left, he was nine and so angry he smashed the mirror in his bedroom with his bare hands. Then he said I must have been really torn up when my dad died. At first, I told him I didn't remember, but finally I admitted the truth. It was my big secret then. I hadn't cried at all—not right after the accident, not at the funeral, not a month later or a year later, or seven years later. Never.

I told him I felt guilty, but I also figured it made sense. It really wasn't my loss, I said, it was Mama's. And I reminded him of what Mama said about Daddy not really wanting me. Maybe Daddy and I didn't have much of a relationship anyway.

Rick insisted on driving out to the cemetery, even though it was after midnight.

"He was your dad." Rick was shaking my shoulders. "You have a right to miss him."

We were kneeling on the grass by the grave. After a while, he stuck my hand on the cold stone, forced my fingers over the engraved letters. "Feel it. It says Beloved Father of Patty. That's you. You were his daughter. This isn't about your mom."

I'd been to this cemetery countless times before, but I'd always just stood there while Mama wailed and prayed and begged God to bring him back. I'd never felt anything except embarrassment. And I didn't want to feel anything—then or now. I jerked my hand away and yelled that he shouldn't have brought me here, it was heartless. But then he grabbed me in his arms and kept saying, "Your dad is dead," until finally I broke down.

For what seemed like an hour, we sat in the damp grass of the cemetery while I sobbed until my throat ached and my eyes felt as raw and sore as if I'd rubbed them in salt. I remembered Daddy, and even though he was away from home a lot, I remembered us doing things together. I helped him plant that garden of daffodils in the photo Mama loved so much. He was the one who used to call me his princess. He taught me how to ride a bike and took me fishing and even built me a beautiful dollhouse. We painted the dollhouse together. Pink with white shutters. A little wooden couch and little wooden chairs. Three little wooden beds: one for the mom doll, one for the dad, and one for the girl.

I was crying because I missed Daddy, but that wasn't all. For the first time, I understood that my childhood had died with him. I'd lost the normal kid I had been, the girl who didn't have guilty secrets, who wasn't afraid to cry because she had nothing to cry about.

When Daddy fell off the roof that day, I was talking to him. I was jumping rope and talking about nothing. And he was listening to me. I remembered him smiling at something I said only a few minutes before it happened.

I was never sure I was innocent. I wanted to be innocent so badly. I tried to be quieter. Sometimes I'd wish I'd wake up and find my lips grown together, become a perfect plum, no seams.

I wasn't innocent. Daddy was gone and he was never coming back. If I didn't have Rick, I'd have nothing.

"Promise you won't die," I stammered, when I could catch my breath. "Please promise me, Rick."

"I promise," he whispered into my hair. He leaned back and grinned. "You know me, I'm invincible."

He loved me. He said so all the time, and the whole time we were together, I was sure it was true. I was still sure when he came to my hotel room in Kentucky. I absolutely believed that he loved me—until Sunday night in the field, when he chased me like a dog. Held me down. Bruised my wrists, my face, my pelvic bone. Scared me.

I couldn't use the word Irene did. I was afraid of that word; it's so ugly. But I don't have another word for what happened. I can't understand how Rick could do this.

As soon as Mama told me he ran into that wall, I was sure it wasn't an accident. What I didn't know—and still don't—is whether he was punishing himself or trying to tell me he was sorry. More than anything, I wish I didn't care. I wish I wasn't remembering all this. I wish Willie would wake up, so I could stop thinking about Rick.

I stand up and go to the window. The storm is still going strong. On the other side of the street, there's a kids' plastic swimming pool, overturned and snagged on the wheel of a car. The lightning is reflecting off all the standing water: in the depressions in the yards, in the potholes, in the curbs. The gutters are doing what they can, but they can't keep up.

I can't wait until tomorrow, when we leave for Topeka. I hate this trailer park. I hate the swimming pool. I hate that field and that ugly farmhouse. I hate all of Omaha.

But I don't hate Rick. I can't hate him, even though I want to so bad. He held me down and put his hand over my mouth and I wasn't even screaming. I just wanted to tell him about the rock, about my hair. I just wanted to tell him he was hurting me.

He slammed into a brick wall at over seventy miles an hour. He could have died. He's Willie's father. But he raped me—I know Irene is right. And now I feel insane because I can't cry or scream or even get mad. I can't do anything other than walk around in a daze, remembering all this.

After a while, I stumble back to the bed, take the sheets off Willie. It's already getting hot in here. If the power doesn't come back soon, it's going to be unbearable.

Willie's still snoring, still fast asleep, even though the rain is even louder on the roof, and staccato; it sounds like it's mixed with hail. Only his eyes are moving. They're darting back and forth behind his eyelids. He's dreaming. He's too young to talk about his dreams, but I know some of them are bad. I hear him cry out in his sleep.

I worry about him so much, especially this week. I wonder what he made of everything he saw last Sunday. I wonder what he made of Rick.

He only asked about Rick once. It was Thursday afternoon, and out of the blue, he said he wanted the new guy to come back so he could sit in that brand-new truck again.

123

When I didn't respond, he asked if I'd told the new guy not to come back here. I said no, but he stomped his foot and said I did. Then he started crying and whining that I shouldn't have done that. "I wike trucks, Mama! I want to sit in the truck!"

He'd just gotten up from his nap, and he was grouchy. Normally, I distract him, but I couldn't. Luckily, Irene was there; she picked him up and took him out of the room; then she and Harry played with him in the backyard. Fifteen minutes later, he seemed to have forgotten all about it.

But maybe he's dreaming about it now. Dreaming about the brand-new truck that was destroyed by his crazy father.

"Poor buddy," I say, as I brush a lock of hair off his forehead. All he has is me. Even if I'm screwed up, there's no way around it. I'm his family.

I have to get some rest, or at least try. When he wakes up, he'll need hugs and breakfast, talk and happiness.

I lie down and close my eyes. I remind myself that he's only two. Soon enough, he'll forget about the new guy, the truck, this trailer. Soon enough, I'll get my mind right and we'll move forward.

At least we only have two weeks in Topeka. And after that, the summer will be over. We'll go back to Kansas City, where we're booked for September. I'll stay with Mama, because she wants me to and because it's good for Willie to have her in his life, and yeah, because I've never stopped hoping that she and I will find a way to be together that will make it feel like being home.

eight

Hurry up and wait. It's always like that with Fred. His time is valuable, ours isn't, unless we're at a gig.

It's Monday morning, Labor Day no less, and here I am, trapped and pacing Fred's reception area. My plans for today included letting Mama take care of Willie so I could sleep in for the first time in months, driving to the lake for a picnic, and maybe renting a video later, if I could think of a movie Willie would like and Mama could stand. I also thought about hitting the Independence mall, since Mama said they were having a big sidewalk sale. But no matter what we did, I wanted to take it slow, relax. I didn't want to think about anything—not Rick, not work, not my future—and I definitely didn't want to have a meeting with Fred.

When he called on Sunday afternoon, we'd just gotten back from Topeka. Jonathan had dropped Willie and me off at Mama's. I'd barely had time to say hello to her and unpack Willie's toy bag when the phone rang. He said he needed to see me in his office right away, at nine o'clock the next morning.

So I dragged myself out of bed and drove Mama's Ford the forty-five minutes to his office in midtown Kansas City. When I walked into the reception area, it was exactly nine o'clock. Fred was back in his office. I could hear him talking on the phone.

I sat down and thumbed through an old copy of *Rolling Stone*. Then I got up and wandered around the room, looking at the pictures. Fred has framed publicity shots of every band he's been involved with for the last thirty years; they cover the right wall and the back wall from knee level to ceiling. Some of the names are impressive. A few of his groups have appeared on one of the Billboard Lists. One had a platinum record that went on to win a Grammy. A lot of the older pictures are signed. "To Fred, who made it all possible," that kind of thing.

The newer band photos are closest to the door. Irene says that's no coincidence, given Fred's reputation for taking on—and quickly firing—new bands. Ours was taken at a club here last winter. It's a very good picture. Fred paid for a top photographer, who took at least forty shots to get this one. Fred says it's "energized" and "sexy."

On the drive over here, it crossed my mind that Fred was going to bitch me out for something, maybe even fire me. I was a little scared, but more than a little hostile. I don't hate Fred, but I certainly don't trust him anymore. The expensive flowers he sent couldn't make me forget how horrible he was that night I froze at the club.

It's now nine forty-five, and I've just made up my mind. If he doesn't come out of the office by ten, I'm going to leave him a note and go. It's a national holiday. Even garbage workers get the day off—why shouldn't I?

When he finally comes out of his office, it's 9:58, and I'm just about to bolt. He apologizes, claims he didn't know I was waiting. Then he smiles and takes my palm in his like we're old friends. He's wearing a suit and tie on Labor Day. This is typical Fred, but it makes me nervous. I withdraw my hand and ask what's up.

He motions for me to follow him in. He sits down at his desk and points to the chair across from him. "I have some exciting news for you."

I exhale and sit down.

"A few weeks ago, I had a long conversation with Jim Peterson. He is right where I want him now. Eating out of my hand." Fred smiles. "He couldn't say enough about the marvelous Patty Taylor. He expressed his fervent wish for you to play his club forever. He said it would be heaven."

"Thanks." I pause for a moment as a depressing idea crosses my mind. "I hope you're not about to say we're going back to Omaha. To me, heaven doesn't include Peterson's trailer."

Fred laughs loudly. Too loudly. It isn't that funny. "Oh, no," he says. "I'm merely expressing my profound admiration."

I nod as he continues pouring on the compliments. Finally, he sits back and folds his hands. "When I said I would get you into a studio, my dear, I meant it. I have the highest hopes for you. You remind me of Darla, as you know."

I smile. "That's great. I'd like to record something. But we need songs, right? Originals?"

"Of course." He leans across the desk and hands me a picture. "And that's where these young fellows come in."

It's a slick band photo: five guys in tuxedos. I've seen them before. They play a lot of the same places we do. Sometimes the club will still have their promo material up when we unload. They're called Mystery Train. They have two guitar players; one of them, Ron, is also the singer. They're one of Fred's older bands; they've been playing the area for more than ten years. I've heard Carl and Dennis make snide remarks about how little talent they have, but Carl and Dennis say that about all the pop bands.

"Ronald knows I want to record you," Fred says, as he points to a cassette at the top of his in-basket. "He's written these songs because he wants to be part of that."

Fred hands me the tape. "I want you to take it with you. Bear in mind that the keys will be changed. And some of the lyrics are inappropriate for a female singer, but Ronald is aware of the problem. He's promised to have revisions before the first rehearsal tomorrow."

I set the tape on the picture in my lap. My voice sounds as confused as I am. "You're moving me to Mystery Train?"

He laughs. "No, no. Mystery Train as such won't exist anymore. It will still be the Patty Taylor Band."

"You mean, when we go in the studio?"

"Yes, and in general. As of tomorrow, Ronald's band will be backing you up."

I lean forward. "But what about our gig? Aren't we supposed to open at McGlinchey's tomorrow night?"

I know we are; Jonathan told us about this weeks ago. McGlinchey's is one of the best rooms in Kansas City. It's also a good room for us since the owner likes jazz. He has us booked for the entire month of September.

Fred waves his hand. "Tomorrow, this week, isn't so important. The time after Labor Day is very slow in the clubs. I can easily put in a replacement. After that, it depends on how the rehearsals progress. When you're ready, of course I'll put you in. The new Patty Taylor Band will be easy to book anywhere."

I stare at him as it dawns on me what he's saying. "You're firing Jonathan and the other guys? Immediately?"

He smiles. "Your success is what's important, my dear. I've been telling Brewer's quartet that for the last year."

"But they have no idea. I mean, you told them they'd be staying at the Balconies. I was there when you called Jonathan just a few days ago."

The Balconies is an apartment complex Fred owns down by the Plaza. The name is something of a joke among Fred's groups—only the apartments on the top floors have balconies, and those are rented out to regular, paying tenants; the bands are always housed on the bottom two floors—but it's considered the best place to stay because each musician gets a furnished apartment with a small kitchen, a bedroom alcove, even a television.

All of the guys were happy when Fred gave them the news last week. It didn't matter to me because I'd be staying with Mama, but I was glad for Irene. She'd be able to cook whenever she wanted. And, as she kept saying, she wouldn't even have to see the rest of them; she'd have Harry all to herself.

"I'll probably get sick of him," she said, but she was smiling. "Damn, this is good news. If old Fred was here, I'd kiss him."

"Calm down, Patty," Fred is saying. His face hasn't changed but his voice is noticeably cooler. "They are installed in the Balconies as promised. I gave Jonathan the keys yesterday . . . Of course, I can't house them indefinitely, but I plan to give them a week to find other quarters."

A week. Dennis might be okay—his parents live in Kansas City—but what about the rest of them? What about Irene and Harry? They can't afford a deposit on an apartment; they spent all their savings last June, when Irene's Honda had transmission trouble on the way to Little Rock.

I rub my eyes and remind myself it isn't my problem. True, the guys have been nicer lately, but only because they fear losing their "meal ticket." And I was seriously considering asking Fred to find me a new group anyway, like Jonathan suggested. I thought about it constantly while we were in Topeka. Fred is just making it easier. And he's offering me a chance to go into the studio, cut a tape of original songs.

Of course I hadn't decided yet. I was stuck on a few points, the biggest being how I could do any of this without Irene. She's a good friend, and more important, she loves Willie. I love that she's part of his life.

"I should tell you that I have an interested party in California," Fred says. "A record executive at a major label. But I've told him he can't have it exclusively." He smiles. "This demo will be too hot to limit ourselves to the offer of one label."

"Wow," I say. It does sound incredible, and I tell him so. Then I take a deep breath. "Well, how long do I have to make up my mind?"

He laughs—and not a nervous chuckle or a little ha-ha—a full-throated, wide-open, completely amused roar. I blink with surprise, but I cross my arms, wait for him to finish. "I do have a say in who I work with, don't I?"

"Yes," he says lightly. "But I can't imagine you would care."

I force my voice to stay calm, ask why he thinks I wouldn't care. He talks in circles, but the upshot is that I have no experience in the business and I'm in no position to judge what's best for myself. Then he hints that it's very unlikely I could even tell the difference between Ron's band and Jonathan's.

I flash to the storage closet in Omaha, when Fred asked if I could comprehend English. Now I know it's true: he thinks I'm stupid.

"I may be new to this," I say slowly, more than a little fiercely, "but I know one thing. I want to work with good musicians." I look at the wall behind him, so I don't lose my courage. "For your information, I care a lot about what I do."

"Patty, you have to be reasonable. Aren't you forgetting all the difficulties you've had with Jonathan's group?"

"No. But maybe we could work those out, if it was best for the music."

"The music," Fred mutters, as he picks up a silver letter opener and taps it against his desk. I can tell he's getting angry. The corners of his lips are turned down, and his eyes are staring a hole through my forehead. "This is all very charming, my dear, but it's beside the point. Yes, Brewer is extremely talented, but I spoke to him only a month ago and suggested that he write songs you could record. Do you know what he told me?"

I shrug, even though I'm dreading this. Fred smiles. "I believe his exact words were, 'I'd rather lick a toilet bowl.'"

It's not fun to hear, but it's Fred's nonchalant tone that really gets to me. And he looks so smug, leaning back, tapping his letter opener—so absolutely confident of his right to decide everything, tell us all what to do. Yet he will freely admit that he's never played an instrument and can't even carry a tune. All of a sudden, I realize I do hate him. Maybe I've always hated him, since the first day, when he made me model three low-cut gowns in the freezing rehearsal room before he would tell me I had the job.

I sit up straighter and arrange my face in what I hope is a confident expression. "Jonathan and I have been working together for a year. I think I know him a lot better than you do. I'm sure he didn't mean that."

When Fred bursts out in a laugh, I wince, though I know it's true: what I said is ridiculous. Yet I can't back down. I want to, I know I should, but my mouth won't cooperate and form the words. Instead, I find myself blurting out that I won't make up my mind about Mystery Train until I've had a chance to confer with Jonathan and the rest of my current group.

He's obviously surprised, but no more so than I am. We both sit quietly for a moment; then he shakes his head and says he'll give me until tomorrow.

I put Ron's tape back on his desk; he tells me to take it. He smiles coldly and says he's sure I'll need it soon, adding in a low voice, "Unless I lose interest in this project."

Now I'm nervous. I say that I really appreciate everything he's done, but he waves me off and picks up the phone.

I have to force myself not to run out of his office. As I slump down in the Ford, I wonder if I really am losing my mind. What on earth have I just done? Why did I antagonize Fred when he was finally giving me my big chance?

I take deep breaths, tell myself it's no problem, I can fix it tomorrow. All I'll need to do is grovel a little: admit he was right, apologize for doubting him, and thank him sincerely for the opportunity to work with Mystery Train. But what if my mouth refuses to cooperate, like it did today? What then?

Something has definitely gone wrong with me. Fred is my boss, the one person I need on my side the most, and I've just defied him. "You really screwed up this time," I say to my reflection in the rearview mirror. "You're such a stupid idiot."

My reflection won't cooperate either. My lips are flat, unmoved; my eyes are still defiant.

"Go ahead, ruin your life," I say to the face in the mirror. Then it hits me how ridiculous this is, sitting in an empty parking lot, talking to myself. I start the Ford.

By the time I get to Mama's, I have myself pretty much convinced that there is no point in talking to Jonathan anyway. I feel very sorry for Irene and a little sorry for the rest of them, but I can't imagine how to change it. Fred wants me in the studio, I want to be in the studio, and Jonathan won't write for me. What is there to discuss?

Willie has already had lunch; the dirty dishes are sitting on the kitchen table. I peek into my bedroom, where Mama is trying to rock him to sleep. When she sees me, she signals with her hand for me to be quiet. I think it's too early for his nap, but I don't interrupt. I know Mama loves to rock him.

I plop down on the couch before I remember the Mystery Train tape in my purse. My Walkman is in my room, but Mama has an old tape player in the kitchen. I'll have to keep the volume low; at least I can get a feel for what Ron has written.

The voice on the tape sounds friendly. I assume Ron is talking to Fred. "We call this first song 'Push Over.' Hope you like it."

It starts with a few loud guitar chords. Then the bass comes in, thumping a two-note line to a pounding drum beat. I don't hear the keyboard player until Ron starts to sing. "I push you/ You push me/ Dealers push drugs/ Waves push dolphins out to sea/ It's the land of the push over, honey/ What I want from you/ Be my little push over/ Let me push all over you."

The words are silly but catchy enough. The music, though, is terrible. There's almost no melody; it sounds like Ron is reciting a cheer for a football team. Or maybe he thinks he's rapping. I remember Carl saying Mystery Train loved rap; the rumor is they even tried a modified rap version of Barry Manilow's "Mandy."

The second tune is better, but still nowhere close to good. It's a slow song, so at least there's a melody, but the refrain is as monotonous as "Row, Row, Row Your Boat." And this time the lyrics are beyond silly; they make no sense. They keep repeating, "Come down to my cabin/ The weekend's meant for two/ Over in Havana/ I like to see it through." But the verses have nothing to do with Cuba or traveling—unless the bit about some girl's "banana yellow pants" is supposed to make us think of Havana.

I tell myself I'm being too harsh. After all, a lot of the songs we do have lyrics that are just as lame. If I can sing "Manic Monday" and "Like a Virgin," I can certainly do these.

By the fifth song, I've realized what the problem is. I've been spoiled by my band. Even when we do something as basic as "Manic Monday," we mess with it a little: add riffs that weren't in the original song, throw in an extra stop or push past the stops already there, vary the tempo of the refrains. Of course by "we" I mean Jonathan. He does all our arranging.

Ron's songs are average pop tunes. Nothing wrong with

them, nothing great about them either. I guess I should be flattered. Fred plans to shell out big bucks for a studio; he's obviously thinking that I'll add the spark to make the record company people pay attention.

I'm wondering if I'm up to the task when Mama comes into the kitchen. She doesn't have Willie and she's smiling with her nap success. I tell her I'm amazed she got him down this early. I don't say I'm sure he won't sleep more than a half hour; he never does if he naps before two.

She picks up Willie's half-empty yogurt cup and throws it in the trash, but I tell her to sit down. I'll clean up. Ron's tape is still playing, but I'm not paying attention, I'm looking at her. Every time I come home, I'm surprised by how old she seems. Her hair has been gray for years, but it's only recently that the skin on her face seems to have crumpled like a tissue. Even her movements are cautious now, like she can't trust her own body. She's only fifty-one, but she's led a hard life. Her doctor has told her many times that if she hadn't stopped drinking, she'd be dead from liver damage.

When I'm finished with the dishes, I sit down across from her, and she lights a cigarette. I wish she would stop smoking too, but I haven't been able to persuade her.

Ron is droning on about a tree that fell in the forest and nobody heard it crash. Nobody cares either, I think, as I hit the stop button.

"I thought I might get the hose out this afternoon," she says, moving the ashtray by her elbow. "It's pretty hot. Willie might like to water the bushes for me."

"I'm sure he would." I smile. "Before you hand him the hose, better make sure all the windows are closed."

She points at the tape recorder. "What was that?"

"Nothing." I rub my eyes. "One of Fred's bands."

I look away from her, let my eyes wander to the back window. The yellow swing she hung for Willie looks crooked. I make a mental note to check the chains, make sure she counted off the same number of metal links on the left and the right.

After a moment, she takes a long drag. "You upset about something?"

"I'm just tired."

We haven't been talking much since I came home. She keeps bringing up Rick, and I don't know what to say. She tried to talk about him almost as soon as I walked in the door, and then again last night after Willie went to bed, and then again this morning over coffee. The first time, I told her, "Come on, Mama, I just got home." The next time, I said, "Can't we forget about him for a while?" And today, I said, "You know I have to meet Fred in an hour. Cut me a break, okay? Don't dredge all this up now."

What she wants is simple enough. I'm supposed to listen while she talks about how nervous she is. And then I'm supposed to reassure her that everything will be all right, like I always have before.

It's simple, but I just can't do it. Not after Omaha.

"What happened to all the pictures of Daddy?" I ask, a minute later. I'm thinking I've hit on a topic she'll like. I noticed yesterday that the photos weren't on the coffee table, where they always are. I figured she was having them reframed, cleaned, something.

"I packed them up, put them in the basement."

"Really?" I can't hide my surprise.

She shrugs. "Willie likes to do his puzzles and coloring on the table. Now he's got some room to spread out."

"Sounds good," I manage, but I have to look away from her. Is it possible she doesn't remember the fight we had about this?

I was seven or eight, and I had a friend over for the first time in months. Everyone wanted to play with Alison because she had dozens and dozens of Barbie dolls. When she suggested using the coffee table for the Barbie doll party, I told her no, but then she said it was creepy to have all these pictures of a dead guy around anyway.

"Your house is weird," she concluded.

I was afraid she'd tell the whole school, so I carefully moved all the pictures of Daddy to the kitchen. I planned to move them back before Mama got home from work, but I was having too much fun. Alison had every Barbie accessory imaginable. Just getting all the dolls dressed for the party had taken hours. I'd lost track of time.

Mama walked in the door and told Alison to leave. Just like that. "Go home, little girl," she said, and Alison started crying.

"You're mean," I said, when Alison was gone and Mama was putting the pictures back on the coffee table. I was holding a tiny pink Barbie shoe that Alison had left behind. I was surprised she hadn't left more things; she'd been in such a rush to get away from my mother.

"Go to your room," Mama said. "Right now."

I should have gone, but I was too mad. I threw the little shoe at her and repeated that she was mean. I told her that every girl in school had a nicer mother than I did.

Then she started crying loudly, just like Alison had. She was crying as she shoved me into my room and shut the door. She was crying as she pushed the heavy cedar chest in front of the door, the way she always did, so I couldn't get out.

I couldn't stop saying it though. "You're mean," I said through the walls. "You're mean," I yelled, when I realized she'd turned on the TV. "You're mean," I said, over and over, until I was dizzy and hoarse and half crazy.

The click of her lighter startles me back to now.

"You sure you're not upset about something?" she says.

I shake my head, and remind myself to focus on the important thing here. She packed up all the pictures of Daddy. I can hardly believe it. Maybe she's ready to move on with her life, finally. And all because she wants Willie to have a place to play.

No question about it, my little boy is doing her a world of good.

When he wakes up from his nap, she insists on getting him. I figure he'll yell for me anyway, but he doesn't. A few minutes later, they come into the kitchen holding hands. He tells me Granny promised to give him a peanut butter cookie.

He's grinning like he's getting away with something. Normally, I make him eat grapes for his afternoon snack.

"You little goofball," I say, and smile. "Your granny sure is spoiling you."

He giggles and stuffs half the cookie into his mouth before he says Granny gave him a present today.

"He was tickled pink," Mama tells me, as Willie dashes into his room to get it. "He must have played with it for over an hour."

When he comes back, he's lugging a black Casio synthesizer that's almost as big as he is. It isn't full size like Jonathan's, but it isn't a toy either.

"You shouldn't have spent this kind of money, Mama. It's not even his birthday."

"I got it at a garage sale down the street. It was only fifteen dollars."

"But still. He's only two. He doesn't need—"

Willie is yelling. He has the keyboard on the floor and he's kneeling over it. He wants me to listen.

I'm surprised he knows how to turn it on. I'm even more surprised when he says, "Jingle Bells," and pushes a button and it plays "Jingle Bells." He plays along with it, hitting random notes with one finger and then taking his whole fist and pushing down five or six keys. When he's finished, I clap and whistle and he's beaming. Then he says, "I sound like Jonathan?" and I tell him yes, he's a good little musician.

"He's been asking me that all morning," Mama says. She glances at Willie but he's hitting buttons, not paying attention. She laughs and whispers, "He even asked me if he looked like Jonathan."

"What did you say?"

"I said yes."

I laugh. "You lied to an innocent kid? How could you, Mama?"

She frowns and crosses her arms. I tell her to lighten up, I was only teasing, but she mutters, "Say what you want, I'd sure rather that boy want to look like Jonathan than look like—"

"Stop," I whisper, nodding at Willie. "I don't want him to hear this."

"Now you're defending that man?"

"No, but Willie does look like him. You know it. And I'm not going to let you imply there's something wrong with that."

I walk over to Willie and sit down on the floor. Out of the corner of my eye, I see Mama stomp out of the room. I know I should follow her and apologize, but I'm not sorry.

Willie is telling me what the buttons do. Then he says he's going to be in my band when he grows up. I smile. "You'll be my keyboard player."

"Me and Jonathan. I sit with him on the big stage."

"Sure, buddy," I say, patting his back.

All morning, I've been forcing myself not to think about how much Willie likes the guys. Even if they don't deserve his affection, it's real and it's understandable: he's known them for almost half his life.

This is another reason Fred's plan is depressing: Willie will have to adjust to a whole new group. Maybe Ron's band will be nicer to him, but I doubt it. If anything, they'll probably resent being turned into my backup band after all those years as Mystery Train, and take it out on my son.

141

I tell myself I have no choice, make the best of it. About an hour later, I listen to the rest of the tape and try to convince myself it's not that bad. And then, while I'm eating a cheese sandwich, I run through all the reasons I wanted to leave Jonathan's band. But it doesn't work; I'm still depressed. Finally, around four thirty, I ask Mama if I can use her car again. I have to talk to Jonathan.

She says yes, and I thank her. I'm digging in my purse, trying to find the car keys, when I realize she's staring at me.

I know she wants to say something. We haven't spoken more than a few words to each other all afternoon.

"Watch yourself," she says, in an ominous voice.

"I will."

"I mean it, Patty Ann. This is the first time you've been home since he got out of jail last June."

"I know."

"And if that parole violation didn't stick, he's back in Lewisville, only thirty miles from—"

"Okay."

"He could show up any time. He could be out there waiting right now, for all you know. You can't just—"

"You think I don't know this?" I snap my purse closed. "God, Mama, I'm not stupid!"

I start to turn around, but then I catch a glimpse of her face. She looks both humiliated and confused, like a little kid whose parents have yelled at him for something he can't even comprehend.

After a moment, I take a deep breath, tell her I'm sorry.

And then I say the rest. I'll be super careful. Don't worry. I can handle this. Everything will be fine.

It works. Her shoulders loosen, her mouth relaxes into a weak smile, as she says she's probably being silly. It's only been three weeks. He had a gun. Of course he's still in jail, right?

"Right," I tell her. And then I force a smile, give her another confident "Don't worry," before I blow Willie a kiss and hurry out the door.

"Get gas," she yells to my back.

I nod, put it on my list. Get gas, be careful, talk to Jonathan. Oh, and make a decision that could affect my entire future—if I even have a future, after the way I acted with Fred. Some holiday.

nine

I wish I could call him first, but I don't know his number over at the Balconies. I don't even know which apartment he's in, but that turns out not to be a problem. As soon as I walk in the carpeted front entrance hall, I hear his piano. It's a tune I've never heard, but it's unmistakably Jonathan, and I follow the sound to the back of the building, apartment 1C.

I knock three times before the music stops. Even then he doesn't come to the door, he just yells, "It's open," and goes back to playing.

When I walk in, I have to be careful where I step. The living room is sparsely furnished and hotel generic, but the floor is cluttered with his equipment, sheet music, fake books and paperbacks, CDs. He's unpacked the essentials, which don't seem to include his clothes. He's still wearing the blue-and-green-striped T-shirt he had on yesterday.

The Fender Rhodes is set up facing the window. I'm about four feet behind him; he still hasn't turned around, when he says, "Check this out."

I'm sure he thinks I'm one of the guys, but I don't correct him. I walk to the couch, sit down, cross my legs. The song he's playing is unusual, even for him. The chords are loud, rich, almost too bright, but the melody is sparse and more melancholy than any piece of his I've ever heard. The combined effect is weirdly haunting, like the background of a dream.

When the last chord fades, it takes me a minute to remember where I am. He rubs his hands together and says, "Did you catch that key change?" before he spins around on his black stool and says, "Oh." His voice is surprised but not unfriendly. "Patty. What are you doing here?"

I tell him I need to talk about something; then I take a breath. "That piece you just did. It's new, isn't it?"

He nods. "I've been working on it for the last few weeks." He leans his elbows on the edge of the piano. "Did you like it?"

"Yes. It's really different."

"Um, I suppose I should offer you something. I don't have any food, but I have Pepsi and beer."

"Pepsi sounds good."

"Coming right up."

When he disappears through a doorway on the right side of the room, I stand up and walk to the window. It's a nice view: the back of the apartment faces Brush Creek. I hear him cursing the ice cube tray, then the slamming of the refrigerator door. When he walks back in, he's holding a half-full glass of soda, like he was in such a rush he couldn't wait for the foam to go down.

It flickers across my mind that he's in a hurry to get me out of here, but after he hands me the soda, he asks if I want to listen to the rest of the piece. "There are three movements," he explains. "What you heard was the middle section. It sounds better in context."

I say, "Okay," and he sits down at the Rhodes, adjusts a few knobs.

"There may be some rough spots." He glances at the wall behind me. "I've never played this for anyone before."

I'm very surprised and more than a little pleased. He's never asked me to listen to one of his songs.

I wish I was back on the couch, but he's already playing; I don't want to move and distract him. The opening is nothing like I expected: it's confident, almost happy. When he asks if I notice the mood is different, I say, "Of course."

"It's this chord progression. It's all dominant sevenths." He plays another few bars. "But when the right hand comes in with the melody, the left hand starts to change. It's not minor, but it's augmented sevenths. It sounds much less certain."

He plays for a long time without speaking. After a while, I'm leaning against the wall, engrossed in the music. When I realize he's back to the part I've heard before, I'm surprised. The sparse melody is so different from the upbeat first part, but it fits perfectly. I don't know how he did it, but it feels like this melancholy was there all along, a part of the happiness, even though you couldn't hear it before.

We're up to the third movement, when he shouts, "All right. Can you hear the chords becoming responsive?"

I have to shout too. This part is very loud. "I'm not sure."

"What I mean is, do they seem to be supporting the right hand?"

"I think so. I mean, they seem sadder now too."

"Exactly. They're not fighting the melody anymore; they're cooperating, giving it more of a voice. It's not simply a harmonic resolution though. I think of it as a deeper resolution, a movement toward compassion."

It seems true. The last few bars are so full and rich that the silence when he finishes is painful, like waking up from a dream of color into a world of only gray.

For more than a minute, neither one of us speaks. Then he turns off the Rhodes and crosses his arms. "What did you think?"

"I've never heard anything like it," I begin. I don't want to gush, but I can't stop myself. "It was wonderful, Jonathan. So beautiful. All those different feelings, like listening to the music of an entire life."

"Thanks," he says calmly, but then he smiles.

He has a nice smile; I've noticed that before, watching him with other people. His face is too pale, his nose is a little bit sharp, but his smile is just right. And right now, his blue eyes look serious, sensitive, and not at all sarcastic. No trace of boredom. No attempt to be cool.

I can't believe I was dreading this visit. We're getting along so well.

Of course I still haven't mentioned the problem I came to discuss. When I remind him we need to talk, he says, "Right," and motions me over to the couch. He pushes some cords out of the way with his foot and sits down on the floor, on the other side of the coffee table.

I have to plunge in and get this over with. I tell him I had a meeting with Fred this morning. I leave out the part about Fred firing them, but I say Fred wants me to record some songs with Mystery Train.

"It's a bad idea," Jonathan says flatly. "I know their leader, Ron Whitburn. He's a hack and a charlatan."

"Their tape isn't very good. But Fred is really putting on the pressure." I force a laugh. "He even claimed you said you'd rather lick a toilet bowl than write for me."

He crosses his hands. His voice is still flat. "I did say that, Patty."

"I figured as much. He said it was a month ago. But I was hoping you'd changed—"

"I refuse to write pop songs. Not for you, not for him, not for anyone."

"But they wouldn't have to be pop. Didn't Fred say they could be jazz, as long as they had crossover potential?"

"Yes." Jonathan rubs his palm against his forehead. "But Fred doesn't understand the problem that presents."

He pauses for a moment, taps his fingers together. "Let's say I agreed. It's not something I've done before, write with lyrics, but it's not impossible. The word crossover is meaningless. It's marketing crap; it has nothing to do with creating art."

His mouth looks like he's just swallowed something so bitter he's resisting the urge to spit. And more important, he seems to have forgotten the topic. He's bitching about Fred: how he always emphasizes the trivial, how he doesn't understand that music is about having something to say, not about promotion and marketing and all that meaningless stuff. At some point, I say, "Fine, forget crossover," to get him to continue.

"All right," he says. "If I wrote these pieces, they would be jazz. They would have to be, because that's what I compose."

"That's okay."

"No, it isn't. I'm supposed to be writing these for you. That's what Fred wants, what you want."

"But Fred likes your music, I think he'd—"

"He would probably go along, yes."

I look at him. "Well, you know I'd go along." I feel a little embarrassed. "I mean, I always like your songs."

"I do appreciate that. The problem is I don't think you'd be capable of singing them."

"What?" I sputter. "You said I wasn't a weak singer."

"For pop. You don't know anything about jazz."

My face is hot, but I snap, "It can't be that hard."

He laughs. "Tell that to Betty Carter. Tell that to Abbey

Lincoln or Shirley Horn. You've never heard of them though, have you?"

"Well no, but—"

"They're jazz singers. And they worked for years to become good. Like Harry and I did, starting when we were kids. Like Carl and Dennis will, if they keep going." He looks at me and shakes his head. "You aren't serious about music, Patty. You have talent, but talent is cheap. You have no devotion, no dedication. To you, this is just a good gig."

I slump into the couch, stare at the wall. I feel miserable, but I can't think of a reply. Even Fred doesn't think I'm serious about music. Apparently, nobody does.

"I'm not saying it's your fault," he says slowly. "You've obviously had a difficult life." He pushes his messy hair back, looks past me. "I realized after what happened in Omaha . . . I can't imagine what it's been like for you."

He's never mentioned this to me before, none of them have, but I've overheard Carl and Dennis talking about it. My "psycho boyfriend," as they refer to Rick. Irene says they have to talk about what happened that night because they're still freaked. Maybe so, but from what I heard, they didn't sound freaked, they sounded amused.

I glance at my hands. "I think I'd better go."

"Are you upset?" He's blinking, confused.

"No." I pause and hook my fingernail in the couch cushion, rip at a loose thread. "I mean, why should I be? I suck, but it's okay. I have a good excuse."

Before he can say anything, the door swings open. Harry

steps inside, says "Hey" to me before he tells Jonathan, "The jam starts at six thirty, man. We need to take off."

"Give me a minute," Jonathan says.

"There's no reason," I say, standing up. "I'm leaving."

By the time he and Harry come out of his apartment, I'm halfway down the hall. They turn the other way, towards the parking lot. Before they disappear, I hear him tell Harry that he can't wait to jam tonight. For a split second, I forget how bad I feel, wonder if he plans to play his beautiful new song. I'm sure the guys will love it.

I'm almost to the front door when I run into Irene. She's been out jogging in Loose Park; she's out of breath, but she manages to say I can't go home until we have a beer.

"I'm not really in the mood," I say, but she takes my wrist and starts pulling me back down the hall. "Come on, kiddo, I haven't seen you for what? Thirty-one hours. It's too weird."

Her and Harry's place is furnished exactly like Jonathan's, but it looks very different. Irene is such a clean freak; she's already unpacked everything. Her beads and silver tools are neatly arranged in baskets on the coffee table. The only evidence that a musician is staying here is Harry's electric bass, propped against the wall by the couch. He must have taken his acoustic to the jam.

Irene says she needs to change out of her sweaty running clothes. When she returns holding two bottles of Coors, I'm staring at the wall. "What are you thinking about?" she says.

"Nothing." It's true. I feel like all my thoughts have been crushed out by what Jonathan said.

We sit on the beige couch and drink while she tells me about an argument she and Harry had last night over who is smarter, Bart or Lisa Simpson on the TV show. "Harry bought the standard line: Lisa is smart because she reads and plays the sax. But that Bart, I said, he's clever. He gets out of any jam 'cause he knows people, he knows the streets. Like me."

Irene is laughing. I laugh too, even though I've almost never seen that show; it's on at the same time I'm putting Willie to bed.

She points to the twenty-inch television across the room and says she and Harry did nothing last night but watch it. "We didn't even have sex." She grins. "Well, not till after the news."

I smile, but when she goes to get another beer, I go back to staring at nothing. "What's the deal, Patty?" she says, as she sits back down. "You look like you lost your last friend." She pauses for a moment, lowers her voice. "You haven't heard from him lately, have you?"

I know she means Rick. I tell her no, he's back in jail. Before she can ask any questions, I say it's a long story; I don't want to get into it right now.

"Okay," she says. "So it must be Jonathan. What did he do this time?"

"I'm not sure," I say. "Nothing, I guess."

I stand up and walk to her window. It faces a popular seafood restaurant. As I watch the couples milling around outside, waiting to hear the hostess call their name for a table, I realize I've never been on a real date. I wonder what it would feel like to get dressed up and go somewhere other than work.

I turn around and look at Irene. "Do you think I'm a good singer?"

"Hell yes." She giggles and purses her lips. "You're better than Darla, my dear."

"For real," I say. "It's important."

"How would I know?" She grins. "I'm just the groupie. But okay, I'll tell you what Harry says. He says you're lucky, 'cause you can succeed without even trying."

"But I do try."

"I'm sure you do, hon. I think what Harry means is you don't work like they do. You know how they're up all night, improving their chops, rehearsing, obsessing. It's everything to them." She smiles. "At this very moment, they're off working and you're here getting drunk with me."

"I'm not getting drunk," I say, but I see her point. I go back to the couch, rub my temples. "It's not all that easy for me. I have a kid, they don't."

"That's true."

"And I'm new at this. Jonathan's been playing for over ten years. Ten years ago I was in grade school."

"That's true too, honey." She looks at me. "But what's this about? Did Brewer say you weren't good?"

I tear at the label of my beer. "You know what? I bet I could sing jazz. All I'd have to do is listen. Fred says I can sing anything."

She laughs. "Listening might help."

"I'm serious here." I wad up the gummy label and stick it

in the empty beer; then I exhale deeply. "At least, I think I am. I want to be serious."

After a minute, I tell her I'm going over there.

"Where?"

"To their jam. I'm going there and tell them I want to sit in and do some jazz."

"Oh honey, it's not just the guys tonight, it's this huge thing at Eliot's sister's farm. Harry said there might be forty or fifty musicians, some of the best jazz players in Kansas City. You know, since the clubs are all closed for Labor Day." Irene pauses. "But Eliot's sister is a singer. I guess you could check her out. She's good; she used to front for Max Adams and his trio."

I've never heard of Max Adams, but Eliot is the guitar player who crashed with the band for a couple of weeks last spring. We were staying in hotel rooms; I rarely saw him. All I remember is that he was always high and always wore sandals, even though it was only fifty degrees. And his clothes were ripped-up rags. Jonathan had to lend him a shirt one night after the club owner complained that Eliot was a bum, scaring off the customers.

"Eliot has a sister with a farm?"

Irene laughs. "You wouldn't know it from meeting him, huh? It's not a farm, farm. It's on thirty acres, but she doesn't have animals or crops, just a big vegetable garden."

I sit up straighter. "Can you show me how to get there?"

"Yeah, I was going over anyway. I told Harry I'd be there around eight." She looks at me. "But are you sure you want to do this?"

"I have to prove to Jonathan that he's wrong." I shrug. "I'm going to listen until I get the hang of it, then get up and sing. Really belt one out."

My voice is confident, even though my stomach is doing flips and my heart is pounding so hard I can feel it against my shirt. But what choice do I have? I can't just let Jonathan tell me I'm not good enough and walk away.

When I call Mama, I'm hoping she'll say she and Willie need me, but she doesn't. She says they're doing fine. There's no way out.

"I'm glad you're coming," Irene says, as we walk out of her apartment. She smiles. "I know you'll pull it off."

I can't smile back; I'm way too nervous. But later, as I'm steering the Ford down a dirt road, trying to keep up with Irene's Honda, I remind myself that this is my chance, I have to take it. I've wanted to be a singer my entire life. I am a singer and a good one too. Tonight, I'll show everyone what I'm made of.

ten

The farm is about ten miles south of Kansas City, outside a suburb called Raytown. The house is so much bigger and nicer than I expected. As we walk in the door, Irene whispers that Eliot's family has money; his father is an investment banker who made a killing in the stock market.

"This place is like a mansion," I tell her.

"Yep." She laughs softly. "Calling this a farm is like calling a millionaire comfortable."

Eliot's sister Lydia doesn't look rich, I think, as Irene introduces us. She has on baggy jeans and a Miles Davis T-shirt, no shoes. She's in her mid-twenties, and she isn't wearing makeup. Her brown hair is cut short and so close to her head it looks like a cap.

Lydia is telling us who's here, but the music is loud; it's hard to hear her. And the names I do catch don't mean anything to me anyway. If Irene didn't have her hand on my arm, I'd probably run back to the Ford. It's stupid, but I'm obsessed with what I'm wearing. I still have on the lime green sundress I wore to Fred's this morning; I didn't have time to change, but also I thought it would be good to be dressed up. Wrong. Every time somebody walks by—always in jeans or tattered shorts—I feel like I'm wearing a neon sign that blinks Outsider.

"There's a spread in the dining room," Lydia shouts. "You hungry?"

Irene shakes her head. "How about you, Patty?"

"No." I feel a little nauseated. It's nerves, but also the smell: the place reeks of weed, tobacco, and patchouli oil. Irene always says that patchouli oil is the musician's all-purpose product because it substitutes for deodorant, aftershave, cologne, even the necessity of a shower.

"I'm going to wander around," I tell them. I'm hoping to find a dark spot close to the music, where I can listen and not be seen.

I wander through room after room, nodding at people I don't know, as the music gets louder. Some of the rooms are almost empty, but others are full of solid, heavy furniture and have walls covered with bookshelves, paintings, thick colorful tapestries hanging from wooden poles. It seems funny that I thought Eliot was so poor he was homeless when he slept on the floor of Jonathan's hotel room in Joplin. I should have

157

known better, since I'd heard Eliot tell Jonathan he'd just gotten back from Paris. In all my time in shelters, I've never met
one homeless person who talked about their time in Paris.

I follow the music until I finally get to the back of the
house, where the jam is taking place. It's an enormous room,
as big as some of the clubs we've played, and it seems even bigger because all the furniture has been pushed against the walls
to make room for the musical equipment. It's so dark I can't
tell how many musicians there are. They're standing all over
the room, facing each other. Those who aren't playing are sitting along the side, leaning against the furniture, smoking cigarettes or joints.

I know Jonathan isn't playing right now. The piano player
has a completely different style—more rhythmic, less melodic—
than Jonathan. When my eyes adjust to the dark, I can see the
drummer and it isn't Dennis. After a minute, I make out
Harry. He's over on the right, playing his acoustic bass. The
guitar player is taking a solo. It's Eliot. He has long red hair;
he's hard to miss.

I'm relieved as I move over to the corner next to a leather
couch. There's so much going on here, no one is going to care
about my dumb dress. I don't know if I'll have the guts to sing,
but I am hoping Lydia will. I want to check it out, see if it's
really as difficult as Jonathan claims. In the meantime, I'm
going to sit back and listen. Maybe I can figure out something
I can use.

The first thing I figure out is that clapping is inappropriate
at this jam. When Eliot's solo ended, I was the only one who

clapped, but not for long. I gave two big claps, then two half-hearted ones, so it would seem like I was only fading out, not suddenly dropping my arms because I'd made a stupid mistake. Clapping is for audiences, but everyone here is part of it: they don't clap, they yell. "Cool." "Damn." "Play it." "Yeah." "Like that." "All right."

After about twenty minutes, Irene plops down next to me and shouts that she hasn't seen any of the guys but Harry. Maybe they left, I suggest, but she says no. Lydia told her they were around here somewhere.

When Lydia comes in, the musicians are paused, discussing what they're going to play next. Eliot sees her, tells her to quit playing hostess and get over here, get busy. She laughs. "I am busy. I'm making sure all these sleazy musicians you invited don't steal anything."

Everybody laughs. Before Lydia leaves, she says she will sing in a little while. "But not 'Satin Doll.' I sang that every night for three years. I vowed never to do it again."

"How about 'Going to Kansas City'?" somebody shouts and the whole room groans. I'm not surprised. Jonathan hates that tune; I've heard him tell the guys that the chord changes are completely uninspired, stupid. Of course it's a popular request in clubs all over Kansas City, so maybe that's why he hates it; maybe that's why they all do. Popular always seems to mean bad.

The music here is good, I know, and I like it, but I don't love it. Even when Jonathan takes over the piano, I still don't love it. He isn't playing his songs, he's playing what Irene tells me are jazz standards. "That's what you need to learn," she says. "The words to one of the standards."

Actually, I realize I already know the words to some of these songs. I've heard them on the radio in the van, when Jonathan tunes in a jazz station. The one they're playing now is called "Body and Soul." I've heard it several times, but only once with a singer. But I remember the words, or at least I'm pretty sure I do. There's no way I could sing it though, not the way they're playing it. Everybody is playing around the tune, over it, under it, and every way they can except straight through it. I can't imagine how a singer could fit in.

When Lydia joins them on the next song, I find out. They play it much straighter. They have her do the verses and the bridge, and then they start taking solos. She doesn't have to do a solo; she doesn't have to do anything but sing the usual words while they back her up. And I do know these words; I can mouth them as she goes along. The song is "When Sunny Gets Blue," and I just heard it yesterday on the way back from Topeka.

She's not a power singer. Her voice is what Fred calls smoky, which means breathy with lots of vibrato. By the end of the song, I realize I don't see what's so great about her. I have a bigger range, better intonation. I'm a better singer; at least, I think I am.

At some point, Irene elbows me in the ribs. "Check out the way Lydia keeps leaning on Jonathan. They used to date when they were in college. The rumor is she still has a crush on him."

"Really?"

"Yeah. And notice how she waited until he was playing before she got up. She definitely has a thing for him."

They do seem to be having a good time together. By the third song, a lot of the other musicians have dropped out: it's just Jonathan, Lydia, Harry, and the drummer I don't know. After Jonathan's solo, Lydia laughs and says, "You're pretty good for a white boy," and the others laugh too. After she finishes the bridge, somebody shouts, "Damn," and Jonathan says, "She's all right for a white girl."

Irene turns to me, asks if I want to hear a joke. Before I can answer she asks if I know how many white jazz players it takes to screw in a lightbulb. I say, "No idea," and she giggles. "There's never enough. Even if you get a thousand of them together, nobody will do it. If they leave the light off, they can pretend they're black."

I smile, but I can't manage a laugh. Lydia's on the verse again and I can hear her going flat on the low note at the end of each bar. I'm better than she is, I'm sure of it now. Yet Jonathan obviously respects her, and he has never respected me, not for one single minute in the year I've worked with him.

Of course she's been to college, like he has. She's probably read all those "fascinating" books he's always telling the guys about. I'm sure she knows all kinds of things, just like his other girlfriend Susan, the one who played chess and wrote poetry.

Irene wants to know if I'm coming along. I was so lost in

thought I didn't realize that the music has stopped, the room is emptying out. "Where?"

"To the dining room. Lydia just announced that she made all this food; everyone has to eat something now or she's going to end this party."

"She's weird," I mumble, and Irene nods. When she stands up, I follow her to the door leading to the dining room.

The house is air-conditioned, but it's warm in here. The dining room connects to a large screened-in porch and Lydia has the glass doors open so that people can fill their plates and go eat at one of the big wicker tables. The crowd around the dining-room buffet is intimidating, and the food looks strange: lots of unidentifiable dips and odd black-purple vegetables, a large bowl of brown gook that looks exactly like mud. Lydia's talking loudly, explaining what each dish is. I hear someone ask where the meat is, and she laughs and calls him a cannibal.

I grab a beer from the ice bucket against the wall and tell Irene I'm going out on the porch. I need some fresh air.

No one is out here yet and it's nice. There are probably a hundred candles sitting on tables and on brass stands along the walls, and in the breeze they're flickering, dancing on the ceiling. I go to the darkest corner, settle in a rocking chair by a wind chime. The noise sounds as soothing as a lullaby.

I'm not sure what time it is, but I know it's late; Willie is obviously in bed. I wish I'd been there to tuck him in. As soon as Irene gets finished eating, I'm going to make up some excuse to leave. This is a waste of time.

"What's this? You all by yourself out here, green dress?"

I look up and see a man standing next to my chair. He's maybe sixty, black, and his voice sounds hoarse like a smoker's, like Mama's. He's not wearing jeans, which makes me like him immediately. He has on gray pants, a bright yellow button-down shirt, and a fancy black hat with a broad rim. When he asks if I mind if he sits at this table near me, I say that would be fine.

He asks my name, and tells me his: Charlie Jubar. When I ask him what he plays, he says, "Alto," and laughs softly. "I guess it's gotta be alto if your mama gives you the same name as the Bird."

He's eating deviled eggs and a pastry dish I don't recognize. After he takes a few bites, he says, "And you, Miss Patty green dress? What's your specialty?"

"Nothing, unfortunately."

"Come on now. I know you're shy, but don't hold back on old Charlie."

"Okay." I smile. "I'm a singer."

"Bet you are," he says, nodding. "Bet you bring 'em to their knees too."

"I wish."

He shakes his head a little, tells me doubting yourself is normal when you're young. "There ain't no perfect music, but you just gotta keep going. I've been playing almost forty years and I sure learned that."

He asks if I know what jazz was like in Kansas City in the mid-fifties, when he first started. I say no, and he says it was a hard time. All the great names were gone: Lester Young had left; Charlie Parker had just died. There were few clubs that wanted anything other than big bands. And smack was taking a huge toll. Half the musicians he knew were sick; his older brother, a drummer, died of an overdose.

I'm nodding, just to be polite, but he narrows his eyes. "You understand about this, don't you?"

He seems like he knows, which is impossible. I never talk about this part of my life with anyone, not even Irene. I feel like saying no, but I can't. His face is too open, sincere. When I mumble yes, he says, "I could tell. You got the look, green dress."

I have no idea what that means, but I can't bring myself to ask. And he's talking again about how hard it was when he started just to keep a band together and keep playing night after night with audiences that talked over your solos and sometimes booed you off the stage.

"That still happens, I guess," I say. I know it used to happen to Jonathan's quartet; Irene has told me some of the awful stories. Once a club owner picked up one of Dennis's drums and threw it out the back door after he told the guys to get packing and they didn't move fast enough.

"Now you're getting my point," Mr. Jubar says. "It's always been hard and it always will be. But you gotta keep the faith. You gotta do it, be it, live it. Keep paying dues till you got the chops to play your heart."

He sits quietly for a moment; then he glances around the room. "Look at all these hungry folks."

I was so engrossed in what he was saying I didn't notice the porch fill up with people. Mr. Jubar is still turned around in his chair, facing me, but every seat at his table is taken.

"You still feeling shy," Mr. Jubar says, "or you want me to introduce you to some of these folks? I think I know 'most everybody here."

"It's not necessary."

"Sure it is." He turns to the guy next to him. "Malek, I want you to meet a friend. Her name's Patty and she's one fine singer."

I sit on the edge of the rocker, so I can see Malek, nod hi. He smiles and says his ax is bass, but it used to be cello. "Ain't much work for jazz cello players, eh, Charlie?"

They laugh, and then Mr. Jubar leans closer, whispers, "Now, that wasn't so hard, was it?"

"No," I say, and smile. I can't believe how nice he's being. "But you haven't heard me sing. How do you know I'm fine?"

"You've been out there long enough, you recognize a fellow traveler. Like I said, Patty green dress, you got the look. You've seen your share of the shit and come back to tell about it."

He introduces me to two more guys before I get nervous and tell him that's enough. I've just noticed the next person at the table is Carl. And the whole band is with him; they're talking to each other and Lydia. None of them have glanced in my direction, thank God. I don't want them to see me; I hope Irene didn't even tell them I was here.

"They won't bite you, girl," he says.

"It's not that," I say quickly. "It's just I already know—"

165

Too late. He's telling Carl to turn around, pay attention, there's somebody he ought to meet.

"This here is Patty. She's a singer, but she's shy as a stray pup."

Carl looks at me for a second before he turns to Dennis. "Who invited her?"

"I did," Irene says. "Chill out."

Carl nods at Mr. Jubar and his voice becomes respectful. "We know Patty. She works with us."

"Well, well," Mr. Jubar says to me. "So you're hooked up with some good players. That's what I wanted to hear." He looks at Lydia. "Patty sings too. Maybe you two gals could get together on something after this food break."

When Carl and Dennis start laughing, I want to kill them. I know they're high, but I'm finally feeling happy for the first time all day. Why can't they leave me alone?

Carl starts to explain that I don't sing jazz, but I cut him off. "Right now I'm doing cover tunes," I tell Mr. Jubar. "Just to put food on the table, support me and my son. But I'm working on some other stuff. Better stuff."

Maybe Lydia doesn't intend to put me in my place. Maybe her question, "Oh, like what?" is just innocent curiosity. But Dennis is laughing again, and Carl says, "Probably the latest masterpiece from Madonna."

It's silly, but I feel like I can't stand for Mr. Jubar to lose faith in me. If only I had a good answer. And then I remember. I do know one great song. And it is jazz. I didn't know that when I learned it, but I've heard it on the jazz station in the

166

van. "My favorite right now is a piece called 'I Loves You Porgy.'" I stare at Carl. "I'm sure you've heard of it. It's by George Gershwin."

"Heard of it." Mr. Jubar laughs. "Now, there's a song for you. I was in New York when Bill Evans played it at the Vanguard. That man had hands. He didn't play a song; he caressed it." He nods at Jonathan, sitting between Harry and Lydia. "You remind me of him, Johnny. Not saying you don't have your own sound, but you got a debt to Evans."

Lydia says, "I'd like to hear this, Patty. Jonathan does a wonderful version of 'Porgy,' as I suppose you know. You could do it together."

It's dark, yet I can tell he's looking straight at me; I can feel his eyes. But I tell Lydia, "I'd love to." I'm nervous but I really think I can do a good job with this song. That contest was citywide, hundreds of singers. I made the first cut, the second cut, and the final cut. And then I won.

Mr. Jubar seems proud of me too, and that helps. He says he was confident Patty green dress wasn't the kind to sit against the wall and watch. We're walking back in when Jonathan stops me, says we need to talk. I say all right, and he motions for me to follow him into the yard.

"What?"

He moves right in front of me, lowers his voice. "You can't do this."

"Why? Because you know I'll prove you wrong?"

"No, because you've never sung jazz and this is the worst conceivable place to start." He takes a breath. "Carl and

167

Dennis aren't even playing yet. They know they have to wait, let the best guys play first. It's the way it's done."

I pause and watch Mr. Jubar disappear through the dining-room door; then I ask if he's considered good.

"Of course. He's a legend."

"Well, he thinks I can do it."

"Have you lost your mind? He's never even heard you." Jonathan lowers his voice even further. "He likes your hair and your dress. Use your head, he's—"

"Everyone doesn't judge me on that basis, you know that, Jonathan? For your information, I won a big contest singing that Gershwin song. And surprise, surprise, I didn't have sex with the judges!"

"Keep it down. I'm not saying he's coming on to you. He's cool, he's deep, I have nothing but respect for him. But he obviously thinks you're pretty and that's why—"

"No. He thinks I'm a human being. He respects me. I'm sure it's hard for you to believe, but it's true."

I've turned to walk back to the porch when he says, "All right. If you're determined to do this, follow me exactly. I'll try to keep you from looking like a fool."

"Don't do me any favors. I don't need your help!"

"Fine." His voice is angry now too. "Go ahead, hang your-self. Be my guest."

He's still standing there as I walk back to the porch and then inside. Irene is talking to some guy, but she pauses and asks what happened to Jonathan. I say, "Who cares?"

When I get into the jam room, a trio is already playing.

Mr. Jubar waits until they're finished, then he waves me over to the piano. He asks if Jonathan is coming and when I tell him no, he says why not go ahead. This piano player's name is Wes, and he'd be happy to play "Porgy" for me, as soon as I'm ready. I smile, tell him I am ready. As Wes begins playing the intro, I remind myself this is no different than the contest. I'd never seen that piano player before and I was fine.

And I am fine for the first few bars. I think I sound good, certainly better than Lydia. I know this song so well; I'm hitting every note perfectly. I wish I could see Mr. Jubar's face, see if he's enjoying this. But then I hear a guy on the side shout to somebody, "Who is this uptight chick?"

Screw him, I think, but my hands start sweating on the mic. The room seems smaller now and strangely silent; I can feel people staring at me. When the first verse is over, I glance at Wes and he looks surprised or disgusted or both. At the end of the second verse, I'm listening to the piano, wondering what on earth I'm doing wrong when I hear the drummer yell to the bass player, "Take a solo, man, before she kills this."

And he does. Then Wes does, and then a horn player who's stepped in. They seem to have no intention of returning to the changes. I'm confused, but I'm not giving up. I'll sing the rest if I have to stand here all night. But when Wes shouts, "So what," I finally get it. "So What" isn't a comment; it's the title of a tune. The tune they're starting to play. "Porgy" is finished, so am I.

I put the mic back in the stand and walk away. I'm not upset, I'm not even angry, I'm just stunned. But when I get to the doorway, I run into Mr. Jubar. He's still smiling, but not at me; he won't meet my eyes. I hear him yell, "That's the way, Garrett," to the horn player as I move down the hall.

Well, obviously Jonathan was wrong about Mr. Jubar's motives. He believed I was a fellow traveler, just like he said. He was encouraging me because he thought I was good. Now he doesn't, it's that simple—although I have no idea why.

I keep walking until I get to an empty room; then I slump down in an armchair. All I want is to be home, but I'm too unnerved to move any farther. My whole body is shaking with a delayed panic. I've been heckled before but I've never been ignored like this. Of course my band wouldn't dare. Fred would have fired them immediately.

My band, what a laugh. I don't know where Harry was, but I caught a glimpse of Carl and Dennis standing behind the bass player, grinning, as I stood there and held my mic and waited for my turn like an idiot.

Thank God Jonathan wasn't there, I think. But almost immediately, I discover it isn't true. He was there, he saw it all, and he's followed me into this empty room to make sure I know he was right and I was wrong.

"I'm sorry this happened," he says.

I glance up to see him standing with his arms crossed, looking down at me. I know he isn't sorry; I'm just waiting for the evidence—and I don't have to wait long. He takes a breath, tells me I got what I deserved. "You can't just walk in here and be good," he says. "That's arrogant."

"I was good! They didn't give me a chance."

He stands there for a moment before he says, "All right. Come with me."

"No."

"Fine. Stay a fake."

"I'm not a fake!"

He shrugs and walks over to a door on the left, opens the door, and goes through it. It's a small room with a baby grand piano; from my chair, I can see him as he sits down at the bench. I wonder how he knew about this room, but then I remember: he used to date the fabulous Lydia.

He looks back at me. "You said they didn't give you a chance. Do you want to sing this or not?"

I don't say yes but I stomp after him. He tells me to shut the door so we can concentrate. I do, but we can still hear the music from the jam. He's tapping his foot to the beat as he pushes back the lid on the piano.

When he begins playing the intro, it sounds much different than the way the other guy played it. It's slower and quieter, but the chords are so lush and rich they fill the room, make it seem even smaller. He's right, I do want to sing to this. It's the only way to make up for what happened, prove to myself I can. But I only get through the first verse before he stops and says, "No."

"No what?"

He glances at me. "It smells. Start over."

"It does not smell! I have ears, Jonathan. I was singing it perfectly. I—"

"It was technically correct, but there wasn't any feeling. It sounded like you were singing the phone book."

"Up yours," I mutter, but when he repeats, "Start over," I do. But again, he stops me, this time after only two lines.

"Jazz is an art. You can't get by on a good range and pitch; you have to care about what you're doing."

"Dammit," I say, but now I'm determined. I have to show him I do care, I can sing this song. But before I get a chance, while he's playing the intro again, Lydia comes into the room.

"So, this is where you're hiding," she says. She sits down next to him. "Everyone's asking for you. Eddie and Garrett want you to sit in on 'Take Five.'" She glances at me, says she feels bad about what happened out there. "Jazz musicians are a tough crowd, especially for singers. You have to convince them you can groove along without taking over the tune. And they're very judgmental if they suspect you're not sincere."

I have no idea what she's talking about. I am sincere; my mind is screaming that I am. But I don't say anything. Jonathan is telling her we're working on the song; she says that's a good idea. Then she looks at me. "I think it helps if you imagine yourself in the role of Bess."

"Bess?"

She smiles. *Porgy and Bess.* That's the opera this song is from. You are Bess singing to Porgy."

Her voice sounds patronizing. Obviously she's surprised I don't know this. The truth is, I didn't pick the song, the contest coordinator did. I remember I used to practice it at the apartment, and when Rick and I were high, we would laugh and call it, "I Loves You Porky Pig."

Maybe this is a problem.

"To sing Bess well," Lydia is saying, "you have to feel as she feels. Bess sings this song to Porgy after she's been raped by Crown, her dangerous former lover. 'Don't let him handle me,' she pleads with Porgy, 'and drive me mad. If you can keep me, I wants to stay here. With you forever and I'd be glad.'" Lydia pauses. "The lyrics are very poignant, don't you think?"

Before I can answer, Jonathan says, "I never paid attention to them before." His voice sounds soft, a little surprised. He's not looking at her; he's looking at his hands lying motionless on the piano.

"Typical keyboard player." She laughs. "Words? What words? All I hear are notes and chords."

She stands up and says she'd better get back. After the door closes behind her, Jonathan says, "We don't have to keep doing this, Patty."

"But I want to." I move closer to the piano. "Go ahead. Start."

"Are you sure?" he says, and glances in my eyes.

Oh, of course. What Lydia said about Bess is making him think about Omaha again. What he calls my "difficult life."

I rock back on my heels. "Just play the damn song, Jonathan." He's still looking at me, and I wave my hand. "Any decade now."

When the cue comes, I sing the first line. Then the second one, the third one. He doesn't stop me. I don't know if this means it's better, I doubt it. Screw him and his stupid pity, I think, but I keep going. I really want to do this. I know I can; I remember at the contest one of the judges told me I won because I sang it with such feeling and passion.

Something was different then. As I finish the first verse, it starts coming back to me. There was a huge, faceless crowd; I was tired and nervous and strung out from the night before. And I was sweating so much I was worried the audience could see wet spots on my blouse. Until the music started, I was seriously considering running off the stage. I'd never been in front of this many people. What if they laughed at me? What if they thought I sucked?

But then I began to sing. And I was all right, because I just sang it to him, the same way I had in all my practices. I couldn't see him but I knew he was right there in the front row, cheering me on.

I didn't know about Bess; I didn't need to. It was all about Rick. The lines about love were directed to him, but so were the other lines. He was the man I wanted to protect me; he was also the man I wanted to be protected from. This is why I sang the song with so much passion. Now I know. I loved Rick, but I was also afraid of him, even then.

I'm up to the third verse when I realize I understand why Mr. Jubar and everyone else thought it wasn't any good. It's just like Jonathan said: it had no feeling. I know this because now that I can feel it, it's killing me.

I force myself to finish even though the last verse is terrible. I don't have enough air to sing; I have to keep swallowing to stop myself from crying. Jonathan is hunched over the piano, playing the end fiercely, his foot pounding against the leg of the bench. I don't know if he's trying to make up for my weakness or if he's so involved in the piece he doesn't hear me anymore. He's still playing after I sing the last word, but then I don't hear him. I've already moved to the door and out of the room. The music from the jam is loud; an alto sax is wailing, screaming a beautiful pain. I wonder if it's Mr. Jubar.

My purse is where I left it in the front hall. A few people are standing there passing a joint back and forth, but I don't know them; I don't have to explain or say good-bye.

The farther away I get from the house, the more the music from the jam becomes nothing but bass and drums. It seems like it's coming from the ground, like it's pulsing from the dirt under my shoes. The beat of the earth's heart.

I don't collapse until I get to the field where all the cars are parked. It's cloudy and dark and my eyes are swimming in tears; I can't see the Ford. I thought I parked it over on the left, next to a large oak tree, but I can't find the tree.

"Shit," I say, as I slump down on the front bumper of someone's car, drop my face in my hands. But then I suddenly feel a man's hand on my shoulder and my heart stops. I think, he's here because I let myself feel this. I conjured him from sadness, pulled him back into my life. I jump up to run, but he moves too and I stumble right into him. When he puts his arms around me, I'm gasping his name and the one word: no.

"It's all right, Patty." His voice is loud, but it sounds shaky. "It's me. Jonathan."

The relief is so strong it leaves me limp, and he holds me tighter to keep me from falling. My face is against his neck; I can feel him gulp before he says, "I'm sorry I scared you."

He's never touched me before. I'm surprised how comfortable it feels. He's thin, but he has a keyboard player's big hands, muscular forearms. He holds me easily but carefully, the way I used to hold Willie back when I thought he was so delicate he'd break into pieces if I ever let go.

A minute goes by. Then another. Our chests are touching; he's breathing deeply and slowly; it makes me feel calmer. I'm not upset anymore. I know I should pull away, but I can't bring myself to. It's nice being in his arms; I didn't expect that. It feels easy and comfortable. Safe.

His messy hair is blowing into my eyes; he moves it out of the way with one hand, but he keeps the other hand on my back. I don't understand why he isn't talking. I don't understand why he hasn't pulled away either.

He brings his face closer as though he's going to say something, but still, he's quiet. He's so close now. Our lips are only a few inches apart. It occurs to me that he might kiss me. After a moment, I'm sure he's going to. I lean forward, just a little, so he can see I'm okay with it. I lean forward, and then it happens: I find myself kissing him.

His lips are warm and firm; they seem to fit perfectly with mine. It has to be a mistake but it doesn't feel like one. It feels like what I've wanted forever, since I first heard him play.

But his hands are on my shoulders. He's pushing me back. And worst of all, he's apologizing.

I stand up straight and roll my lips together so tightly they hurt. Thank God it's dark. He can't see that my face is burning.

"I can't do this, Patty. It's important that you understand. I don't want—"

"You don't have to explain," I whisper, as I move back. He drops his arms, and I have to will myself not to run away from him. I already look ridiculous; I can't make it any worse.

"Just listen," he says, but then he stops. Someone is walking down the hill from the house, calling him. It's Carl.

"Hey, man, I've been looking all over for you."

I quickly step back behind a car. Carl can't see me, but there's a break in the clouds now; I can see him as he walks up to Jonathan. And there, on his left, I spot the tree I was looking for. I feel so stupid; the tree, and the Ford, are only about fifteen feet away.

"We're up, dude. They're ready for us."

"Cool," Jonathan says. "I'll be there in a minute."

"What are you doing out here?" Carl laughs. "Turning into a werewolf?"

"Go on," Jonathan says flatly. "I told you I'll be up in a minute."

"Okay," Carl says. Before he turns back to the house, he yells, "Jubar said he'd sit in, man. This is gonna be cool."

He listens until Carl is gone. Then he peers into the darkness, whispers, "Patty?"

"I'm over here." I inhale. "But I need to get home."

The sky has turned pitch-black again, but he's coming

nearer anyway, following my voice. I tell him to go back to the jam, I'm fine.

"Wait," he says. "This is important."

I'm almost to the Ford, but I stop. I'm terrified he's going to say something about what just happened, but of course I'm madly hoping he'll say something to make me feel less like a stupid little girl with a crush he doesn't share. But no. He stays a good arm's length away. I can make out his shape, but not the expression on his face. His voice grows cool, distant. It's taking everything I have not to cry.

"Look, I've changed my mind. I will write songs for you."

That's it. He exhales and waits for me to respond.

"Great," I manage.

"But you'll have to work very hard. My music is sacred to me, I won't let it be butchered."

"I will work hard," I tell him. And after a moment, when he doesn't say anything else, I mumble good-bye and hop in the car.

I start the engine, and the radio comes on, blasting the jazz station. I was listening to it on the way here, trying to convince myself I could sing jazz, I could impress Jonathan.

Well, I impressed him, all right.

All the way home, I can't imagine how I'll ever be able to face him again. But later, sitting on my bed with the saggy mattress and ugly, brown corduroy spread, the same bed I've had since I was a kid, I finally realize this is good news, no matter what his motive is. Jonathan is a fabulous composer, and I'm going to be recording with him. Of course I feel like a complete fool now, but I'll have to get over that. If he changed his mind because I freaked out and threw myself at him, fine. If he changed his mind because he feels sorry for me, also fine. I have Willie; I'll do anything it takes to succeed. Do it, be it, live it, like Mr. Jubar said. That's my new motto. I can eat this embarrassment, of course I can. I can handle this. I can handle anything.

eleven

When I was pregnant, I was positive the baby was a girl. The intake clerk at the shelter told me, "You don't have morning sickness all day long with girls." Margaret, who ran the place, said, "You're carrying too low for a girl." I nodded, but when I was alone, I told Willa not to bother with their opinions.

Her name was Willa because Daddy's name was William. She didn't look like Rick or me; she had red hair and pale green eyes and skin so white it seemed unnatural. But the oddest part was, she always wore a hat. Sometimes it was a pink-and-white baby bonnet, other times, a floppy black beret, a shiny yellow rain hood, a boring baseball cap. Whenever I imagined her, even when I dreamed about her, the hat was there, as inevitable as her arms and legs.

I joked that maybe she was covering up a bald spot, but Margaret didn't think it was funny. "It could be an omen," she told me. "You better figure out what it means."

Margaret believed in everything: omens, reincarnation, psychics, tarot card readers, astrology, and of course Catholicism. The shelter for pregnant teens was founded by the Catholic Church.

I wasn't sure what I believed; still, what Margaret said made me nervous. And it got even worse when I was eight months pregnant and Margaret took me to Lou, a fortune-teller in a dingy basement downtown, who told us, "Hats are a sign of movement. Hats always mean someone is going away."

Willa wasn't even here, how could she go away? I was fighting back tears; I asked Lou if she meant Willa was going to be born sick, maybe even die. She said she wasn't sure, could be yes, could be no. Then she asked about the baby's kicks. Too few kicks are bad, but too many kicks could mean the baby was fighting the life I was offering it.

"We gotta run now," Margaret suddenly announced. When we were back outside, blinking in the sun, she whispered, "I wouldn't worry about it. Lou's darned cards said Richard Nixon was innocent too."

It wasn't until after Willie was born that Margaret mentioned the omen again. He was 8 pounds 11 ounces, 22 inches, and healthy as could be, not even much jaundice. But Margaret concluded it had been true, after all. Willa went away, and Willie took her place.

I loved him more than I ever loved her. She was just a dream; he was tiny fists and milky breath and such earnest little struggles. I was amazed at how hard he tried. Just getting his thumb in his mouth completely wore him out.

I felt bad for calling him Willa in the womb. For the first few months of his life, I made a point of telling him how glad I was that he was a boy. I knew he couldn't understand the words, but I thought of them as corrective, like braces or shoes.

He was eighteen months old when I finally realized why I'd been so sure he was a girl, and why that girl always wore a hat. It wasn't supernatural, but Margaret was right, it did have a meaning. I was trying to solve one of my biggest worries. If the baby was a girl, and if she had all the hats she needed, it wouldn't matter that she didn't have a father.

The winter after Daddy died, I was the only girl on the playground without a hat. Daddy had never bought me hats before, but I was in the second grade and I knew it was all connected. If only I had a father, I wouldn't be standing here with my ears freezing off. If only I had a father, I'd be running around with a warm, toasty head, like everyone else.

I bought Willie hats and he pulled them off. I loved him as hard as I could, but at eighteen months old, he was already hungry for the affection of a man.

The first day he went with me to Fred's office, he kept running over Fred's ugly shoes with his Thomas the Tank Engine, hoping Fred would stop talking, notice him. And from the beginning, he wanted so much from the guys. We'd only been on the road a couple of weeks; we were in a band house in Fort

Smith, Arkansas, when he threw a fit because he wanted one of them to take him in the backyard: not me, not Irene. Of course they didn't pay any attention. It was early afternoon; they'd been up all night. When Willie's crying got loud, Dennis put his hands over his ears and Carl turned up the CD.

They weren't being cruel, they just didn't see him. Irene says it's true for most men: they don't really notice kids until they have their own.

The first time Willie asked where his daddy was, I got him a book at a flea market called *All Kinds of Families*. I made a big deal about the page with a single mother. "That's just like us," I said. "A mama and a little boy." It embarrassed me, but I threw in, "Look how happy they are."

When he asked again, it was a few months later and the book wasn't an option. I'd thrown it out after the spine came off when Willie tried to tear out a picture of an Amtrak on the grandfather page. He put the question more directly, too. He asked where his daddy lived. "A long way from here," I said quickly. When he was still sitting there, waiting, I forced a smile. "I bet he would like to see you, buddy, if he could. I'm sure he'd be proud of what a big boy you are."

That satisfied him, but I know that any day now, he'll ask again. The older he gets, the more questions he'll have. He'll want to know where his daddy is and what his daddy is like. Most important, he'll want to know why his daddy never comes around.

And how will I answer him? This is what I'm wondering as

I listen to Mr. Gerald Boyd. Mr. Boyd is Rick's parole officer. He is calling to tell me that Rick wants to see Willie. Actually, "wants" isn't even the word. Rick is pleading with me to let him see Willie. And Rick has offered to do it any way I want—at the house, at a McDonald's, wherever I feel most comfortable.

What I'm wondering is how I will tell Willie, when he's older, that I said no.

Mr. Boyd has already explained that his job is to make sure Rick is successfully integrated into the community. And it's a proven fact: men with families are much less likely to end up back in prison.

It's a Saturday morning, a little after eight thirty, and I'm exhausted. Jonathan meant it when he said I'd have to work hard. For the last few weeks, since the jam at Lydia's house, the two of us have been rehearsing every night after the gig at McGlinchey's. Most times, we go until three or four in the morning, trying to get ready for the studio. Of course I still have to get up with Willie at seven thirty, eight if I'm lucky. I try to nap when he does, but it's not enough. Yesterday, I put Willie's Duplo car away in the microwave.

When I got up about fifteen minutes ago, Mama told me I had two phone calls: Fred and Gerald Boyd. I already knew what Fred wanted, and I decided to avoid him.

He did seem thrilled when I first told him Jonathan had agreed to write songs for me. He claimed that Mystery Train was only an idea but this was what he really wanted, that when he put this group together, he knew we had talent and "sexy energy." But when he showed up at our rehearsal on Tuesday, he was obviously annoyed. He doesn't see why we're spending all our time practicing jazz standards. "The Patty Taylor Band isn't a jazz group," he reminded Jonathan. "You're supposed to write for her, not turn her into a white Billie Holiday."

Jonathan didn't argue, but he also didn't answer when Fred asked if he had any original songs ready. Since then, Fred's called me every day, and every day I give him the same answer. Not yet but soon, I'm sure. And no, I'm not worried.

I assumed Gerald Boyd was a music store salesman trying to hawk a new Peavey PA, or maybe a club owner trying to go around Fred and get us in cheap. Whenever we're in Kansas City I get calls like that, even though Fred's secretary swears she doesn't give out my phone number.

I figured Boyd would be an easy no thanks. How wrong I was.

He does seem like a nice guy. He tells me his background and it isn't anything like I expected. He has a degree in social work. He used to work with teenage mothers; he says he knows how hard it can be to raise a child by yourself.

He coughs. "Are you receiving AFDC?"

"What?"

"Government assistance."

"No, I've supported Willie since he was born."

"That's quite an accomplishment. But I'm sure you could use some financial help."

"Maybe," I mumble. Mama is plopped down at the

kitchen table, staring at me and smoking. She's already mouthed, "Who is it?" but I shook my head.

"Rick is aware that he should be paying child support," Boyd is saying. "He's been putting aside money from every paycheck for the last month."

"Paycheck?" I whisper. "Isn't he in jail?"

Mr. Boyd gives me a long explanation of why they decided not to revoke parole even though they found a gun in Rick's truck. Basically, it came down to Rick's statement, which convinced them that he's changed; he's sincere about wanting to straighten up.

Boyd believes Rick's accident really affected him. He tells me that Rick's had a job since July—it was a condition of parole— but Rick was rarely there. Since the middle of August, though, he's shown up every day, and his supervisor is impressed with what a hard worker he is. And just last week, Rick moved into a new place outside of Lewisville. He told Boyd he wants a fresh start away from the people he used to associate with.

I haven't been awake long enough to process all this. Mama just scribbled, "What's going on?" on the front of an envelope, but I turn away, stand up, and pull the phone to the refrigerator. I need some juice or soda, something. My mouth is so dry it feels sunburned.

All we have are boxes of Willie's apple juice, but I get one out, drink it while Mr. Boyd reiterates that Rick does not want to cause me any trouble. He'll see Willie whenever it's convenient. He'll let me supervise the visits; he'll comply with any and all conditions, as long as he gets to see his son.

"I have to go now," I finally say. I'm still in my sleep shorts and ratty T-shirt. I want to take a shower, get dressed. I want to get away from Mama's stares.

"Rick has some problems," Mr. Boyd says slowly. "I don't want you to think I'm not aware of the things he's done. But the issue is what's best for your child, now and in the future."

"Yes, but—"

"My sense is that Rick really cares about little William. I wouldn't suggest visitation if I thought he was capable of harming him."

He pauses as if he's waiting to hear what I think. I'm not thinking though; I'm remembering that day in Omaha, when Rick took Willie out to the truck. Willie was so excited he took off running down the driveway. Long before he got to the street, Rick caught up with him, grabbed his hand. As he lifted Willie into the truck, he kissed him in the middle of the back, but quickly, as if he didn't want anyone to notice or object.

Mama is chain-smoking and the tops of her house shoes are shaking; she's wiggling her toes like she always does when she's nervous. I tell Boyd I really have to hang up. He thanks me for talking to him; then he lowers his voice, says there's one more thing I should know.

"Rick's counselor and I believe the car accident was a suicide attempt." Boyd coughs. "The transition from prison has not been easy for him. I hope you'll consider giving him a chance."

"Shit," I whisper, as I put the receiver back. Mama wants to know what happened, but I shake my head. Willie is in the kitchen now too.

He's wearing the goofiest outfit. The pants are blue-and-white striped with little ducks on the pockets. I got them last spring; they're almost too small. The shirt Irene bought at a garage sale in the middle of Oklahoma. It's tie-dyed, mostly orange, and it says Gimme Shelter.

I smile. "I guess you dressed yourself, huh?"

"Yep," he says. I lean down to give him a hug, but he squirms, says he's got to go.

"Where?"

"I a fireman." A few seconds later, he comes back in. "Call me if you got a fire. I put it out for you, Mama."

I smile, tell him I'll be in the shower. "But I promise I'll yell if a fire starts in the tub."

"You're not going to tell me what's going on?" Mama is standing too, blocking the doorway.

"Just let me get dressed first."

"Okay," she says, exhaling loudly, giving me a look like I just spilled milk all over the floor.

Even if it irritates her, I have to have a minute before I can discuss this. I know I'll have to reassure her but I have no idea how.

When I pull into the parking lot of the Evans strip mall, the car in front of me has a bumper sticker that reads: LIVE IN THE MOMENT. Thanks for the advice, I think, and scowl at the back of the driver's head. I've had all the moments I can stand today and it's only three o'clock.

I figured Mama would be upset, but I didn't expect her to

lose it. On the one hand, she's in awe of law enforcement people and thinks if a parole officer feels Rick should visit, I may
not have a choice. On the other, she believes we have to do
whatever it takes, including taking Willie out of state, even
out of the country, to keep Rick from coming near him.

She still has no idea that Rick has already been near him.
She thinks the parole officer was playing detective, tracking
down me and Willie as part of his job.

We spent Willie's nap discussing it, getting nowhere. The
fact that Rick is his father means absolutely nothing to her.
I'm not surprised; I know she never understood what Daddy
meant to me. He was her husband, first, last, and everything
in-between. Being my father was just another aspect of their
marriage, a part of his relationship to her.

Before we left for the mall, I told her not to worry, I'd come
up with something. She nodded, but then she looked in my
eyes and said, "You better get over him, Patty Ann. If you
don't, I guarantee you'll live to regret it."

I was so angry I could feel it in my teeth, but I couldn't yell,
Willie was there. I scooped him up and hurried to the Ford;
after a few blocks, I managed to calm down and think up a
bribe. The Baskin-Robbins is right next door to Custom Cuts.
I promised if he's good I'd get him a double dip of chocolate
with sprinkles.

We're in the beauty salon now. I'm sitting in the plastic
chair, watching Willie snap and unsnap the pink and orange
curlers in the big blue bucket by the dryer.

"It's beautiful," the hairdresser says. She's standing behind me; she has my hair bunched in her hands. "Are you sure you want to do this?"

"Yes," I say, but I look away from the mirror. I can't watch it happen.

When it's finished, I still can't handle more than a quick glimpse. I told her to cut it very short, close to my head, and she did. I was hoping it would make me look older, but it doesn't. My face seems so exposed. From the side especially, I look like a big-faced, overeager kid.

But it's certainly a change. I only hope Fred doesn't have the same reaction as Willie.

"Don't wike it," he sputters. He's standing by the chair, shaking my elbow. "Put it back."

"I can't do that, buddy."

He leans down and grabs a piece of hair from the filthy floor. He sticks it on my shoulders and when it falls off, he stomps his foot. "Glue it, Mama."

The hairdresser laughs. "Your mom looks glamorous."

I smile at her. "You really think so?"

She shrugs. "Seems like everybody's doing it nowadays. Some of those actresses get their hair so short they look like cancer patients."

Great. I pick Willie up and carry him to the register. He's almost in tears. I have a coupon for a ten-dollar cut but the cashier points out that the fine print says good until September 15. Today is September 21, and it's twenty dollars, not counting tip.

After I pay for the haircut, I have nineteen dollars left in my purse. I figure what the hell, might as well spend that too. I buy Willie his ice cream and then go into the music store, find a tape of Nina Simone.

Almost every night, Jonathan mentions the name of some great singer I've never heard of. "The key to jazz is listening," he always says. It's his mantra. He means listening to the other musicians on stage and listening to the giants of the past.

I want to be serious about music, but it's turning out to be more expensive than I thought. In the last few weeks, I must have bought a dozen tapes.

The Gimme Shelter T-shirt is smeared with chocolate, so are Willie's arms, legs, face, even his ears. When we get home, Mama is making dinner, banging pots like she's trying to scare away intruders. I put Willie in the tub and put the new tape in my Walkman. I'm surprised. With most of the others, I've had to work to see what's good about it, but I love this from the very first piece. This Nina Simone has incredible tone. Her voice is powerful, deep, but controlled too; it's not like a storm, it's softer, like snow.

I have to turn the tape off when I get to "Porgy." I still can't stand to remember how stupid I was that night with Jonathan.

Thank God he's never mentioned it. And whatever his motive, our work together is going just fine. I know I'm getting better, he knows it too. He's even started to praise me like he does the guys.

It's only one word, but until recently he'd never said it to me. I used to watch Carl and Dennis beam when they heard it; Harry would just nod, but he was obviously pleased.

Occasionally I'd hear him say it to the radio, to a CD, even to himself—but never to me.

"Yes," he says, and sometimes he smiles; sometimes he slaps his hand on his knee. "Yes," he says, and it means this is good, I like this. Or even you are good, I like what you did.

The guys are also beginning to compliment me. Just last night, Harry smiled and said I'm really getting the "swing" down. I said thanks, but I was thinking about all the time Jonathan had spent teaching me to emphasize 2/4 instead of 1/3, to go across the bar, to slide into a note and then stretch it out or cut it off abruptly, to back away from the obvious accent.

I'm learning so much from him; sometimes I feel so grateful I could kiss him. Ha-ha.

Even though we're spending more time together than ever before, he always manages to keep his distance—literally. If I move over to his piano, he leans the other way. If I follow him to the bar, he walks back to his table, even if he doesn't have the drink he came for.

Since Labor Day, the one and only time we got closer than three feet apart was in Fred's office. He had to sit next to me because there was no other chair. I sat as rigidly as I could; I didn't even cross my legs because I was afraid I'd accidentally brush against him and confirm what he seems to suspect: that I'm just waiting for the opportunity to jump him.

The only place I want to jump is into my bed. I'm so tired from all this rehearsing I can barely lift Willie out of the tub. But it's after six. I have to get ready for the gig tonight.

At least I won't have to spend much time on my hair.

I can't believe Mama hasn't even mentioned I cut it off. When I'm all dressed and ready to go, I screw up my courage to ask what she thinks.

"You've always been pretty," she says, and shrugs. "Even when you were a kid, everybody told me how pretty you were."

She's never said this to me before. I'm too surprised to do more than mumble, "Thanks."

"You could be bald and be pretty." Then she frowns. "You'll always have men running after you. You're lucky."

I kiss Willie good-bye and leave. It isn't until later that it hits me how odd it is for her to call me lucky about this, given how panicked she is about Rick.

It's been exactly eight days since Gerald Boyd's first phone call. Just a little more than a week—but Mama's nerves have gotten so bad, I don't know how to deal with her anymore.

The strange part is she was there when Boyd called back yesterday; she heard me tell him I'm definitely not ready for Rick to visit Willie, but it didn't help. She's just positive Rick is about to storm the house. She checks and rechecks the doors, stands dinner plates up in all the windowsills, gets mad at me when I take the plates down in my room even though I've told her I'm afraid they'll fall off and hit Willie in the head.

She's mad at me a lot now. I'm still exhausted from all this rehearsing, but she doesn't offer to let me sleep in, doesn't cut me any breaks. Before I'd even had my coffee this morning, she was bugging me about taking Willie to some cousin's farm.

"Without me?" I asked. As much as Willie likes her, he still cries if I'm gone too much, and she knows it. It would break his heart to leave me, not to mention what it would do to mine.

"You come too. Just for a while. Lay low until we see what that killer is gonna do."

"Lay low?" I forced a laugh. "This isn't a movie. I can't call Fred tomorrow and say, oh, sorry, I won't be at the gig, I'll be busy lying around. I mean, lying low."

"I don't see how you can joke at a time like this." She frowned and scratched a mosquito bite on her upper arm. "You talk like your dumb job is more important than that little boy's safety."

Dumb job was just silly, but the rest was irritating as hell. I don't think Willie's safety is important? This from the person who was so drunk she passed out holding a cigarette when I was in fourth grade. If I hadn't woken up and smelled the burning carpet, we both would have died.

I told her to back off and she did, but not for long. I was washing Willie's juice mug when I heard her grumble that she was really surprised at me.

I spun around and looked at her. "Why?"

"All this time, I thought you regretted being with that man. Now I wonder if I was wrong."

"Well, no need to wonder anymore, because I'll tell you right now, you are!" I paused and glanced in the living room, where Willie was doing his Busy Town puzzle on the coffee table. "How could I regret it?" I hissed. "If I hadn't been with him, Willie wouldn't have been born."

If she had something else to say, I didn't hear it. I threw the dishrag in the sink, then sat down next to Willie to help with the puzzle. A half hour later, she stomped out without saying a word. Of course she took the Ford—it's her car, not mine—even though she knows I need to take Willie to Kangaroo Park. I've been promising for a week.

It's called Kangaroo Park because there's a twenty-six-foot-tall concrete kangaroo with a slide coming out of its mouth. It's six long blocks, but Willie makes it without asking me to carry him. He loves this park.

It's unusually crowded for a Sunday morning, but I don't mind; I can use the distraction to stay awake. I'm pushing Willie on the toddler swings; on his left side, there's a pale, thin girl with bright orange hair, and the woman pushing her is making conversation. She asks Willie his name and introduces him to the little girl, Miranda. She turns to me, remarks about the great weather.

It is gorgeous today. It's finally cooled down; whenever there's a breeze, I wish I'd brought my sweater. Both Willie and I are wearing what he calls our "spy glasses." I got them on sale in Little Rock; they're sunglasses but they reflect like mirrors. Willie likes to pretend they make us invisible.

Miranda just turned three. She's telling Willie about her birthday party, how her daddy made a treasure hunt in the backyard. At first, I'm not sure he's paying attention. He's facing straight ahead, in the direction of the kangaroo slide. But then he announces that he's going to have a birthday party too, with a super big treasure hunt. "My daddy will do it," he says, "if I want."

He's said things like this before, not often. Of course I understand. I would have lied too, when I was a kid, if everyone hadn't already known my father was dead. Usually I tell myself it's not much different from his bragging about how strong he is or how gigantic our nonexistent car is. Today, though, it feels like the world is conspiring against me.

And it just gets worse. Maybe Willie has overheard Mama and me arguing, I don't know, because he's squirming in the swing seat, obviously uncomfortable that Miranda is talking so much about her dad. Her daddy is tall, she says. He buys her anything she wants. He always gives her a glass of water at night. He has a real important job.

The woman explains that Miranda is going through a father phase. "When he leaves for work in the morning, she screams, 'I don't want you, I want Daddy.'" She laughs a little. "Is this the thanks I get for quitting my job to stay home with her?"

I make myself smile at her before turning to Willie. "You want to go on the slide now?"

He says yes, and I unbuckle the swing and put him down on the ground. But he doesn't walk over there; he stands next to the metal post of the swing set. He looks so silly with those sunglasses on, his bottom lip pushed out in an obvious pout. I say, "Let's go," but he doesn't move. Then he yells to Miranda, "My daddy has the bestest job."

Miranda's mother smiles. "What does your daddy do, Willie?"

Now his little chin is quivering. He hates it when he's confused. "Come on, buddy," I say, but his hands are clinging to the posts, he won't budge. I'm sure he's about to cry, but finally he shouts, "I not telling," and runs away.

The woman is apologizing, but I can't listen, I have to run after Willie. He's at the back of the line for the kangaroo slide. When I get there, he yells, "I'm big. I do it!"

I lean down. "You can't go on that slide alone. You know it's a rule."

"I big," he says, and now he is crying. But he won't let me pick him up. And he still wants to go on the slide alone; he says he'll hit me if I try to climb with him.

"No, you won't." Willie never hits; he hasn't since he was a year old.

He says he will hit me, I say he won't, all the while he's crying so loud that the other kids in line are staring at him. Finally an older boy turns to me, asks if my "baby" is okay. Willie is so insulted he throws himself against my legs.

"Can I pick you up now?"

He doesn't answer, but he doesn't resist. After I lift him in my arms, he snuggles against my shoulder, buries his face in my neck. His cheeks are hot and his little chest is shaking with sobs.

"Poor buddy." I rub his back, walk around with him until he feels heavy. I point across the park at a weeping willow tree. "Let's go over there. See how pretty it is?" He shakes his head, but I whisper, "I bet we can hide under all those branches. Be spies."

It's cold under the tree, and wet, I discover, as soon as I sit down on the dirt. But the tangle of thin branches is fascinating to Willie. He's clumping them in his hands and then letting them go, watching them slowly spread out again. When he tires of that, he begins to pick off the tiny leaves and rub them against a rock he found by the tree trunk. I ask him what he's doing and he says, "Spy stuff."

After a while, he's banging a twig against the rock, and I'm watching Miranda and her mother walk out of the park. Now they're leaving. Now, when the damage is done.

I don't need anyone to tell me this is a sign. I can't keep putting it off; Willie has a right to know who his father is, even if he never sees him again. Of course he's too young to really understand, but at least he'll have something to say when faced with a kid like Miranda. He can brag about his daddy's truck.

I take it slow. I start with the trailer, then that day at the pool, and finally the new guy who let him drive. "Remember him? His name was Rick?"

He doesn't answer. It seems I may have taken it too slowly. He has his back to me, I'm not sure he's even listening. But I go ahead and say it. I figure if he isn't listening, it's another sign. A good one.

I force my voice to sound calm. "That guy is your daddy, buddy."

To me, it's like a crash of thunder, the sky tearing in two, the opening of the earth beneath my feet. But Willie is banging the stick like nothing happened. Either he didn't hear or he doesn't really care. Thank God.

He's spotted a ladybug crawling by the rock, and he has his hand down flat as he tries to coax it onto his finger. His voice sounds so sweet. "Come here, wady bug. Wady bug." But the bug won't come to him. He asks why and I tell him the bug doesn't understand he won't hurt it.

"I wanna go home," he says.

That makes two of us, I think. After I hand him his sunglasses, put mine on, I pull back the branches of the willow tree. But he only makes it out of the park before he holds out his arms and whines that he's tired. He needs Mama to carry him.

I was stupid; I should have brought his stroller. I'm out of breath from hefting him after only one block. He's squirming, too, and tugging on my ear lobes. Ever since I cut my hair, he's fascinated with my ears.

At least he likes something about my short hair. When Fred saw it his only comment was, "It will grow."

I make it another block, and another. It's getting easier; I must be getting a second wind. When he asks why I don't have the "rings" on, we're only a block from home. I've already decided to make him a microwave pizza and get him down for his nap as quick as possible. I can't wait for my own nap.

"Because you pull them." I laugh. "I can't wear earrings around you, you little goofball."

He pushes my lobes up tight against my ears. I pretend I can't hear him. "What'd you say? Huh? What?" while he giggles.

"He gots a ring," Willie says, as he pokes his finger on the hole in my ear.

199

"Who does?" I'm not paying much attention. I can see the house now. No Ford, Mama's not home yet. Only a few more minutes and I can shove the pizza in and collapse on the couch.

"Daddy."

His voice is so confident, that's what stuns me. He doesn't sound like he just learned this; he sounds like he's known all along. He's leaning back, grinning, so I force a smile. "Rick does have an earring, you're right. Good memory, buddy."

"Rick."

"That's his name, remember?"

"I know!" he says, and puckers up his face in a silly frown. Then he chants, "Rick, Daddy, Rick, Daddy," until I feel like I'm losing my mind.

But now I'm unlocking the door. Willie runs into our room, turns on his synthesizer. The pizza will be ready in two and a half minutes. Maybe I'll feed it to him, to get it over with quicker. A half hour, tops, and I'll be back in the only place I want to be: my bed.

While he's eating, I remember to tell him that we shouldn't talk about Daddy to Granny yet. Daddy will be our secret for a while.

"Like spies," he says, and I nod, but I hate doing this to him. I wish I could tell her how it really is.

Willie's just fallen asleep and I'm halfway there when the phone rings. I race into the kitchen so the noise doesn't wake him, but my hello sounds like a curse.

It's Jonathan, calling to tell me that Fred just called him. It seems Fred can't wait anymore. He plans to drop by McGlinchey's this evening, to hear what Jonathan's written. We need to have a band meeting right away.

I yawn and tell him Mama isn't here, I don't have a car. He pauses; then he says fine, he'll pick me up.

"Do you have anything yet?"

"More or less. I'll be curious to see what you think."

His voice sounds hesitant, even a little nervous. I've never heard him sound like this before.

Since he won't be here for forty-five minutes, I go back in our room, lie down next to Willie, but it's useless now. I'm way too nervous myself.

twelve

McGlinchey's is one of the nicest rooms we play. The table-tops are thick mahogany; the light fixtures are solid brass. Even the women's bathroom has fancy flowered wallpaper and an overstuffed couch that's so comfortable I've learned to avoid sitting on it, it's too hard to get back up. Still, it's a bar, and being in any bar on a Sunday afternoon is vaguely depressing. The windows in the front don't bring in enough light, the bottles of booze lining the wall seem sleazy, a little sad, and the whole place feels scrubbed with silence, like the halls of an empty grade school.

Or maybe I'm depressed because of what Jonathan just said. On the drive over, we didn't talk at all. I thought maybe he was annoyed because the Ford was sitting in the driveway when he picked me up. I tried to call him when Mama came home not ten minutes after he called, but it was too late; he'd already left his apartment.

At least I didn't have to bring Willie with me. It would be hard to deal with him and deal with our problem.

Jonathan does have a song, but he doesn't have lyrics. "None that are worth using anyway," he adds, nodding at his open briefcase, where I can see a stack of crumpled notebook paper at least two inches thick.

All the guys are already here. Dennis and Harry are sprawled out on the stage floor. Carl is sitting on a chair by the PA; his hair is wet and he's blinking at the overhead lights like he just woke up.

"You're a composer, man," Carl is saying. "You shouldn't have to deal with this lyric bullshit." Dennis chimes in, bitching about what Fred has suggested Jonathan write.

"Patty's forte is the heartbroken girl," as Fred put it. "But give it a hint of sex. Let her come off as hurt but hot." When he saw me, he faked a bow. "No offense intended, my dear."

Jonathan is sitting behind his Rhodes. After a moment, he says he's going to play the melody of the piece. At least he can let us hear this part.

The melody seems perfect. It's pretty, and surprisingly simple. Of course the guys will improvise around it, but it sounds like exactly what Fred wants. It's catchy but still good. And it's not just in my key, it sounds like it was written specifically to take advantage of my strengths—the longer notes are all on the low end, where I can cut the vibrato, and avoid my weaknesses—no sudden jumps above high C, thank God.

"It's great," I tell him.

Harry smiles. "It kicks butt."

"But she can't sing it," he says. "Not without words."

"Maybe a scat thing would work," Dennis says. "Doo wop, doo wop, doo wop."

Carl laughs. "I've got it. Just sing 'bite me' over and over. Send old Fred a message from us."

I shoot him a dirty look, but he shrugs. "Brewer is an artist, Patty. He writes because he has something to say. He can't fart out some commercial dog shit just to please Fred."

"But if he doesn't come up with something, the studio is canceled. For me, and for you guys too. Fred won't keep his deal if we don't do what he wants."

This is the way it was presented to them: if Jonathan writes for me, Fred will record and promote their instrumentals. They fussed a little until they realized Jonathan wasn't going to write pop; he was going to teach me jazz. "I guess you're not as big a sellout as we thought," Carl said, and smiled like he'd just given me a compliment.

It's about fifteen minutes later, and Jonathan has played the song twice, but no one has any good idea for lyrics. Dennis has just come up with the brilliant suggestion that we make the song about owls. All of them are laughing when we hear a phone ringing.

Carl runs into the little storage room behind the bar to answer. He probably thinks it's his latest woman, the one Irene calls mouthy—not because she talks too much, because of what she supposedly does for him in the backseat of his Camaro, during breaks, to relieve his tremendous artistic tension.

When he comes out and says, "It's for you," I know it has to be Mama.

"Why do I hear those boys laughing?" she says. "I thought you had to rehearse."

Her voice sounds as suspicious as if she caught me in a lie. "We're discussing the song," I say, and blink. "What's wrong?"

"There's a car sitting right in front of the house. I've never seen it before and I know it ain't from around here."

"A car? What—"

"It's him," she sputters. "I'm positive. Good Lord, what if he's here to take Willie?"

"Calm down," I say. "Did you actually see Rick?"

"No, I ran in here and called you, but I—"

"At least go look at the driver. Please!"

She mutters that isn't necessary, but I hear her drop the phone on the table, and then a thumping like she's stomping across the room. After a moment, she comes back. "It's gone now. But I know it was him."

"Oh, Mama." I'm so relieved I let out a laugh. "Don't you think you're being a little paranoid? I mean, why would Rick drive up, sit there, and drive away? Especially when he knows his parole officer is in contact with us?"

"You tell me," she snaps. But then she says, "I don't know why I'd expect that. You never tell me what's going on."

I slump down on a can of pretzels, wondering what on

earth she's mad about now. When I finally get up the nerve to ask, she hisses, "Willie told me."

"What?"

"He's seen his daddy." Mama's voice is a spit. "It sounds like they had a load of fun together too. They played with his cars. They even ate spaghetti."

"Shit."

"Oh, that ain't the half of it. He said you told him y'all are going to live together in a big house. But I can visit if I want."

"I did not say that. Willie loves to pretend, you know he does. I would never—"

"But you did eat spaghetti with that killer? You let him be in the same room as your sweet little boy?"

There's no point in denying it. She isn't giving me a chance anyway.

"You promised you'd stay away from him, Patty Ann. You promised you wouldn't let Rick Malone come near that innocent child!"

I pause and rub my forehead. I know it's just stress, but my head is pounding so hard I can barely think.

"Look, Mama," I whisper, "there were circumstances I couldn't control. That's all I can tell you right now."

"He showed up and you couldn't resist? Is that what you mean by circumstances, young lady?"

Her voice is quiet, but the disgust is unmistakable. She sounds exactly like she used to when she would call me a slut. I'm too hurt to argue. I tell her she has to stop it or I'm going to hang up.

"Oh," she yells, "here we go again."

"What?"

"You know what." I hear her take a deep drag of her cigarette. "This is the way you used to treat me when you lived with that man."

"The way I treated you?" I burst out in a laugh, but it's so bitter and loud, it sounds like I'm choking. "How about the way you treated me? Do you ever think about that part? Do you, Mama? Huh?"

I know I'm going too far, but I can't help it. It's like all of a sudden, I'm back in the truck with Rick, remembering when she screamed that Daddy hadn't wanted me to be born. And it's all blending together. Her slamming the whiskey glass against the wall, Rick pushing me down. Her calling me a brat, him telling me to relax as he—

"I was your child! You were supposed to take care of me, not the other way around. And you know what? If you'd been there for me even once, my whole life might have been different. Rick wouldn't have come looking for me in Omaha because I never would have gotten involved with him!"

I don't really believe this. Just this morning, I told her I don't regret being with Rick, and it's true. But I don't care. I'll say anything to make her stop torturing me. It works, but too late. Now she's quiet. Now, when I've already made a fool of myself.

Jonathan is standing in the doorway of the storage room. I don't know how long he's been there. Maybe the whole time.

Ever since that night at Lydia's, I've been trying to prove to him that I'm not a mess. And I was making progress, or at least I thought I was, until now.

Dammit, I think, as I turn around and tell Mama I can't discuss this anymore. Before she hangs up, I whisper that I'm sorry. She doesn't respond.

There are tears standing in my eyes as I put down the receiver. Most people would look away, but not Jonathan. He stares right at me as I wipe my face on my shirt sleeve.

"Are you all right?"

"Of course."

I want to walk out of the storage room—get away from him—but he's blocking the doorway. Then I realize I don't hear the guys laughing anymore. When I ask what happened, he says they went out to get some food.

I exhale. "Great. I come all the way over here and they cut out."

"I thought you would need some time."

This might seem sweet if he didn't look so uncomfortable. His arms are folded tightly across his chest; his face is arranged in what I'm sure he thinks is a concerned expression, but actually looks slightly ill.

I put my hands on my hips. "The only thing I need right now is a good tune. Can we please get back to work?"

He says okay, and we go back on stage, presumably to discuss our lyrics problem. But as soon as he sits down behind the piano, he says, "I can't do this, Patty. I'm sorry."

"But you have to. I mean, you said you would." I stop because my voice sounds whiny, desperate. I sit down on the stool and point to his briefcase. "Isn't there anything in there we could use?"

"Unlikely. Ninety percent of it is my usual rants against the simpleminded trash that passes for art."

"Well, a rant might be okay."

"How could you sing it? You don't believe that most people don't care about beauty or meaning." He smirks. "That they don't care about anything but the petty trivialities of their miserable lives."

I pause, wondering if Fred's call is the reason he's being so negative. "Charlie Jubar told me the reason you need chops is so you can play your heart."

"Jubar is cool. Very deep."

"Okay, but where is the feeling in what you're saying? It seems like it's just hatred."

"Hatred is a feeling, Patty."

"But there's nothing beautiful about it."

"I disagree. I think there is beauty in appropriately directed rage. At least it isn't complacent." He pauses. "But you see my point."

"Not really."

"I'm supposed to write words for you. Something you can feel. But what you've lived through I can't begin to express."

Oh God, not this again. "I'm really not as bad off as you seem to think," I say firmly, crossing my arms. "But I don't want to discuss my personal life. Like you just said, it's trivial."

He laughs a little before he says, "Maybe you should write the words yourself."

"Yeah, right."

"I'm serious. Many singers write their own lyrics." He plays a loud minor chord. "Why don't we give it a try? I'll play the song again, and you follow me. Make up words as you go."

"I can't."

"That's a start. I can't," he says, as he plays the first two notes of the melody. "Now what?"

"I mean, I can't come up with words."

He plays the first line, repeating what I just said. Then he smiles. "It's interesting, but I think Fred is looking for something more accessible."

I cross my legs. "Come on, Jonathan."

"Good. It sounds like Clapton. Lay down, Sally. Come on, Jonathan."

"Ha-ha."

"That's the refrain? 'Ha-ha.' It's simple, and that's always good. But it may not play with the crowd. They may feel you're laughing at them."

I don't say anything but I smile. He's still playing. "What's next?" he shouts.

"You're nuts."

"You're nuts," he repeats. "Is this a musical allusion to Joe Cocker's 'You Are So Beautiful'? You are so nuts, so nuts, to me-e-e."

Now I'm laughing. "Wait," I say. "We need to add something romantic. Something like 'I love you just the way you are,' except it should be 'I love you in spite of the way you are.'"

"Good," he says, and repeats it, but the way the melody

210

goes, the accent falls on the word 'spite.' "Riff on that now," he says. "Spite is one of my favorite emotions."

"I've noticed," I say, and giggle. "But I think it's a little boring."

"Boring?" he says, and fakes a frown. "You've cut me through the heart."

"Hey, that part goes perfectly with the first line. You've cut me through the heart."

I'm still giggling as I stand up and walk next to him, lean my elbows on the top of the Rhodes. "You've cut me through the heart. But I'm still alive. You've got plenty of spite but only a plastic knife."

I sing the same thing again before I notice he's not laughing anymore. He's not smiling. Even his back is straight now. Stiff.

"I was only joking."

"I know." He's still playing, but it's so soft. "It was funny."

"Then what's wrong?"

He doesn't answer, he just continues to play. When he goes to the refrain, he adds the chords. I'm starting to realize this song is more than pretty. At times, it sounds as delicate as a butterfly wing, but at other times it's so full of feeling that I have to force myself not to stare at him. I'm not sure if I can do this justice, but I can't wait to try. Even if the lyrics aren't great, the song will more than make up for it. The song is so wonderful; the words could be as inane as Ron's.

I'm still thinking about this when he says, "Maybe this part should be something romantic as well." His voice is flat. I can't read the expression in his eyes. "How about, 'When I kissed you, I was thinking . . .' fill in the blank."

I can feel my cheeks burn. "Are you asking me to tell you—"

"'When I kissed you, I was thinking . . .' what's next, Patty?"

"I wasn't thinking," I whisper. "It was a mistake."

"All right. 'When I kissed you, I wasn't thinking.'" He smiles, or maybe it's a smirk. "I doubt Fred will find that sufficiently romantic though."

He plays another line. I look at him, unable to believe he's making fun of me. He hasn't in so long.

"Perhaps I should fill in the blank," he says, after a moment. "When you kissed me, I was thinking of the night we drove out of Springfield. We'd just gotten fired, remember? The club owner was an imbecile, even Fred thought so. We had to pack up and leave for St. Louis even though it was after midnight."

"Why did you think about that?"

"You fell asleep in the back of the van. I watched you in the rearview mirror. The side of your face was smashed against the window."

I force a laugh. "That's great. Really romantic."

"It was." He's not playing anymore and his voice is so quiet I can barely hear him. "It was the first time I admitted to myself that I wondered what it would be like to kiss you."

I'm still leaning on the Rhodes, and I suddenly realize how close we are. Our feet are almost touching under the piano. I can hear him breathing. But I stand up straight, take a step back. "I don't understand why you're telling me this."

"When you kissed me, it had nothing to do with me." He's

looking down at his hands. "You were thinking about him. You were afraid of him."

He pauses, but I can't speak.

"Or maybe I've misinterpreted it," he says slowly. "I've also considered the possibility you're still in love with him." He glances at me and shrugs. "The point is, I knew you would think it was a mistake in the light of day."

"So you were doing me a favor? That's what you thought?"

"No, I was protecting myself." He smiles a little. "I like anger, but I don't like pain."

"No one likes pain, Jonathan."

"But some people handle it better than others. You, for example." He hits a chord. "Wait, here's a romantic story for you. A woman and a man have been together for a long time. She says she loves him, he thinks he could love her. But then his father has a heart attack. His father is in the hospital, the doctors say he might die. The man hates hospitals, has ever since he was a kid, when his sister died of leukemia. He can't go to the hospital; he can't talk about it to the woman he's supposed to love. Even when his father recovers, he runs away from the woman and never calls to tell her why. What would you think of a man like that?"

I look at him closely. "You did this?"

He nods. "To Susan, when my dad got sick." He plays a trill. "I'm still not sure why."

I knew his father had a heart attack not long before I got with the band, but I'm still surprised. I never heard about what happened to his sister, though I realize I do know her name. Claire. One of his saddest songs is called "Remembering Claire, Age 9."

I pause for a moment. "Maybe you were afraid to see Susan. She knew you. She'd make it impossible to hide the fear."

"I don't know what I was afraid of. I'm just telling you I don't handle pain very well. I avoid it, and when I can't, I run from it." He smiles a half smile. "I'm not brave like you."

"I wish you would quit saying that. It really isn't true." I take a breath. "You know what? Sometimes I feel like I'd give anything to run away from all this."

"This?"

"Everything." I look at the brick wall behind him. "Rick, my mother, Fred. The studio. My life, I guess."

He's standing too, and walking towards me. "Patty, I'm sorry."

I shake my head. "It's okay." Now his eyes are kind. Too kind. I'm afraid I'll cry. "I'm just tired."

His hands are on my shoulders. When he starts pulling me to his chest, I say, "I'm all right. You don't have to—"

"Close your eyes."

"But—"

"Just close your eyes and listen. I did write something. Tell me if you could sing this."

He feels just like I remember. I don't want to relax here, but I can't help it. It's so comfortable being in his arms.

"It was the wrong script," he says softly, "the wrong time. You had drama with him, but never the rhythm oceans know, never the rest that surrounds the note, giving it meaning."

He shifts his weight to his left foot. "That's a first verse of sorts. Then the chorus is, 'You start a rumor in your mind, and the words become a chain, each link obscuring, the possibilities that remain.'"

I look at him, and he shrugs. "At least it rhymes. Fred might appreciate that." He takes a breath. "I have a lot more, but I'll just give you one phrase. Another rhyme. Close your eyes again. This is from the last verse, when you realize you want something different." He whispers, "Not that play with lines too slow, but me, waiting in tomorrow."

He pauses. "It may sound corny but I didn't write it to please Fred."

I want to tell him how touched I am, but I can't speak. He's leaning forward and this time, I know he's going to kiss me.

It still feels like what I've wanted forever. His mouth tastes like peppermint; his messy hair feels unexpectedly soft in my hands. And he's touching me so gently. His fingers feel like I imagine they would when he's playing a ballad, when he lingers on each note like it's not just an insignificant part but the truth of the whole piece.

At some point, he whispers that he likes my hair. Then he laughs a little and asks if I remember the fight we had this summer when I was thinking of getting it cut. I say yes, but I can't remember why I was so mad. At this moment, I can't imagine ever being mad at him. The wrong script. This is how he looks at what I did with Rick. Just three little words. As innocent as a mistake.

thirteen

Irene is trying to get me to admit I'm in love with him.

It's the next Sunday, and we're in her Honda, headed to the mall. She begged me to come with her to pick out some fall clothes. I should have known she just wanted to get me alone and pump me for information.

Willie is in the backseat. I tried using him as my excuse for not talking even though he's totally absorbed in his book, *Things That Go Zoom*. The truth is, I can't talk about this yet. It still feels too new, too fragile. We haven't even slept together, although Irene keeps teasing that that will change tonight, when I go to his apartment for dinner. I've told her to cut the crap, but it keeps flitting through my mind that I really should get some new underwear at the mall. Just in case.

"I'm your best friend, kiddo," Irene says, as she turns out of Mama's neighborhood. "If you can't tell me, who can you tell?"

I look out the window. "Maybe I'll tell my mother. Ha-ha."

"You know, she didn't say hi to me or jack squat just now," Irene says. "I felt like screaming, hey lady, I've taken care of Willie for a long time. I'm part of the family. Don't act like I'm dirt."

"Well, I am her family and she's barely spoken to me all week."

"I'm really beginning to think you should move out. You don't deserve this kind of abuse, honey. And apartment 1D is about to open up." She winks. "Right next door to Jonathan."

"I guess I'm going to have to." I lower my voice and glance at Willie. He's making machine noises. Vroom. "I hate to do it to her though. She'll miss Willie so bad."

"But what is her problem? She can't be this pissed just because Rick sent you some money. It's like she's gone crazy."

"I know," I say. It wasn't even Rick who sent the money, it was Gerald Boyd. But it was Rick's check, the first installment of his child support payments. An amazing sum, to me at least. Six hundred and eighty-five dollars.

Still, I thought about ripping up the check. And I offered to rip it up when Mama started freaking. She didn't want me to do that though; she wanted me to use the money to leave Kansas City.

She's sure I'm going to break down and let Rick see Willie

again. And even if I don't, she says, Rick will take the decision out of my hands.

"I saw a TV show about this. Fathers steal babies all the time. And sometimes the law helps 'em out. Ask that Mr. Boyd you're so fond of, he'll tell you even criminals have rights to their kids. For all we know, that killer will end up getting custody."

I tried telling her Rick would never take Willie, but she wouldn't listen. "I can't believe you're still in denial when it comes to that man!"

I hate the word denial. Even though Mama learned it in AA, I've never heard her apply it to herself, only to me.

She didn't stop yelling until Jonathan showed up to take me to McGlinchey's. He's been picking me up all week. I figured she would see us holding hands as we walked to the van, so I told her I was dating him. No response. Nothing about my life seems to matter to her now. Nothing except what I'm going to do about Rick.

I wish I knew. I told Irene what was going on with Rick because I wanted her advice, but she didn't have any. "What a mess," she said, and then she changed the topic to what really interests her right now. Jonathan and me.

Jonathan and me. It still sounds so strange. Of course the guys think it's beyond strange, but they didn't snicker and laugh when they found out, like I expected. Far from.

Carl was the first to say what was written on all their faces. "I hope you know what you're doing, man. That ex of hers is classic psychopath. If he finds out you even touched Patty, he could come after you and cut off your hands."

Jonathan shrugged this off, but I felt like someone had dropped an anvil on my chest, making it difficult to breathe. All week, I've had to force myself to keep repeating what Boyd said about Rick having straightened up. Not that Boyd couldn't be wrong, but he's the professional. He's spent hours and hours with Rick, as he keeps telling me.

"He really is a great guy," Irene is saying. "I know I used to bitch about what a weirdo he was, but I was just kidding around. Harry says Jonathan has more integrity than anybody he's ever met. I can definitely see why you're in love with him."

"I didn't say I was."

She frowns. "Boy, you're a tough nut to crack."

I smile but I don't say anything. I'm thinking about him now, and the last week. It has been great, and so unlike any other part of my life. The intense closeness we've had on stage is only part of it. He talks to me—about music but also about the newspaper or a book he's reading or the way the sky looks outside his window. He listens too, like what I think really matters. He calls me Pretty Patty when we're alone. He says I'm the first thing he thinks about in the morning and the last thing before bed.

Of course I'm in love with him. It feels like I've been in love with him forever, since I started singing jazz, since I heard him play, since he was born and I was born, and even before.

We're almost to the mall. I've pretty much decided that I need new underwear anyway. Nothing too fancy. Cotton in pastel colors, maybe with some flowers. And some perfume, too. Just in case.

• • •

"Isn't It Romantic" is playing on his stereo as I walk in the door. He has a beige blanket spread out on the living-room carpet, with a coffee mug full of daisies in the middle, and a bottle of red wine. "The food is coming," he says, and smiles. "Chinese. An occasion like this is too important for mere pizza."

Before I sit down, I call Mama. Willie was crying when I left, and holding out his arms for me. She told me to leave anyway, and I did, but I'm still worried. He never does this anymore.

"Is he okay?" I ask her. I hear the TV blaring cartoons. Then I hear Willie laugh and I feel so much better.

"He's my grandbaby, Patty Ann. I think I know how to take care of him."

"I didn't mean—"

"Don't worry about us," she barks, and hangs up.

When I come out of the kitchen, Jonathan has poured us each a glass of wine. "Everything all right?" he says.

I tell him yes, because there's nothing to say. Mama is mad at me, and that's not news. She's always like that now.

I don't really like wine, but I take a big swallow, hoping it will help me calm down.

"You smell nice," he says, kissing my neck. He leans back and smiles. "Do you notice anything different about me?"

The only thing I see is how adorable he looks, but that's not different.

"I cut my hair," he says, and turns around.

It's true. It's still not short by any means, but it's shorter than it was. Almost as short as mine.

"It looks good, but why?"

"I thought you would like it." He raises his eyebrows. "And this way, Irene can't call me Beethoven anymore."

I laugh. "You know about that?"

He laughs too, and moves closer. "Not the composer, the dog. I heard."

I take another gulp of the wine before we start kissing. A few minutes later, we end up lying on the blanket. He pushes the mug of flowers out of the way with one hand; the other is on my stomach. It's so much more intense than I expected. The food hasn't even arrived yet.

"All week, I've been thinking about this," he says. "I don't mean just the physical act. With you, I want it to be philosophical, spiritual, and emotional. The union of our souls."

His hand is inching up my shirt. Now I wish I'd thought to replace my raggedy bra, too.

He's touching my breast and it feels so good, but something is telling me to hold back. Don't do this with him, it could ruin everything.

I'm saved by the delivery guy. Jonathan jumps up to answer the door. I'm not hungry but I act like I'm starving when he suggests we heat it up later.

"Sorry," I say.

"It's fine." He squeezes my hand. "We have time."

He eats three plates full while I'm still picking at my first. He's talking about a new sax player he heard on the radio today. I'm listening, but I'm also trying to figure out what's wrong with me.

"What are you thinking?" he says, as he stands up to change the CD. I've eaten a half-dozen bites of rice and half an egg roll; I can't stuff in anymore. He's already cleared away the cartons and the dishes.

"Nothing much."

He sits back down and looks at me. "Are you nervous?"

"A little."

"We don't have to do this. If you're not ready, I'll understand."

"That's sweet. The thing is, I don't know if I'm ready."

He picks up my hand and kisses my palm. "The only way to find out is to start. But I'm not a brute. If you want to stop at any point, I will."

"I know." I gulp. "I think I might be a brute though."

"What?" He looks like he's going to laugh but then he looks closely at me and stops. "Of course you're not a brute. You're elegant and womanly, the very definition of the not-brute."

"But I'm not like you. I don't even know what it means to have philosophical sex."

He does laugh then but it's gentle. "Patty, you really do blow me away. You're incapable of being anything but real." He kisses my forehead. "All I meant was that I want it to be special with you."

"I want that too."

"Well, then?" He nods at the stereo. "Listen to the man."

The man is Johnny Hartman, who's becoming one of my favorite jazz singers. The song is "They Say It's Wonderful."

I smile and pull him closer. I hold his face in my hands as we move back down on the blanket.

By the time the phone rings, I have my shirt off, and we're both out of breath. He says he isn't going to answer, but I tell him it might be Mama. "Something could be wrong with Willie."

"Right," he says, and stumbles up to get it.

He says hello, then rolls his eyes and mouths the word "Fred."

After a minute, when he's still talking, I flip through my *Jazz for Beginners* book, lying on Jonathan's floor. I finally showed it to him last week, and he told me it was a great book to start with. "You have good instincts," he said. "You're obviously really smart, Patty. Don't worry, you'll catch up."

I beamed like I'd won the lottery.

I put the book down, go over to him and reach around the back of his waist. "Hang up," I whisper, but he shakes his head. He looks away from me. He's listening intently now and his mouth looks tight, mad.

Fred doesn't know about us; we both agreed it was none of his business. This is why when I hear Jonathan mention my name, I'm stunned—and even more so by what he says.

"Patty and I would rather quit."

"What?" I whisper.

"Then call her yourself," Jonathan says. "Be my guest." He slams down the phone.

223

"What was that?"

"The Almighty has decided that the piece isn't marketable as is. He said the lyrics are too complicated for the average consumer."

I'm really surprised. Fred seemed happy last night when we unveiled the finished version of Jonathan's tune right after the last set at McGlinchey's. We'd been working on it all week. I sang the lyrics with "he" and "she," like a story, rather than "me" like Jonathan wrote them. The bartender and the waitresses applauded, so did Fred. He told me I was better than Darla, usual stuff.

"He thinks you sang it wonderfully, but the piece itself is flawed. The average consumer. Jesus, he's such a moron."

I'm back on the blanket, but Jonathan is pacing back and forth, almost knocking the mug of flowers over every time he passes. Obviously it's time to put my shirt back on. I turn away from him to do it. He doesn't come closer or object.

"If you don't change them," I finally say, sitting up straight, "then what?"

"I don't know. You heard me tell him we'd quit first."

"You mean not go in the studio?"

He looks at me. "No, I mean quit. The end. Finis. We don't work for Fred."

"But who do we work for?"

He shrugs. "Even if we starve, we're better off than letting that idiot treat us like slaves in his puppet dictatorship."

I lower my voice. "I don't think I can starve, Jonathan."

"That was only a figure of speech. I worked for years without a manager and I was fine. I couldn't buy clothes or records or gas, but I ate. Sometimes it was fried flour and water, but it was food."

"I have to buy clothes though. And I have to buy vegetables and fruit and meat and vitamins. I have Wil—"

"I don't think you understand. Fred isn't telling me to make a few minor changes; he's saying the lyrics are unacceptable."

"That sucks, but—"

"You told me you loved what I wrote. Were you humoring me, Patty? Is that all this was?"

On the next pass, he finally kicks the mug of flowers over. As I stand up and move to the couch, I watch the water spread over the blanket like a shadow.

"I do love the song," I say, and force my voice to sound friendly. No matter how it looks, we're not having a fight. We can't be. "It's just that I have Willie to consider. He can't wear last year's clothes. He can't eat flour and water."

"And what are you going to teach him? That art is irrelevant? That having no principles is acceptable as long as you have a convenient excuse?"

"I hope not. But I can't teach him anything if I can't feed and clothe him and take him to the doctor when he's sick."

He isn't saying anything so I rush ahead. "I won't be able to do this road crap much longer, Willie will be in school. I have to do everything I can to succeed now, while he's still little. Put some money in the bank. Even be able to help him go to college."

"College is vastly overrated."

225

"That's easy for you to say. You got to go."

He doesn't respond. I lean back on the couch, watch as he stomps back and forth on the blanket, running his hands through his hair until it looks as messy as usual.

Okay, we are having a fight, but still, I tell myself it's not that bad. We can patch this up. Somehow.

Finally he spins around and looks at me. As he speaks, the side of his left hand seems like it's slicing the air.

"While I was trying to write lyrics, I kept coming up against the idea that even if I wrote something great, you would reject it if Fred said it didn't have the potential to be popular. That you wouldn't defy him no matter how narrow-minded he is, how stupid and shortsighted."

"But I just told you why. I understand how you feel, I just don't have the choices you do."

He shakes his head. "I'm sorry, but this is not what I expected after all the work we've done together in the last month." He glances in my eyes. "It certainly isn't the way I want you to be."

"The way you want me to be?"

"You know what I'm saying."

"No, I don't."

"Everything about us seemed different, but I told myself it was only appearances. I told myself that deep down inside, we were the same. That you might be my true soul mate."

"I thought that too," I whisper.

"Then it seems we were both equally deluded."

"You don't mean that," I stammer, even though I know he

does. His lack of response is the proof. That and the distance between the couch and the wall he's leaning against. It's only ten feet but it seems enormous suddenly, unbridgeable.

But it can't be true. Yes, we're having a terrible fight, but we can work it out. I can change this back. Make it like it was only a few minutes ago, when I was in his arms on the blanket, amazed at how wonderful it felt, how lucky I was.

If only I knew what to do. I'm so nervous; my mind can't come up with anything except I'm sorry. And I'm not sorry, that's the problem. I respect the way he sees this. It's part of what I love about him, that he has high standards, that he believes in what he does so much. I also understand why he wants me to see it the same way, but I just can't. Do it, be it, live it, yes—as long as it doesn't hurt my baby. Music is wonderful, but Willie is my heart. Music makes me feel alive, but he is the reason my life makes sense at all.

When I finally force myself to stand up, part of me is still sure he'll try to stop me. And after I tell him I'm leaving now, it feels like my whole body is straining to hear his no.

But it doesn't come. He looks every bit as sad as I feel, but he doesn't move. Doesn't even say good-bye.

I miss the exit to Evans, and it's after ten—and way after Willie's bedtime—when I finally make it to Mama's house. When I pull into the driveway though, every light in the house is on. And Willie's still awake. I can see his shadow against the curtains, running back and forth like it's a party.

I feel like throwing something. Mama used to let me stay

227

up all night when I was a kid, but with Willie, she's always treated bedtime like this huge deal. I've even lied to her about what time he goes to bed on the road, just to avoid hearing another lecture on the importance of kids keeping regular schedules.

Maybe Irene is right, maybe she is going crazy. Irene isn't the only person who's noticed how weird she's been acting. Two of the neighbor women just asked me yesterday if she's okay. Mama used to come to their morning coffees but now she won't even wave at them. They thought maybe she was sick. I told them no, she's fine. She's just tired, I said. She has a lot on her mind, I said. I told Joan, her AA sponsor, the same thing, when she called and asked why Mama missed the weekly meeting.

"You know why," she said, when I asked her why she didn't go. I pretended to ignore the rant that followed about my letting Rick see Willie, have spaghetti with him. "You opened that door," she's said, several times. The door to the past, she means. My response has been to roll my eyes or tell her to back off or something, anything, other than really think about what she was saying.

I'm getting out of the car—cursing this day, wishing so badly I didn't have to deal with her now, when what happened with Jonathan is still too fresh and painful to think about—when a sickening possibility crosses my mind. I can't believe I didn't think of this before. But it's not true. It can't be. Anything but that.

I run up the driveway and onto the front steps, but I'm still telling myself it's not possible. I'm already looking forward to how stupid I'm going to feel, running like this, when I see that everything is fine. Mama is mad at me, but that's it. Nothing worse.

And then I walk into the living room and see her. She's standing by the television, and there's no way to deny what's going on. She has the bottle in her hand. It's Jim Beam, her favorite, and it's half empty. There's another one almost empty on the coffee table, only a few feet from where Willie is chasing his ball.

I feel like I've just stepped off a cliff. Of course she's drinking—it explains everything. All the anger and how tired she looks and even that she's fallen asleep three times this week "forgetting" to change Willie's diaper. But how could she be drinking? How could she, when she knows it will destroy our lives?

"Baby," I whisper, leaning down to pick up Willie. He seems fine, but my breath is coming in short gasps as I think about all the things that could have happened. What if she'd passed out? What if she'd dropped one of her stupid cigarettes and burned the house down?

He's in the same blue-and-yellow-striped T-shirt he had on when I left, even though it's stiff with dried grape juice.

No wonder he's napped so well all week. He's completely exhausted. As soon as I have him in my arms, his head falls on my shoulder and his legs go limp as he lets out a deep breath like he can relax now, he's finally where he belongs.

"I want you to know it's happened." She's shaking the bottle at me. "You think I'm so damned funny! Well, the joke's on you, missy."

"I don't want to hear it." I turn away from her. My voice is as disgusted as I can manage, even though I'm swallowing back a sob.

"He came to see Willie, just like I said."

"What?"

"That's right! Your two-bit movie star." Mama is yelling so loud, I'm sure the neighbors can hear. She kicks at a green truck on the floor and it rolls under the coffee table. "He wanted to give him this stupid thing."

"Truck," Willie says softly.

My first response is relief. If Rick was here, then maybe it's not her fault. Maybe he made her do this somehow. I imagine him holding her down, pouring the bottle down her throat. She's begging him not to. Saying she'd rather die than endanger her grandson.

But I know it's just my imagination. I know before I ask her why she let him in.

"I didn't. I'm not stupid! I told him he can go to hell in a rowboat without a paddle. I told him if he put one foot in my house, I'd call the cops and have him put away for life." She smiles at Willie, but it's a syrupy, cloying smile. "He saw the truck, so I had to let Malone give it to him. But I slammed the door in his face."

"So you were already drunk?" I know she's been at it for a while. She has that glassy-eyed look I recognize so well.

"I ain't drunk now," she says, putting the bottle down with a start, like she didn't realize it was in her hand.

Tomorrow, I'll know what to do about this. Tomorrow. "Let's go to bed, buddy," I whisper.

"I can put him to bed." She drops her hand on his arm. "Give me my baby. My sweet little Willie."

He's still awake, and he's snuggling into me, hard. It occurs to me that he's afraid of her. My teeth are clenching to keep from yelling. "Stop it," I hiss, and move towards my room.

She gets there first though, and blocks the door. She keeps telling me to give him to her. "I'm taking care of him, not you," she says. When I finally tell her we'll have to leave then, we'll spend the night at Irene's, she says, "No you won't." Her voice is a triumphant squeal. "You think you can drive any time you want, but it's not true. It's my car. If you take it, I'll call the cops on you."

"Granny is just joking," I tell Willie. I'm rocking back and forth on my heels, praying he'll be asleep any minute. He's slept through rehearsals before. If only he could sleep through this.

She comes so close I can smell the whiskey on her breath. "I don't care if you get arrested, Patty Ann. Everything is about you. You, you, you, always the little princess. I'm sick of it!"

"Please, Mama, shut up. You need to shut up." I already can't imagine ever trusting her with Willie again. If she goes much further, we'll lose it all. "You don't mean any of this."

"You don't know what I mean." She points a finger at me, but her voice turns halting, a little teary. I've heard this shift a thousand times. Back and forth: anger, self-pity. This is the past. I can't believe we're here again.

Even what she wants to talk about is the same.

"I want to tell you something about when I met your daddy," she says, after a moment. Her finger is still in the air.

231

I couldn't care less about this right now. I shake my head.

"He was in love with that Evelyn."

I look at her. "What?"

"Yeah, he wanted to marry that slut instead of me. Isn't that the funniest thing you ever heard?" Her eyes are darting around the room; her voice is shrill. "He only changed his mind 'cause I got pregnant. He wouldn't even sleep in my bed, 'cause he thought I tricked him."

She's crying now, sudden, angry tears.

"No matter what I did, he wouldn't give me a chance. He'd come home and walk right by me, looking for you. He didn't even want me outside with him when he was doing his chores. He'd take his little princess anywhere, but not me."

I think of all the times she wailed for him to come back. All the times she told me how happy they were.

I'm surprised, but I also feel like everything makes more sense now. All those memories I had, sitting with Rick in the cemetery that night, of Daddy and me. The fact that I've never remembered a single time when he and Mama touched each other. Even the pictures are all of him by himself or him with me, never the two of them.

Maybe I would feel sorry for her if she hadn't kept this from me for so long—and if she wasn't screaming that she'd never had anything because she sacrificed her life for such an ungrateful little brat.

I'm finally able to get past her, but my whole body is shaking as I go into my room and push the door shut. I turn the lock in the knob, and she screams for me to open this door. She's pounding on it, yelling to let her in.

Willie has his hands over his ears. I put my hand on the door, willing her to stop. Stop. Stop.

My bedroom door at the old house was cracked. She cracked the wood, doing exactly what's she doing now. I used to wonder what the people who bought the house thought when they saw that door. Maybe they thought we were crazy. I didn't care though. That was the past.

When I turn around and see him sitting on my bed, I'm not even that surprised. Of course Rick's here. This isn't now anymore. Now ended when I walked in the door and found my mother stinking drunk.

His arms are crossed; his eyes are looking straight down, staring at the mess of Willie's crayons on the rug. He's wearing the same black shoes, maybe even the same jeans he had on in Omaha, but there's one difference. He has a deep gash running along his hairline to his left temple, not open but not a scar yet either. The only sign of his accident.

He's standing up. Apologizing for startling me. Explaining why he crawled in my open back window—easy to do, I remember, since I took down Mama's dinner plate.

"I got here, Sylvia was like this." His voice is quiet, urgent. He nods at Willie. "I thought I should stay until you got home. Make sure he was okay if she passed out."

Sylvia. He had a lot of ugly names for her, but he always called her by her real name when she was drunk. Even the way he's acting is exactly the way he used to: shy, almost afraid, as if her being like this reduced him to being a kid again with his own drunken mom.

I'm so confused, but I manage to whisper, "I want you to leave now."

He nods again. Before he can move though, Mama is messing with the lock. She has a master key, I forgot about that. It's her house. Even this room is hers, she tells me, as she pushes open the door and then lets out a hysterical laugh when she sees Rick standing there.

Her face is white as bone, but her voice is dripping with sarcasm. "Well, well, well. If it ain't the killer. I should've known you'd be here, waiting for your little slut." She turns to him and laughs. "Guess what? You can have her for all I care."

"Mama, stop."

"Everybody loves the little princess." She leans against the door frame. "Go on, take her." She turns to me. "I don't want you in my house no more."

She always threw me out—that's how our fights ended. It was as if getting rid of me was the solution to some problem she couldn't name. The problem of her inability to love me, it seems now. The problem of having a child you can't stand to look at, much less care for.

I've been trying not to look at Rick, but when I turn away from her, he catches my eye. I look in his big brown eyes, just for a moment, but it's enough. This is what he knows about me that no one else does. This is the thing we've always had in common—the ugliness at the root of our families, the lack of love, the hopelessness.

"But you don't get to have my grandbaby, too. You got everything, you always have, but you don't get him!" She moves right next to me. Her arms are thrust out. "Give me my boy."

I keep blinking, wishing so badly to see her standing up straight and saying she doesn't mean it. She doesn't just care about my father or my son; she cares about me, her daughter.

The other reason I'm blinking is so I won't be blinded by tears.

"Daddy," Willie mutters, half asleep, pointing his chubby finger at Rick. He's just showing me he remembers, but it feels like fate.

I know it's a mistake even as I grab the diaper bag and Willie's beagle. It's a mistake, but that doesn't mean there are any other options.

Jonathan was wrong, that's all there is to it. It isn't a script and it never was. It's my life.

fourteen

The first thing I feel is his fingers on my ear lobes. He's flipping them back and forth. His voice is higher than usual, excited. "Waked up, Mama. I gots to show you."

"What?" I say, and yawn. My chest hurts, but then I realize why: he's sitting on it, bouncing up and down.

"Toys," he shouts.

"Hold on," I say, but he's crawling off me, dangling his legs over the side, scrambling off the bed. "Come back here, buddy," I yell. No response. "I mean it. I want you where I can see you."

The room is light even though the curtains are pulled closed. It's so tiny I feel like I could reach both walls if I stretched my arms out. At the end of the double bed, there's a green plastic lawn chair with a pair of jeans and a faded gray T-shirt hanging off the back. The closet door is half open. I can see a pile of Rick's clothes stacked on the floor.

Willie peeks through the doorway and grins. "I in here, Mama. The toy room!"

I manage to sit up and then stand, but I feel like a limp rag. I must have slept all of an hour last night. But I make my way into the next room, and I can't help smiling. He's sitting in the lap of a gigantic white stuffed bear. It has a large red bow around its neck; Willie's head doesn't even come up to the bottom of the bow. On his left side, there's an expensive-looking wood train set, a racetrack, and at least fifty little cars. On his right, two more bears and a stuffed elephant, a Fisher Price garage set, a blue ball as big as he is, and a bunch of action figures.

The toy room is what it is, all right. There's a twin mattress in the opposite corner but no other furniture, not even a chair.

"I wike this motel!" he shouts, as he jumps up and grabs a truck from the pile of cars.

"We need to change your diaper, buddy. Let's see if we can find some." The diaper bag had only one diaper. Mama must have taken the rest out, God knows why.

Willie ignores me, but that's okay. I need to use the bathroom, get a drink.

The bathroom is off the bedroom I came from. It looks clean, but there's only one towel and no paper cups. I run the faucet until it's cold, scoop up handfuls of water to drink. I'm splashing my eyes and cheeks when I hear Willie screaming.

He stepped on the wooden caboose; he has it clutched in his hand and he tells me he hates it now. He's not wearing shoes or socks. The bottom of his foot is angry red but not bleeding. After I get him calmed down, I convince him to come with me, explore this place. What if there are other toy rooms?

He takes my hand and puts on a goofy, mysterious grin. "Spies," he says, and I nod.

It doesn't take long. The house has a kitchen, but there's nothing in it but cabinets, an old stove, and an even older refrigerator. The living room seems much bigger than Mama's, but maybe it's only because it's empty, too, except for what looks like a brand-new TV sitting on the floor, next to the radiator. There's another bedroom with nothing in it but a few empty U-Haul boxes.

What Willie really wants to explore is the outside, but I tell him we can't until I find his shoes. From the front door, the outside seems as big as the house is small. The yard, as Willie calls it, is an immense woods. I can hear a creek, but I don't hear any cars. If I didn't see tire tracks in the dirt path, I wouldn't believe Rick had driven us here.

It's Rick's new place, the one Boyd told me about. To get here, we had to go through Kansas City, then Lewisville, then maybe ten miles north on roads I didn't know. Rick promised he would just drop us off and leave, and he kept his word. He opened the door, pointed us back to the bedroom, and then disappeared, after saying he'd see us in the morning.

I didn't expect it to be so beautiful. The air feels cold and still, and the smell is clean, woodsy. Most of the trees are still green, but one of the oaks has a solid orange band of leaves at the top, like a hat; another has tiny splotches of red on each leaf, as though it rained paint last night instead of water. If it wasn't so cold, I'd leave the door open. I do push back the curtains in all the rooms, hold Willie up to the window in the bedroom so he can watch the squirrels scrambling up the branches. His diaper feels like it's soaked up a swimming pool. When Rick gets back, I'll have to ask him to get some. All our exploring turned up nothing in the way of diapers or clothes.

But he thought of it already. He also got breakfast. A few minutes later, he comes in holding a grocery sack in one hand, a McDonald's bag in the other. The food smells wonderful, but I don't say anything as I take the sack from his hand, get out a diaper from the pack of toddler Pampers.

Willie is still in the bedroom. He has the giant teddy on the double bed and he's telling him a story. He fusses while I'm changing his diaper, but when I'm finished, he goes right back to the story. It's "Goldilocks and the Three Bears," or what he remembers of it.

Rick is on his knees, spreading napkins on the living-room floor. He lays out a sausage biscuit and hash brown patty for each of us. When he turns around and looks at me, I go to Willie, tell him breakfast is ready. He says he's hungry, but when he gets in the room and sees Rick, he throws himself on my leg.

"What is it, buddy?" I ask, as I pick him up. "You know who that is, don't you?" I turn around so he's facing Rick, but he won't look, he pushes his face against my shoulder. "Remember?"

"Daddy," he sputters.

"That's right. And Daddy got you a sausage biscuit. Your favorite." His little arms are glued around my neck. "Let's sit down. You can be on my lap."

"No," he yells, and points back into the bedroom.

Rick is staring at us, but I shrug. "I have to see what's wrong."

Willie won't tell me until I shut the door. Even then, he wants me to hold him on the bed. And he's whispering. "Daddy is wike Shredder."

Shredder is the bad guy on the Turtles cartoon. I wish I could laugh. "Your granny told you that, didn't she?"

He nods, and then it all pours out. Not about Rick though, about me.

Granny told him I was going to leave him forever and run away with Daddy. And he didn't want me to go. He wanted to be with me. He cried and cried, but Granny told him to be quiet. Granny told him good boys don't cry. He wants to be a good boy.

I want to scream.

"I was just at work, baby. Your granny misunderstood. I would never, ever leave you." I pause, take a breath. "And you know who bought you all those toys out there?"

He shakes his head.

"Your daddy."

While he's thinking about this, I lift up his shirt—the blue-

240

and-yellow-striped one with the juice stain. I wish I'd thought to grab some clothes. "He also brought us here last night, so I could give you a big belly kiss."

He's laughing now. After a moment, I say, "You want to eat?" He's at the door trying to open the knob before I'm even off the bed.

Rick looks relieved. He's already finished his food, and while we're eating, he talks to Willie about the toys. Obviously, he wants to make the same point I did, because he mentions that he's bought a couple of toys every week for the last month and a half. Since the middle of August. Since the last time he saw Willie, in the trailer in Omaha.

I can feel his eyes on me, but I look straight ahead.

Willie has a mouth full of hash browns when he asks Rick why he doesn't have any chairs to sit on. He thinks it's funny. "You gots a TV but no chairs or tewaphone."

"I just got this place a few weeks ago. I planned to fix it up before you saw it, but I didn't get a chance."

This seems to satisfy Willie. He picks up the little plastic cup of apple juice and asks me to open it for him. Then he babbles about the toys, trying to figure out which is his favorite. When he runs off to look at them again, Rick starts wadding up the napkins and food wrappers and talking about the house. He says he knows it needs work, but he plans to paint it, inside and out. And he's going to put down carpet. "It'll be better for Willie." He smiles. "Softer if he falls on his little butt."

I stand up and walk to the window, put my palms flat against the glass. It still feels cold even though it has to be midmorning. Everything about the last twenty-four hours seems like a nightmare. We're supposed to have a rehearsal today, our first in the studio. Fred said he was putting us with the best sound people in town. The guys were so excited on Saturday night, when Fred made the announcement. Even Jonathan didn't flinch when Fred said he was going to bill us as "Patty Taylor and Jonathan Brewer, popular jazz." "Popular?" I asked, and he just smiled.

Rick comes up behind me and says he figured the country would be good for Willie. And it's only ten miles from his job. The drive isn't bad. I turn around, look at a deep scratch on the floor. "I appreciate you helping me last night, Rick, I really do. But it doesn't change—"

"I have to show you something."

He starts down the hall, and I think he's going to the toy room, where Willie is. But instead he goes into the other bedroom, the one that has nothing except for the U-Haul boxes. I stand in the doorway, watch as he picks up one of the boxes and moves it to the middle of the floor. I can tell from the way he lifted it that the box isn't empty, after all.

"Look," he says.

I walk closer, but I'm still not close enough to see inside. He must know I don't want to be too close to him, because he takes a few steps back. Now I come forward, and on the top of the box, I see our old straw welcome mat.

I can't help it; I kneel down and pull it out. Underneath, the box is full of bundles of newspaper. I pull out a chunk and unwrap a ceramic salt shaker in the shape of a cow.

"Is the pepper in here too?" I say, grabbing the next thing.

"I'm not sure," Rick says.

I take another bundle and unwrap my Campbell's soup mug. I got it from the company for free. I had to save labels for almost a year.

I pull out one thing after another, line them up on the floor. Glasses and cups and plates. The cow pepper shaker. The snowman cookie jar I bought for our first Christmas together.

I haven't seen any of these things since the night Rick was arrested.

It happened after midnight, in Kansas City, down by the river. Of course I didn't know anything at the time; I didn't even realize he hadn't come home yet. When the cops came banging on the door, screaming that they had a search warrant, I was asleep. They wouldn't tell me what Rick had done or where he was. They cuffed my hands behind my back and forced me to the floor.

I had to lie face down in only my T-shirt and underpants. They told me not to say a word, and I didn't, not even when they ran a knife through my stuffed Snoopy, the only thing from my childhood I'd been able to sneak out of Mama's house. I remember thinking it was like being in a war, so much screaming, so much noise. I heard breaking glass, crashing dishes, the rattle of pans bumping across the kitchen tile. The dresser drawers cracking as they smashed them on the ground. A perfume bottle shattering when they dropped it in the bathtub. An explosion when they turned over the stand with the television.

It lasted at least two hours, and it felt like years. When they were finished, our apartment looked worse than if it had been hit by a tornado. A tornado is a random act of nature; it usually spares some things, but this was the work of determined, angry men. Nothing had been spared here.

This is what I always thought anyway. I never went back there. After the police were done questioning me at the station, I went to Mama's, and when she threw me out about a week later, I went to the Lewisville shelter, and a few weeks after that, I ended up downtown, in the Catholic home for unwed mothers, where I stayed until Willie was born. I knew the police had turned the apartment into a crime scene, but that wasn't the only reason I didn't go back. I was afraid if I had to look at all those things I loved broken to pieces, it would break me.

I'm picking up the cows when Rick tells me how he got these boxes. One of his friends went through the apartment, packed up everything that wasn't damaged, and put it all in storage. It's been there the whole time he was in jail, and last week he rented a truck to pick it up.

I'm still too stunned to say anything. In these boxes are three years of my life. All of my life with him.

Willie is yelling that he's ready to show us his favorite toy. He runs into the room, then over to me and pulls on my arm, but he really wants Rick. He's looking at him, but he's too shy to ask. "I bet I know your favorite," Rick says, walking towards him. "The train."

Willie shakes his head, but he lets Rick take his hand, lead him across the hall. I hear him giggle and say, "It's a surprise!"

I walk to the doorway, listen as Willie tells Rick why the elephant is his favorite. Rick is looking right at him, nodding as Willie runs around, talking about one toy after another.

I'm still holding the cows, remembering the day I got them at a garage sale. Rick was out somewhere with his friends, and I had the Lincoln. I had finally gotten my driver's license, at seventeen. I was still nervous about driving alone, but I had to get out of the house for a while.

When I told the old woman running the sale that I wanted those cow salt and pepper shakers, she asked if I cooked much.

"Not really," I said. "But I'm trying to learn." I felt bad because I knew I wasn't trying very hard. I would find a recipe in my cookbook, buy the food, and then let it spoil. Part of the problem was that Rick was almost never there at dinnertime. I kept thinking I'd cook for myself, but then I'd just eat crackers from the box and watch TV.

"You have plenty of time," she said, and smiled and patted my arm like she was my granny.

I was touched by her friendliness, but I thought she was wrong. Time was the one thing Rick and I didn't have. We couldn't keep living like this. Most days, I thought it was unlikely I would live to be twenty-one. Even if I did, I was terrified Rick wouldn't be there with me.

The things I bought for the house were so real, so permanent. I think that's what I loved about them: they never changed. The snowman cookie jar was the same the first Christmas, when we were happy, as the last, when he was so busy cutting and bagging dope that he never spoke to me all day.

I carefully put the cows on the floor and walk into the toy room. Rick is playing with Willie, and I sit on the floor with my legs crossed and watch them. The sun is streaming in the window, and they're pushing cars around the track. When Rick says, "I hope I don't run into anything," Willie quickly shoves four cars right in front of Rick's car. Rick makes a screeching sound and tells Willie he needs better brakes.

I look away when I find myself thinking about his accident.

While Willie is arranging the train cars, Rick tells me about his job. He says he's working on the loading dock at the plastic factory in Lewisville. It's boring, but there's lots of room to move up. And he gets to drive a forklift, he says to Willie. He gets to lift huge wooden crates that weigh thousands of pounds.

Willie loves this idea. He says he wants to drive the forklift with Daddy.

I'm still surprised how easy it is for him to call Rick that.

After a while, Willie says he wants to ride the blue ball, and Rick puts him up on top of it, then sits down in front, holding the sides of the ball, trying to keep him steady. He smiles when Willie manages to roll off the ball and right into his lap. Rick gives him a quick kiss and Willie squirms away, but he's grinning so big you can see all of his little teeth.

Willie is starting to get bored with the toys when Rick suggests they tear down the wallpaper in the kitchen. He says it's disgusting; I don't think it looks that bad. The purple flowers are a little too big, but the floor-to-ceiling vines are pretty. It has turned yellow here and there, but it might be washable. The only tear is in the corner, hardly noticeable.

It certainly looks worse an hour later. Rick is using a sharp knife, but it's too thick to fit easily between the paper and the wall; Willie has a plastic fork from McDonald's. There are patches of torn wallpaper and other places with globs of dried adhesive. The exposed wall is dingy, institutional gray. Willie's contribution is a knee-high line of rips going all the way around the kitchen.

But I have to smile as Willie kicks his way through the sheets of paper on the floor. I can't remember when he's been this excited.

They both have their shirts off. It's still cool in here, but Willie insisted he was sweaty too.

Rick waits until Willie is in the toy room, checking on his teddy bear family, to ask what happens next. I start to tell him I need to be at a rehearsal, but then he says he doesn't mean today.

"I got this place. I bought all those toys. I let Boyd take child support out of my checks." He doesn't turn around. The muscles in his back are flexing like an obscene grin. "I'm his father, Patty. I want to be in his life."

I knew this was coming, but I'm still not ready. I hear Willie laughing down the hall. I take a deep breath, and finally tell Rick he's right. He is his father, and if he's really straightened up—really and truly—I guess he could start supervised visits with Willie.

"Visits?" he says, and turns around. "That's what you think I'm talking about?"

"Well, Gerald Boyd said you—"

"Come on, Patty." He shakes his head. "You know what I want."

"No, I don't," I say, but it's a lie. I do know. Maybe I knew it last night, when he was sitting on the bed at Mama's. Certainly I knew it this morning, when I woke up in this place, so much like the kind of house we used to talk about living in someday. Way out in the country. Far away from my mother and his mother, far away from his friends, far away from all our problems. A real home.

I'm so confused; I can't think of any reply when he looks into my eyes and holds my gaze. "You know the best thing for Willie would be to live here. Me, you, him."

I exhale and look away from Rick, but it doesn't help. The package of Pampers he bought is propped against the wall, and it reminds me of what I always wanted for Willie. What I dreamed about in Kentucky, why I woke up in tears because I knew Willie would never have it. A normal life. A place where he could spread out his toys and stay. Permanence.

Willie is back, holding the elephant, laughing and kicking his way through the sheets of paper on the floor. "Look, Daddy," he shouts, a moment later. He's picked up a long strip and wrapped it around his stomach and chest. "I a wall."

Rick laughs. "You're having fun, aren't you, buddy?"

Willie nods and repeats that he loves this motel. Rick

smiles. "I was just telling your mom that you guys should live here with me. How does that sound?"

Willie is still tangled up in wallpaper. I'm not sure he understood what Rick was saying, but he says, "Yep!"

I've never seen him so happy. Does it matter that I don't love Rick? If Rick has really changed, then Willie deserves to have him in his life. Willie deserves a father who loves him.

I'm still thinking about this a few minutes later, when Rick puts Willie in the air, spinning him around like a top. Every few circles, he leans Willie over so I can kiss his nose. Willie is laughing a high-pitched, joyous giggle. But then Rick changes the game. He doesn't hold Willie out; he suddenly leans over and kisses me, hard.

When I jerk back, I know Willie is looking at me. I force a smile, but still he says, "Don't, Daddy."

Rick laughs. "You jealous I kissed your mom?"

Willie squirms until Rick puts him down; then he runs over, throws his arms around my legs. When I pick him up, he fingers my earlobes. As Rick walks closer, he sticks his arm out, repeats, "Don't, Daddy. Mama don't wike it."

"I'm okay, buddy," I say, but I'm peering into his face, wondering if the sadness I see is real or a reflection of mine. How could he know?

"I wanna go home," Willie suddenly says.

Rick tries to distract him but it doesn't work. He has no interest in the wallpaper now, no interest in playing cars. And every time Rick comes near, he holds his arm out. He won't let Rick get close to me. "Mama don't wike it," he keeps saying.

I hold him closer and breathe in his hair. I know what he's doing and I can't believe it. He is trying to protect me, my tiny boy, who doesn't even understand what he's protecting me from.

All of a sudden, it hits me with the force of a slap, how stupid I've been. His father is a man who forced me to the ground, bruised me, put his hand over my mouth. Of course Willie wouldn't want this for us—even if he's too young to say why. I remember the intensity of a child's feelings. I would have done anything for Mama. She never understood what she had in her daughter's love.

Rick is standing very still, chewing on his bottom lip. I take a breath and force my voice to sound light. "Maybe we should get going. It has to be almost lunchtime. I have a rehearsal this afternoon, like I told—"

"He's two years old, Patty. He doesn't get to decide."

"He isn't deciding," I say firmly. "I am."

"So this is it? I do all this shit for you and you just walk away?"

His voice isn't loud but it's undeniably angry. Even Willie senses the change and mumbles, "Home."

I look at Rick, turning my eyes at Willie. "We really can't talk about this now."

"When can we talk about it? After I take you back?" He smiles a mean smile. "You'll call me up sometime, just to talk?" He takes a step closer, shakes his head. "I've given you plenty of chances, Patty. I tried to talk in Kentucky but you threw me out. I begged you to talk in Omaha but you ran away like I was a dog about to bite you."

Willie whispers, "Mama," and I pat his back.

We argue for a while—or at least Rick does. I'm pretending to listen, nodding like I understand, trying to keep him calm. When he finally grows quiet, I think it worked. He's come to his senses, realized he can't talk like this around a two-year-old.

But then Willie repeats that he wants to go home, and he asks me to call the big guys to pick us up. "I pack my toys in the van," Willie says. "I take them home."

"We don't need to do that," I say quickly, but it's too late. Rick grabs the elephant off the floor, shakes it by the throat, as he shouts that the toys are staying here, so are we.

"Stop it, Rick! You're scaring him."

"I not scared," Willie screams, but his body has gone so rigid it's hard to hold him. He has his hands out and he's trying to grab the elephant from Rick. "You hurt it! You hurt it!"

"Rick! Please."

It doesn't last long, but it seems like forever.

"Here," Rick says, exhaling as he hands the elephant to Willie. He shakes his head. "Jesus, I'm sorry."

He is. I can see it in his eyes, in the way he has his hands stuck under his armpits, like he's determined to control them, like he's ashamed of what they just did, what they're capable of.

But Willie won't even look at him. He hasn't grown up with kindness mixed with cruelty. He sees no reason to forgive.

I'm walking down the hall, trying to comfort Willie, when I see all those things from our apartment lined up so carefully on the floor. It seems sad to me now, how much those things meant to me.

All I wanted then was to hold on to what I had. Nothing in my past had taught me that change could be good.

I've changed, Rick. This is what I told him when he showed up in my hotel room in Kentucky, and it was so true. Maybe the truest thing I've ever said to him.

I hold Willie closer, gently rub his back, as I realize the other thing I told Rick was true too. There's someone else now, I'm sorry. There's someone else, the first person in my life who it doesn't hurt me to love.

fifteen

The enormity of the mistake I've made is beginning to dawn on me, but I have to believe I can fix this. I'm not a little girl anymore. I can stand up to anybody for Willie's sake, even Rick.

Poor baby, as soon as we walked into the toy room, he burst into tears. He cried and coughed and hiccupped and finally fell asleep in my arms. When I put him down on the twin mattress, he rolled over on his side and stuck his thumb in his mouth. His other fist was still glued around the elephant's trunk.

After I shut the door behind Willie, I went straight into the living room. Now I'm standing in the doorway. Rick's about five feet in front of me. Of course he knows I'm angry, but he chooses this moment to ask why I cut my hair.

"It was so beautiful. It felt like—"

"That's none of your business."

He pauses for a moment. "All right. Are you ready to talk to me now?"

"There's nothing to talk about. You're going to take us back to Kansas City."

He shakes his head.

"Yes, you are," I say firmly. "You're taking us back and then you're going to leave us alone. And I'm not talking about this week or this month, I'm talking about for a long time. Willie's too little to deal with this kind of crap."

"It's never gonna happen." His voice is quiet. "I can't live without you, Patty. You know that."

"It is going to happen." I take a breath. "Because if it doesn't, I'll have to tell your parole officer."

His eyes narrow. "What are you talking about?"

"I'll tell him about Omaha, all the stuff you did. The drugs, the gun, threatening to kill Jonathan."

"No, you won't." He walks closer. "I know you. You haven't talked to anybody about that night." He smiles. "You're good at keeping secrets, remember?"

I used to say this when we were first together and he had to go out with his friends. I wanted to be with him all the time. I wanted him to take me along, trust me. Usually he'd just laugh and tell me I was cute. Once he put his lips on my ear: "You want me to tell you a secret? I love you so much, sometimes I dream of building a big cage to keep you in. No other guys would ever see you. I'd feed you from my hand, look at you naked night and day."

I feel like I'm going to throw up. He's right, I'm still keeping his secrets; otherwise, why didn't I tell Boyd any of this before? Why didn't I even mention that Rick had shown up in Kentucky and Omaha?

But I rock back on my heels, insist I will tell him now. I'll tell him everything, even what Rick did to me.

His voice is soft. "What did I do to you?"

"You know what it's called."

"Yeah." He puts one finger on my throat, traces a line around my neck. "With other girls, it's just screwing. With you, baby, it's always love."

Without even thinking, I reach up and slap him across the face. And then I finally say it. "Rape." I say it again, louder, knowing for the first time that I've forgiven myself for letting him touch me, wanting him to comfort me.

His mouth looks flat, depressed, but he isn't arguing. It feels like freedom. I'm standing up to him, telling the truth. By the time I notice the tic on his left eye beating like the tail of a rabid dog, he's already grabbed my arm. He jerks me around backwards, puts his other hand on my shoulder, and starts shoving me down the hall, past the room where Willie is sleeping, into the back bedroom. He throws me on the bed and he's on top of me before I can move.

"It was love," he hisses. "Now I'm gonna prove it to you. I'm gonna take it slow. Make it like it used to be."

I'm squirming and fighting him, but he quickly pins my arms and my legs, pushes my shirt up with his teeth.

"I hate you!"

"No, you don't." He smiles and licks my chest. "I remember. You want this as much as I do."

He already has his pants unzipped when we hear the knocking. He mutters a curse and jumps up, goes to the window.

"Boyd. Shit, what is that little prick doing here?"

I've jumped up too, but before I can get to the door, he grabs my arm.

"If you leave this room, I'll have to kill him."

"Let me go."

He puts his hand under my chin, pulls my face so I am looking in his eyes. "I don't want to kill him, but I can't let you talk to him, now can I?"

I push him off and reach for the knob.

"Go ahead, Patty. Just so you understand, I'm not going back to jail. As soon as you walk through that door, I'll have to go out there and blow Boyd's brains all over the front porch."

I still don't believe him, but I'm afraid to keep arguing about it. Boyd might leave. "At least let me go in with Willie," I say slowly. "If he wakes up, he'll be scared."

He walks me down the hall and into the room; then he closes the door behind him. I press my ear to the keyhole and recognize Gerald Boyd's voice immediately, probably because he's saying my name. He wants to know if Rick has seen me.

"No. I'm just getting ready for work." Rick sounds so sincere. "Did something happen?"

"Her mother called me around four o'clock this morning. Apparently, she'd been calling every police department for a hundred miles. She wanted your phone number, but I told her you didn't have a phone yet." He coughs. "It was difficult to follow what she was saying, but from what I could gather, her daughter and grandson have moved out."

"Damn."

"Have you spoken to Patty at all?"

"No, GB. I thought about going over there, but I remembered what you said."

"That's good," Boyd says. "If you do hear from her, I'd advise you to—"

Boyd is still talking, but I've heard enough. I can't risk going on the porch. I don't believe Rick would kill Boyd, but he might beat him up. He might start screaming and scare Willie. But I've just thought of another possibility.

I rush to the window facing the back of the house. I open it slowly, quietly, and listen for a moment. I can't hear Boyd or Rick. If I crawl out quietly, they won't hear me. I can run into the woods and then circle back around. As Boyd drives away, I can flag down his car.

I pick Willie up and his eyes snap open. I whisper that he has to be very quiet, like the best spy in the world. He must hear the urgency in my voice, because he doesn't cry, doesn't even groan. The window isn't wide enough to hold him and crawl through, but it's low to the ground; it's easy to stand him on the grass and then scramble out backwards. He's blinking in the bright sun, but he still isn't making any noise.

I grab him and take off running. His arms are squeezing my neck; his bare feet are thumping against my sides, echoing the loud beat of my heart. We go deep into the woods, but I can see the sun sparkling on the tops of the trees, and I guess that the dirt road is to the left, along the creek, directly north. If only I'm right.

I keep running until I'm soaked with sweat. I can't pause for breath or even to take off my sweater; I'm afraid Boyd will leave before we get there. When I get to the clearing, there's nothing and I'm sure I'm lost. But then a few minutes later, I hear it. An engine. An old brown Jeep is coming down the hill.

I hug Willie to my chest and pant, "We made it, baby. We did it."

He whines that he wants to get down. I laugh with relief.

Boyd has seen us and jammed on the brakes. He unrolls the window, but I shake my head and run to the passenger side.

"We need to get out of here," I say, after I fling open the door. He doesn't say anything as I jump in. Willie is squirming on my lap.

"What's wrong?" he says slowly, as he puts the Jeep in park. "Who are you?"

His voice is the same. It has to be Gerald Boyd, but he looks like a high school kid. He has a mass of brown curls and a round face and eyes that are so wide they look like he's stuck being surprised. His body is soft like Humpty Dumpty's. He has on gray sweatpants and a shirt that says Drugs Aren't the Problem, Poverty Is.

This is the guy who was so sure Rick had changed. Oh God.

"It's me, Patty Taylor. We talked on the phone, remember?"

"Wait, Rick just told me—"

"Just drive, okay? I'll tell you everything as we go."

I turn my head, glance out the back window. Willie is kicking my legs, whining that he wants out of this car. I don't want to say it in front of him, but I have to make Boyd understand. "Look, he threatened to hurt you. I don't think he'd do it, but—"

Boyd's voice is incredulous. "Rick threatened me?"

"Just go."

But he won't. He has to know what happened. He says he's been working with Rick for the last month and a half. He can't believe Rick would hurt him or anyone. Rick's worked too hard to get his life back on track to screw up now.

His stupid, innocent eyes are looking right at me. I feel like slapping him. "Please! We have to go!"

And then Willie says it. "Daddy." His finger is pointing at the back window. I look, and Rick is running down the hill. Boyd looks too but still, he doesn't make a move to get us out of here.

Rick flings the door open, grabs Boyd by the shoulders and yanks him out of the car. He throws him down on the road and jumps into the driver's seat. The window is still open. I think he might just drive away, leave Boyd lying there blinking with surprise, but then he pulls a gun out of his pants.

The gun makes my mouth go dry. I didn't see the Reebok bag anywhere in Rick's house. I didn't expect this.

It's different than the one in Omaha. It's silver instead of black, and it shines like it's never been touched. Boyd is stand-

259

ing. His voice is conciliatory but not afraid, even though his eyes keep glancing at that gun.

"Listen to me, Rick," he says. "Whatever the problem is, we can work it out. There's no reason to overreact."

"Oh yeah?" Rick says. "We can work it out?" I've never heard him sound this way. His voice isn't cold or harsh; it certainly isn't angry. It isn't even flat, because a flat tone still has resonance. He sounds like I imagine a dead person would sound. He sounds like someone who is capable of anything.

I'm thinking about jumping out of the car when he turns to me. "Sit right there. Don't move." He turns off the Jeep and grabs the keys; then he tells Boyd to wait for him across the road—to talk.

Willie is sniffling. I know he wants to cry. He has one of my earlobes, but he's not flipping it back and forth, he's holding on tightly.

I yell to Boyd to run, but he just looks at me. Rick tells me to shut up.

"But you don't want to do this." My voice is a plea.

"No, I don't." He opens the door.

"Then—"

"Then what? Go back to prison? Lose you?" He steps out, but he's still looking in my eyes. "I don't think you understand how miserable I've been for the last three years. I told you I'd do whatever it takes to have you back." He slams the door. "Now you'll see I meant what I said."

As Boyd and Rick walk off into the woods, they look like two friends going fishing. I can hear Boyd's voice, and it sounds oddly comforting, as if Rick is his brother, in trouble, yes, but not really a danger. I flash to when Boyd told me he was aware of the kinds of things Rick had done. He meant the drugs. He meant the gang stuff: beating up people who couldn't pay, brandishing knives and guns, all the threatening and posturing that goes along with dealing. Of course he didn't mean murder. As far as Boyd knew, as far as I knew, Rick had never killed anyone.

It hits me with a jolt: Boyd is trying to talk Rick out of shooting himself. He thinks Rick is suicidal, just like he told me on the phone. This is why Boyd doesn't seem afraid. This is why the last thing I see is his hand on Rick's shoulder before they disappear into the trees.

Willie has let loose now, wailing and sobbing and kicking. I've opened the glove compartment, looked under the rug, praying that Boyd has another set of car keys somewhere. If only I knew how to hot-wire a car, I could go get help. Rick knows how. I saw him do it years ago, I don't remember why.

"Ssh," I tell Willie.

I'm holding him close, trying to calm him down, when the shot comes. It sounds far away, but it echoes in the quiet woods, disturbs the birds. It's followed by two more in quick succession. A few minutes later, Rick comes walking back. The gun is put away now. He gets in the Jeep and starts the engine without looking at me.

Willie stops crying then, distracted by the fact that Rick is driving backwards up the hill so fast.

"Where the other guy?" he asks, when Rick stops in front

of the house. I look at Willie, pray he really doesn't know.

"He had to leave," Rick says. His voice gives nothing away, but I notice blood splattered in the hairs of his arm.

Rick lets Willie honk the horn before he tells me to take him inside. "I'll be back in a few minutes." He touches my face. His fingers smell like smoldering metal. "Don't run off again. If I have to chase all over the woods looking for you, I'm gonna be really pissed."

I'm trembling so hard I can barely walk. When Willie runs into the toy room and starts lining up the train cars, I slump to the floor and put my hands on my face to stop my teeth from slamming together.

If only I'd stayed in this room, Gerald Boyd would still be alive.

"Choo-choo," Willie says, after a while. It sounds half-hearted though, as if he's forcing himself to play his usual games in this horribly unusual place.

Rick said he'd be gone for a few minutes but it was really almost an hour. I kept thinking we should run, but I was afraid as soon as we tried, he'd come back.

He went all the way to Lewisville and returned with Zeb. They're in the kitchen; we're sitting on the living-room floor, watching television. Rick turned on the set and told me to sit still. I'm holding Willie on my lap, straining to hear what they're saying. Every time a food commercial comes on, Willie reminds me he hasn't had lunch yet.

He sees nothing strange about being in a house with a man

he doesn't know. He's already asked if that big guy plays the drums.

They did something with Boyd's body and the Jeep. Now they're discussing whether Rick has to leave town. Zeb thinks Rick has no choice, but Rick keeps saying no. If the cops come by, he can lie his way out.

"Mama, I don't wike this show."

I whisper, "It's the only channel out here."

"I don't wike this motel."

"Ssh," I tell him. I think I hear something outside.

"I want that," Willie says, pointing to the screen. My ears are straining to make out the sound. It's tires, I'm sure of it. Someone is coming.

Rick hears it too. "I'll take care of it," he snaps. As he walks to the door, he tells me to keep my mouth shut. He nods at Willie. "Trust me, you don't want this to go bad."

When he flings open the door, I can tell from the way his shoulders loosen that it isn't a cop. But then he takes out his gun, points it straight ahead, and says, "You have exactly five seconds to tell me what the hell you're doing here."

"Patty's mother is worried about her. I told her I would come here and see if Patty was all right."

It's Jonathan. I can feel my stomach in my throat. Willie heard him too. He's leaning over, trying to see, babbling Jonathan's name.

"Is that right?" Rick steps back and lets Jonathan inside, but he takes a long look at him. "And how did Patty's mother know where I live?"

"I don't know."

He's obviously telling the truth. Rick is standing still, probably thinking, like I am, that Boyd must have given Mama the address when she called for the phone number. I flash to a few hours ago, when Boyd was standing on the porch and Rick called him GB. It's still impossible to believe that Rick did this. I can hear Mama screaming "the killer." It feels different now, knowing she was right.

"Why you?" Rick finally says, and takes a step closer. His voice is a hiss. "Why would Sylvia ask for your help, piano player?"

"I'm a friend of Patty's." Jonathan sounds matter-of-fact, as if Rick wasn't holding a gun on him.

"Oh yeah?" Rick says. "A good friend?"

"I don't want her to be hurt." Jonathan is facing Rick. He hasn't looked in my direction, even though Willie keeps calling him. "If you feel the same way, I think you should let me take her home."

My lungs feel tight; I can't catch my breath.

Rick laughs a short, harsh laugh. "You do, huh?" He puts the gun in his pants, but then he pushes Jonathan by the shoulders, hard. "Do you know who you're talking to? Didn't they tell you how close I came to blowing your brains out?"

"We got issues here." Zeb is standing in the doorway, scratching his chest. "Come on, man. This little shit ain't the problem."

Rick says okay, he's coming, but he tells Jonathan not to move or he'll have to break his neck. Jonathan doesn't say anything until Rick is gone. Then he looks at me and whispers, "Are you all right?"

I nod. "Mama really called you?"

"No, I called you." He waits a moment. "This morning. After I realized that hurting you over a song I wrote for you was more irony than I could tolerate." He smiles a half smile. "But I'm flexible. If Fred prefers the word 'stupid,' I'll go with that instead."

I can't smile back. "You have to get out of here."

He glances in my eyes. "So do you."

The conversation in the kitchen is getting loud. Rick still insists he doesn't want to leave Kansas City, even though Zeb keeps telling him a parole officer is almost as bad as a cop. Rick's voice is very tense though. Maybe he's starting to realize how serious this is.

Willie is crying with frustration. No one is listening to him. The TV is all scratchy. I won't let him off my lap. He's bored, he's hungry. He wants to go home.

I look at Jonathan. "Will you do me a big favor?"

"Of course." He takes a step forward, shoves his hands in his pockets. His voice grows so soft. "But don't ask me to leave you with him. I can't do that." He smiles weakly. "Porgy wouldn't do it, and neither will I."

I have to swallow hard to keep my voice from breaking up. "Bess didn't have any kids, did she?"

He doesn't answer, but I know the answer has to be no. If Bess had had a little boy, she wouldn't have asked Porgy to keep her safe, but to save her little boy. And she would love Porgy so much for that, even if she never got away.

I wish I knew the story better. I don't know if Bess gets away from Crown; I don't even know if she lives.

I take a deep breath and call Rick from the kitchen.

"I think Zeb is right. We should leave."

He stares at me. "What?"

"Boyd's office is probably already looking for him. He may have left a log with your address." I inhale. "And Jonathan's agreed to take Willie to Irene's, so we can get going."

"No way," Rick barks.

I release my hold on Willie, stand up, and go to Zeb. "Tell Rick he can't take a little kid with him. He's not thinking right."

I've never been this bold with Zeb, but I tell myself he's just another guy in a club. Make eye contact, like Fred says. Smile. Make them think every word that comes out of your mouth is just for them.

"It's true, man," Zeb says to Rick. "What do you care anyway? Shit, you've been telling me for weeks how great it was to get her alone in Omaha."

I want to scream, but I can't even flinch; Zeb is looking at me. And grinning. He sticks his thick tongue out, slowly licks his top lip. When he finally turns back to Rick, I glance at Jonathan. His face is expressionless, but I've spent a year on stage with him, I can see how upset he is. But he can read my face too, pleading with him to go along. Rick has a gun; Zeb does too. There's no other choice.

Even Willie seems to understand. He's run over to Jonathan; he's patting the hole in the knee of Jonathan's jeans.

266

"Fuck it," Rick says, and grabs my arm. "Let's go."

I look at Jonathan, nod a little. He bends down to pick up Willie. He does it awkwardly, tentatively, but once he has him in his arms, he holds him close, pats his back the way he's seen me do a hundred times.

Willie seems confused but not upset. He's waving bye. As Rick pulls me out the door, Jonathan glances in my eyes and mouths the word "cops." I don't want to scare him but I can't resist mouthing back "hurry."

sixteen

I don't have Willie. My mother is a drunk. I'm sitting in a car with Rick and his friend, going God knows where. All of the talk is ugly and meaningless. Whenever I catch a glimpse of people in other cars, I feel an ache of envy for what I imagine they're saying and doing and most of all, where they're going: the mall, a movie, over to friends.

This is the way my life used to be. That I've ended up here again is frightening, but what really stuns me is how sure I used to be that there was no alternative. Other people could have normal lives, but not me. All I could have was Rick.

We're in Rick's Nissan, but Rick asked Zeb to drive. There are only two doors; I'm sandwiched in the back between Rick

268

and Willie's car seat—there's no way I can escape. But of course I will escape, and soon. Now that I don't have Willie, it will be much easier. My arms are killing me from lugging him through those woods. My mind is exhausted from worrying about him.

Before we left, Zeb had the bright idea of shooting out both tires on the right side of Jonathan's van. I'm sure Jonathan will still get Willie out of there: the dirt road is all downhill, and he's very resourceful when it comes to moving the van. But hurrying is out of the question now. By the time he gets to the cops, we'll be miles and miles away.

Rick is holding my hand so tightly my fingers ache. He's already whispered this is all my fault. If only I'd done what he told me to do, we'd be sitting with our kid right now.

Even Omaha is my fault, he says, when Zeb gets out to make a phone call. Yes, he knows he hurt me—and he's been punished enough, he still has headaches from his car accident—but he couldn't help it.

"I was in prison, Patty. It had been three years." He looks at me. "I tried banging other girls, but it didn't change it. It had to be you. You're my wife."

His voice is quiet; his big brown eyes have gone soft like he's just told me the most romantic thing in the world. I can't take any more of this. I say I'm tired and close my eyes.

I hear Zeb get back in the car, but I don't open my eyes. I'm telling myself over and over that I don't belong here. Even if I can't get away physically, my mind can take me somewhere else. I can imagine the future. I can dream up a different life.

At first, it's hard. All I can see is Boyd's hand on Rick's shoulder as he walked to his death; all I can hear are recriminations of what a fool I was to think that Rick could have really straightened up. But then I force myself to concentrate on the last song I heard. It was on the way home from Jonathan's last night. I had the jazz station playing. It was one of my favorites, Betty Carter singing "Lover Man."

I focus on the song until the daydream begins. After a while, it's so clear I forget where I am, I don't even feel the pressure of Rick's fingers. It's winter, my favorite season because everything seems so much cleaner and brighter in the cold. I love to walk outside, follow the steam of my breath. But I'm not outside now. I'm in an apartment. I know it's at the Balconies, but it's not Jonathan's place or Harry's, it's mine. Mine and Willie's. His toys are strewn all over the floor. It's dark now though, and very late; the gig is already over. Irene has left; Willie is asleep in the bedroom. The Betty Carter song is playing softly in the living room. I see Jonathan's stereo on the floor. He keeps it at my apartment, so we can do just what we're doing now: sitting on my couch, listening to this great music.

When we start touching each other, we're so in sync with the music that everything we do is part of it: our rhythm is the same, we play off the melody with our kisses. It's like a solo except it's two people instead of one. Two people playing a riff that fits perfectly with the song and is still absolutely their own, and so full of feeling it leaves them both breathless and in awe.

The magic comes from listening, like Jonathan always says. The two of us listen to the music and each other, and when it's over, we listen to the silence. We sit in the silence for a long time, knowing there's nothing to be afraid of anymore.

After he kisses me good-bye, I go into the bedroom and snuggle up to Willie. Sometimes he cries out in his sleep, but tonight he doesn't. In the light from the winter sky, his face looks as sweet and peaceful as the baby he still is.

I worry about him a lot, but tonight I tell myself he's going to be fine. At least he's growing up surrounded by music, surrounded by people who believe that making something beautiful is what gives meaning to life. And I know he'll never have to feel that he was an accident. Even though he doesn't understand it yet, I've already started telling him the truth: that he was pure gift.

Of course if I'm lucky, he'll never realize how true that really is. He won't remember his father and especially, he won't remember this day. He'll never have to know what a miracle it is that anything good could come of the mess that was me and Rick.

It's almost dark, and we haven't even made it out of North Kansas City. We've spent the afternoon in an abandoned warehouse down by the river. There's one window with metal blinds; I've sat slumped in a corner, watching as a streak of sun moved across the dirty floor and up the gray wall and onto the ceiling before it finally disappeared.

The room seems so quiet now. All afternoon, it was packed

with the sweaty bodies of Rick's friends, dealing with this crisis. Everybody is gone now except Rick and Zeb. They're dividing up a wad of cash. Rick hasn't told me where we're going, but he did say he has enough money to go anywhere he wants.

I've already tried telling him I'm starving, but he ignored me. Of course he knows I could easily escape at a restaurant. It doesn't matter though. Wherever we go he'll have to deal with traffic lights, other cars, pedestrians. All he has to do is stop once and I can make a run for it.

But first, I have to get him away from Zeb. It should be simple enough. One of the other guys left Zeb's car in the parking lot, and everybody's expecting him soon—I heard a couple of them joke that he'd better show up at the bar quick, they want their damn money. He seems to be in no hurry to leave though. We're sitting at a small wooden table in the corner; he has his enormous feet propped up on the table, next to a rifle, and he's taking swigs from a bottle of gin. And talking. Every time Rick says we'd better get going, Zeb makes another comment about some business he's planning or some woman he wants or how terrible it was that he had to spend three years in prison.

Rick has had a few drinks from the bottle too, but it hasn't relaxed him. He's holding my hand tightly, and all his comments are curt, detached.

When Rick finally says we have to take off, Zeb drops his feet to the floor, sits up straight in his chair, and tells Rick there's one more thing they need to discuss.

He pauses for a moment, and then lowers his voice. "I know why you did your PO, man."

"Oh yeah?" Rick laughs harshly. "And why's that?"

Zeb doesn't answer; he just folds his thick hands on the table. His knuckles look gnarled and ugly, like they've been broken and healed wrong.

"She's fucking you up," he finally says, cracking those ugly knuckles. "I think you better get rid of her."

I can barely breathe, but Rick sounds more surprised than angry. "That's not your concern."

"Come on, man, you wanna end up back in Boonville? I guarantee this bitch is gonna put you there if you don't—"

Rick snaps, "I'm not in the mood to listen to this shit."

"You gotta listen—" Zeb begins, but Rick is already standing up. He pulls me up too, and we're halfway to the door when Zeb repeats, "You gotta listen, man."

His voice sounds menacing, but it's the other noise that makes Rick turn around. It's a metallic click, the cocking of a gun.

"Why don't you sit back down?" Zeb says, and smiles. He's holding the rifle, pointed right at my chest. He waits until we're back at the table before he nods at Rick's jacket pocket. "Give me yours."

Rick sits very still for a minute before he slides the gun across the table. Zeb picks it up, sets it on the floor. The rifle barrel is resting on his knees but his hand is still on the trigger.

"If you kill her," Rick says slowly, "I swear to God, I'll cut out your heart."

"I'm not gonna kill her." Zeb takes a long swig from the bottle. "But she's caused enough trouble. We're gonna let her go and then get the hell out of here."

My palm is wet but I'm not sure if I'm sweating or Rick is. But he laughs. "This has to be a joke."

"You can't keep this little bitch with you anymore. It's too dangerous."

"Don't push me, asshole," Rick says. "I'm warning you—"

Zeb slams his fist on the table so hard the gin bottle turns over. I watch the stream form, spill on the floor, as Zeb says softly, "Shut up, man. This is for your own good."

I bite my bottom lip, watch as Zeb sticks the barrel in Rick's face and tells him to give me the car keys and let go of my hand. Now. Rick doesn't move for what feels like forever. He turns around to face me as he holds out the keys, watches me put them in my pocket. His mouth is flat, but his eyes look stunned.

"Go ahead," Zeb says, looking at me, smiling a mean smile. "I don't give a shit who you tell. We'll be long gone."

I stand up, but I don't move. "Do it," he says. "Get the hell out of here."

It sounds like he means it, but there's another note in his voice that doesn't fit. I turn around very slowly. He can't really be letting me go, but why hasn't he shot me already? What does he want?

I keep listening. I hear Zeb breathing loudly through his mouth. Breathing and waiting. Waiting to see if . . . what?

All of a sudden, I get it. I run to Rick, fall on my knees, and throw my arms around his legs. The crying is genuine though; I'm so afraid. "I can't leave," I sob. "I don't want to live without you."

Rick's hand on my hair is soft, tentative. "Patty," he whispers. "Jesus."

Zeb sits quietly for a moment before he smiles and lowers the rifle. Rick blinks with surprise.

"It was a test," Zeb says, setting the rifle on the floor. He shrugs. "She passed."

"What the hell?"

"I had to do it, man. She could rat us out and we'd all be back in jail."

"You motherfucker."

"Don't be pissed. Like I said, it was for your own good. It turns out the bitch does love you. You're safe and so are we."

Rick has pulled me up on his lap, but I'm not crying anymore; I feel like I'm in shock. If I'd taken one more step, Zeb might have killed me.

At first I think Rick is in shock too, but then I realize he's just more furious than I've ever seen him. Even ten minutes later, when Zeb is smoking a cigar, talking about some friend of theirs, Rick hasn't said one word. Zeb doesn't seem to notice. I know he can't see Rick's eye tic drumming a frantic beat when Rick smiles and very casually asks if he can have his gun back before we go.

As he pushes me off his lap, I know what's going to happen, but Zeb still has no idea. He's wearing the same overconfident grin when he hands Rick's gun to him.

It flashes through my mind that it was true what Gerald Boyd said: Rick has changed. He always had a terrible temper, but Zeb is one of his oldest friends.

I hate Zeb, but I still don't want Rick to do this. It's too crazy, too dangerous. What if Zeb starts shooting too?

I put my hand on his arm and tell him I really want to leave now. My voice is begging him, but he pushes me off. He pushes me so hard I fall, and he doesn't even glance over to see if I'm okay. This has nothing to do with me.

The sound is so much worse than I imagined. Each shot slams into my ears like a fist. In between, I hear screaming and cursing, but I can't tell what's happening; the lightbulb went out with Rick's first bullet. I'm crawling along the floor, trying to find the way out. I know Zeb is shooting too. One of the rifle blasts was so close it knocked me over.

When Rick finally yells that we have to get out of here, I'm stumbling along the opposite wall, trying to feel my way to the door. He doesn't have to tell me he succeeded. The burning smell is mixed with the nauseating odor of blood. The air itself feels heavy with smoke and death.

He pulls me by the arm as we go down the hall and through the door. The parking lot is deserted, but it's not dark; the lights have come on. We've made it to the Nissan. Rick seems to be in no hurry to get in. He's breathing hard, stretching his fingers like they hurt. I can see the sweat glistening on his face.

He has all the money. It's shoved into his jacket pocket, but he takes it out, checks that he didn't drop any on the way. I'm not surprised that he took it off Zeb's dead body; I'm not even surprised that he thought to do it. Nothing he does surprises me now.

After a minute, he puts his arms around my shoulders, leans down and kisses my forehead. I want to pull away, but I can't. I'm afraid I'll fall if he lets go.

"I'm cold," I mumble.

He cups my cheeks in his warm hands, says we should get into the car. I still have the keys. I'm swaying as I lean against the bumper, reach into my pocket. My jeans feel damp, but I still don't understand. It's Rick who sees it. There's blood streaked across the gold lion-head key ring.

He gasps a curse and opens the door, helps me into the passenger seat. He kneels down, finds the hole in my jeans. It's to the left, below my waist, and small, but when he unzips my jeans and pulls them open, my whole side is covered with blood.

It doesn't even hurt. It seems as unreal as the rest of this.

"What a difference a day made," I whisper. It's the refrain of a jazz song that just came into my mind, and it seems so weirdly appropriate, I almost laugh.

Rick runs around to the driver's seat, starts the engine. He hands me a pile of napkins and tells me to hold them on the wound. I try, but I'm shaking so hard I can't keep my hand still.

"I'm really cold."

He turns the heater to max, adjusts all the vents so they're facing me. After a moment, he leans down and says he wants to examine it. Maybe he can tell how bad it is now that I've sopped up some of the blood.

"Don't let him handle me and drive me mad." It's that line from "Porgy," and when I hear myself mumbling this, I do laugh. Rick looks at me like I'm delirious. Maybe I am; maybe that's why I can't stop thinking in songs.

The napkins are so wet they're dripping on the seat, but he insists the wound isn't as bad as it looks. The bullet didn't exit, but judging from where it went in, it didn't hit anything but muscle and tissue. No major organs.

He's trying to sound confident, but his hands are trembling as he grabs the flannel cover off Willie's car seat, folds it into a square, and holds it against my side. It seems like only a minute before the cover is soaked through. I nod when he says, "We better get this looked at."

He already has the car in gear. Before we're halfway down the block, he's going fifty miles an hour.

I'm still hearing songs. They're flying through my mind as fast as the Nissan is flying down the street. Right now, it's the first verse of "My Funny Valentine." Jonathan and I have spent hours on this song. He plays it like it's a mischievous child, like you have to sneak up on the chords or they'll get away from you. I sing it like it's the oldest trick in the world I just can't help falling for.

"Hang on," Rick says.

The pain has started; it feels like a flame searing through me, jolting me every time I move. But it's not too bad until he takes a corner too sharply, and I lunge into the passenger door, let out an agonized shriek.

"Oh, Christ." His hand is tightened into a fist. He's punching the steering wheel. "I should have killed that asshole as soon as he started talking about you."

He waits a few minutes before he glances at my side again. I'm still holding the flannel cover, even though it isn't helping. I can feel blood oozing onto my fingers, dripping down my wrist.

The music is leaving me. I want it back, but all there is now is pain.

"I promise, I won't let anything happen to you," Rick is saying. "I can't let anything happen to you." His voice is breaking up, but he swallows. "Don't you remember? You're my real girl."

I'm concentrating hard, telling myself this won't get much worse. I have no idea what time it is. It seems like we've been in the car for hours, but I'm sure it's just the pain. We have to be almost at the hospital though. I know there's a hospital somewhere in North Kansas City.

I've been forcing myself not to look at the street—the buildings are going by so fast it makes me feel sick, and I can't risk throwing up—but when he stops a few minutes later, I glance out the windshield, expecting to see paramedics rushing out with tubes to make the pain go away. And a blanket, so I won't be so cold. A drink of water. I'm so thirsty; it feels like my veins are choked with sawdust.

But all I see are other cars. We're stuck in traffic. It takes me a minute to recognize where we are: the entrance to the highway. We're finally leaving town.

He doesn't deny it. He says he knows a good nurse; he's

going to call and have her meet us somewhere. "If we go to a hospital, they'll ask all kinds of questions. A gunshot wound has to be reported. They'll take me away from you, put me back in jail. I can't let that happen. Not now, when I just got you back."

His voice sounds thick and strangled as he says he doesn't see any choice. He rambles on and on about how I won't die, before he reminds me of our wedding vow. Death will never come between us. If one of us dies, the other will too. "I meant that. You don't have to be afraid. Whatever happens, I'll always be right there, taking care of you."

He's pulled my hand to his face; he's crying on my fingers. I'm not upset. I'm not even surprised. He will never let me go; this is the only end he can imagine. Rick and Patty Forever. Even my life doesn't matter compared to that promise.

We're on the highway now, going up a hill. The traffic is still bad. The eighteen-wheeler in front of us can't get enough momentum, and Rick is crawling close behind at only a few miles an hour. This could be my only chance. I know he won't pull over, and I don't think I'd survive jumping out of the car. But I can move my leg. If only I can do it quickly enough, before he knows what's going on.

I have to bite the inside of my cheek to keep from crying out, but it works. As I stomp on his gas-pedal foot, he yells, "Patty, what the he—" and then we both fly backwards, hear a thump and the sickening sound of metal against metal as the Nissan plows right into the back of the eighteen-wheeler.

He's not hurt; neither am I, although my side is on fire.

He's cursing and punching the dashboard, but he thinks I was just being stupid and scared, trying to force him to hurry.

The truck driver has turned off his engine, but Rick has no intention of getting out and swapping insurance cards. He slams the car into reverse and floors it, but the wheels just spin; the front bumper is trapped under the back of the truck.

It won't stay trapped for long. He's working the gas pedal; the car is starting to sway and rock when I fling the door open, pull myself out of the sticky seat, and onto the highway. The pain is terrible; I want to run as far as possible, but I can't even stand. I collapse to my knees, manage to crawl until I'm on the shoulder of the road. When I realize Rick has freed the Nissan, I howl with frustration, sure I've tortured myself for nothing. He's already yelling my name, telling me to get back into the car. In another minute, he'll be dragging me back to the two of us.

The pain is searing through my side; it drains me of any thought other than relief. I curl up in a ball, look up at the sky. There's a full moon; I hadn't noticed that before. It's so bright. I can't remember seeing one like this since that night so many years ago, when Rick and I went to the party and I climbed up on the bridge.

I know I need to do something, but I find myself just staring at the moon, trying to remember a line. There are so many jazz songs about the moon; Jonathan and I were just talking about that a few days ago. There's "Fly Me to the Moon" and "How High the Moon," of course, but also "Moon Rays," "Old Devil Moon," "No Moon At All," "Moon Love," and

"Carolina Moon." And those are just the ones with moon in the title. We agreed there had to be a hundred others with moon in a line.

Including the one I'm trying to think of now. Why can't I remember?

Rick is out of the Nissan. I hear him apologizing to the truck driver, offering to pay damages. His voice is so smooth as he explains that his wife fell with a knife in her hand and he's trying to get her to a hospital, but she's lost so much blood she's getting hysterical.

The truck driver says I need an ambulance, but Rick insists we can get there quicker in the car. He even talks the driver into helping him carry me back. They're both standing over me, when I finally hear it. "Got a moon above me, but no one to love me." That's the line. It's from "Lover Man," and it was part of my daydream earlier today, when Zeb was driving and Rick and I were in the backseat.

I remember Betty Carter's voice, so strong that every note seemed a proof of her desire, a display of her will. Betty Carter would never curl up and die on the side of the road. She's a power singer, and so am I.

Rick is bending down when I take a deep, painful breath and shout at the top of my lungs, "Help! He's trying to kill me!"

His voice only falters a little. "Patty, you know that's not true. Come on, now. You need to see a doctor."

But the truck driver takes a step back, says through clenched teeth, "Maybe we should wait for the authorities."

I shout again, just as loud, the same words. I don't know if it's me or the accident that's attracting the small crowd. I see emergency blinkers first, then feet, then faces. A man and a woman. An old guy who reminds me a little of Fred. Another guy, young, who's much bigger than Rick.

They're forming a cautious circle around me. My pants are hanging open and there's blood on my side, on the road, smeared all over my hands. But I tell myself it's like being on stage. I just have to keep them here, watching, until the police arrive.

Too bad for Rick that he emptied his gun in the warehouse. All he has is his voice now, and it's no match for mine. Every time he tries to speak, I shout him down. I tell these strangers that he's crazy. He doesn't love me and never has. He wants to let me die.

I can see the confusion in his slack, open lips, the pain and betrayal in his beautiful eyes. But it doesn't change a thing. It was just this morning when I told my little boy I would never leave him, and I'm not about to break that promise, even if I have to shout down the moon.

epilogue

Whenever I asked Irene if he'd been caught yet, she told me not to worry about anything but getting better. She kept all the newspapers out of my room, convinced the doctors to tell the police I wasn't up to being questioned. The police didn't really need me anyway. They'd already found Boyd's body. They knew about Zeb, but it was Boyd they cared about. He was a parole officer, one of their own. He was the reason they didn't hesitate to fire when Rick reached into his jacket for a gun he didn't have.

He died from a shot to the heart. Irene thought that would bother me most. Even Mama worried it might make my recovery take longer, though she was the one who finally told me. I told her I had a right to know, and she said I had a point. I think she also knew I'd hang up on her if she refused.

She's back at AA; she says she wants to make things right again. I don't know if it's possible, but she says she understands why I can't see her just yet, why Irene is taking care of Willie. She says we're lucky nothing any worse happened. We're lucky to be alive, both Willie and me.

The doctors say the same thing—I'm lucky. Zeb's bullet shattered my spleen and ripped through an artery. I could have bled to death before I got to the hospital.

I've been here over a week, but I hope to be out soon. I miss Willie so bad, sometimes I wake myself up at night, calling his name. He misses me too, but not too much. Irene says the guys are bending over backwards entertaining him. A few days ago, Dennis let him hold a drumstick and bang the cymbals while they were rehearsing. When Willie came to see me during visiting hours, he couldn't stop talking about how he got to be up on stage, playing with the big guys.

They've all been nice to me: calling to find out how I am, dropping by to see if I feel like talking. Carl even brought me flowers with a get well card. Underneath he'd written, "We need you back, Patty. It's too boring, having no one to make fun of." Then he drew a stick man smiling and signed it, "Your friend, Carl."

The only person I haven't heard from is Jonathan. Irene said he was camped out in the waiting room during my surgery and didn't leave the hospital for almost twenty-four hours, until I was out of intensive care. She also says he's hanging out a lot with Willie, that they're really tight after that day they spent together. She says sometimes when Willie's crying, Jonathan's the only person who can calm him down. "All he does is talk to him, but it works. Damn, I wish it was that easy for me."

Irene thinks he feels guilty because he couldn't keep me from getting hurt. I don't know if she's right, or if he's hiding from the pain of the hospital and everything that's happened to me. I certainly don't blame him; I'd hide too if I could. But I miss him, especially in the evenings, when visiting hours are over and I'm alone. I find myself thinking about him a lot, and hoping he misses me too.

Of course Fred has been by several times. He thinks the band might get some publicity out of all this. He's also excited that I've agreed to write the lyrics for the next piece. I told Irene it was just the painkillers talking, but the truth is, I want to do this. I don't know if it was Jonathan's idea or Fred's, but it's a good one. And the song I'm supposed to write for is perfect; I already have the tape. I've been listening to it constantly on my Walkman, hoping the first line will come to me.

Irene just called to say she and Willie will be over when they finish lunch. Right now, the orderly is taking me to the hospital roof to get some air. It's hospital policy that I have to stay in a wheelchair, and I don't protest, even though I'm dying to walk.

The roof is almost deserted. The sky is overcast, and an October wind is picking up. No wonder the scar on my knee is throbbing; it always does when it's about to rain.

He pushes me to a patio table. I brought a notepad and a pencil; I told him I'm just going to write a letter. It sounds like tempting fate to say I'm going to write lyrics.

A half hour later, I must have scratched out fifty tries. This is harder than I thought. I know I want the song to be about Willie. Being his mother is the most important thing I've ever done and the reason I could even think of writing lyrics. But it also has to be about Rick, I've realized, even if I don't want it to be.

Ever since Mama told me he was dead, I've been seeing him as he was at the schoolhouse, the first night we made love. I see him holding out his arms and smiling like we had the rest of our lives to feel just like this. I can't believe he's really gone. Of course I'll never forget the hell he put me through, but the loss of what he could have been stuns me like a blow.

By the time Irene and Willie show up, I've crumpled up a dozen sheets of paper. The first few raindrops are falling. Willie knows he can't jump on me, but he runs over and puts his arms around my legs.

"Mama, do you wike my hat?"

It says Fender, and it's Carl's cap, or at least it was. Willie says Carl gave it to him.

"I love your hat," I say, and then ask Irene to lift him to my lap. Willie sits very carefully, remembers not to lean against the bandage across my side.

His legs dangle like he's already grown an inch. And he's not wearing a diaper. Irene bought him Ninja Turtle training pants and he's determined to use the potty now. I wanted him to be trained, but already I miss the chubby bottom, the clean smell of baby wipes.

Irene is pushing me in, with Willie on my lap. The rain is coming down now. He's giggling because he loves the wheelchair. He's already asked if I get to take it home with me.

I kiss the back of his neck and wonder if I'll ever find words big enough for all the things I want my song to do. I love the idea that it would be there for Willie when he's older and needs to know what happened to his father. I want it to tell him the things I can't about what Rick was like, what we were.

I want my song to say everything perfectly, and so it says nothing at all. I tell Irene this lyric writing thing is a real pain. She laughs and says maybe if I just had more painkillers.

We've already rounded the corner on my floor when I see Harry and Carl at the other end of the hall, and standing next to them, shuffling his feet nervously, Jonathan. His hands are shoved in his pockets, and he looks for all the world like a man who'd rather be doing almost anything than standing in this hospital.

But here he is anyway. And when Willie scrambles off my lap to run to him, Jonathan leans down with his arms out, as if it's the most natural thing in the world now, him catching my son.

We're almost to the end of the hall when it hits me that maybe I've been going about this lyric business the wrong way. Maybe it's just like what Mr. Jubar said before I understood what jazz would come to mean to me: there is no perfect music. All you can do is keep trying, keep improvising. And playing your heart is what you're really after, not perfection.

Willie is waving down at me from his perch on Jonathan's shoulders. I wave back, thinking that the next time I see Charlie Jubar, I plan to tell him it's as true for motherhood as it is for music. Maybe it's true for all the things we love. Playing your heart is what you're after, when it seems easy and especially when it feels impossible. Playing your heart when it's breaking and soaring, and hardest of all, I know, when it's both at the same time.

acknowledgments

Simon & Schuster has been a dream publisher for me; I don't know how I got so lucky. I wish I could thank everybody who has helped me at S&S, but the list would fill many pages. First and foremost then, my heartfelt thanks to Amy Pierpont, adorable gal, brilliant editor, dear friend. To the entire amazing team in New York, especially Louise Burke, Liate Stehlik, Maggie Crawford, Seale Ballenger, Barry Porter, and Marisa Stella. To the fabulous Lisa Keim, for her good humor and insistence on sharing her umbrella and for bringing my books out into the world. To my wonderful publicist, Hillary Schupf, for her tireless efforts on my behalf. To the hardworking folks at Riverside for the beautiful lunch. To George

Keating, Terry Warnick, Desiree DeAscentis, Elizabeth Monaghan, Greg Anastas, Barb Roach, and David Eining, for treating a newbie so generously at the trade shows. To Tim Hepp, my hero, who drove me all over Pennsylvania to sell books and even wrote me my very own rap tune.

A thousand thanks to all the fabulous booksellers who hosted me on my tour. Hope to see you again this time. To the many readers who wrote me with their thoughts. To the lovely people at Goldberg McDuffie, especially Lynn Goldberg and my pal, Megan Underwood, for their wisdom, experience, and unfailing enthusiasm. To Kevin Howell, coolest guy and George Burns stand in, for giving me miracles and keeping me sane.

My biggest hug of gratitude and love to Marly Rusoff, agent and goddess, whose ceaseless championing of my work has quite literally changed my life. Mihai, Judy, Lisa, Marly— now it's my turn to buy the steak.

Finally, to the friends and family who have stood by me during the writing of this novel: Melisse Shapiro, Sara Gordon, Michaela Spampinato, Elly Williams, Pat Redmond, Gretchen Laskas, Alix Rabin, Howard Tucker, Melladi and Pat and all of the Tucker clan, Ann Cahall, Jim, Jeff and Jamie Crottinger, Emily and Laurie Ward, my best girls. To Minnie Tucker, in loving memory, for your faith in this project and me. And to Scott and Miles, my true family, my real home.

A CONVERSATION WITH THE AUTHOR

OF *SHOUT DOWN THE MOON*

YOU'VE TRAVELED WITH A BAND YOURSELF. IS THE NOVEL AUTOBIOGRAPHICAL?

I did travel with my husband's band when we were first together. We went across the Midwest and the South, playing little clubs and hotels, and even staying in trailers. Once we had to sneak out in the middle of the night because the club owner refused to pay our hotel bill. Not fun. I incorporated some of these experiences in the novel, but the story itself is fiction. I have a son but he was born later, after we had settled down. The road is such a hard life; I don't know if I could have done it with a child, the way Patty does.

PATTY IS AN INCREDIBLY BRAVE CHARACTER. DID YOU KNOW ALL THE DIFFICULTIES SHE WOULD FACE WHEN YOU STARTED THE BOOK?

No, and actually, I'm very resistant to making any of my characters suffer. Sometimes I find myself unable to write for days when I realize something bad is about to happen to one of the people in my books. Of course you have to let these things happen or you don't have a story. You have to let the plot go in whatever direction it wants to go, even if that means your characters will go through tragedy. In Patty's case, I was fairly confident that she would figure her way out of the mess she was presented with. I knew her love for Willie was a powerful force she could draw upon to free herself from all the darkness in her life.

SPEAKING OF WILLIE, HE'S ONLY TWO YEARS OLD, YET HE'S A FULL-FLEDGED CHARACTER IN HIS OWN RIGHT. WAS IT DIFFICULT TO WRITE A CHILD?

Oh, I enjoyed every minute with Willie. He's one of my favorite characters, and the scene with him in the park was my favorite scene to write. I wanted to make him a strong presence in the novel because he's such a presence in Patty's mind—and the story is told entirely from her point of view. Patty is always aware of where Willie is, what he needs, what he feels, and this awareness is what keeps her connected to the present, even when her past most threatens to overwhelm her.

SHOUT DOWN THE MOON IS LITERARY FICTION, BUT UNDENIABLY SUSPENSEFUL. DID YOU SET OUT TO WRITE A SUSPENSE NOVEL?

No, but I'm always pleased when people tell me they couldn't stop turning the pages. I remember something I heard about Thomas Hardy, that he supposedly asked only one question of his readers: "Did it hold your interest?" I love this because it expresses so well what I think the first job of the novelist is—to keep the reader in the story.

My books always seem to start at the same place: with a character in trouble. In Patty's case, a big part of the trouble was Rick, and Rick involved her in a very dark world. But what's unusual, I think, is that here the criminal's girlfriend is telling her own story. Patty is making us know her as more than her involvement with Rick: as a mother and a singer and a woman finding her voice.

YOUR FIRST NOVEL, THE SONG READER, IS ALSO ABOUT MUSIC AND MOTHERHOOD. WHY DID YOU RETURN TO THESE THEMES?

I think of *The Song Reader* as about what music mean to listeners, and *Shout Down the Moon* as about what it means to performers. A subtle difference, especially as Patty was a listener before she was a singer, and even at the end of the novel, it's when she hears songs playing in her mind that she is reminded she can escape from Rick, and live a better life. In both books, a child is the motivation for a woman to find a place for herself in the world. Music is my passion, and being a mother is the most important thing I've ever done.

ANOTHER COMMON THEME IN THESE NOVELS IS THE DESIRE FOR STABILITY AND HOME. BOTH LEEANN [THE NARRATOR OF *THE SONG READER*] AND PATTY TALK IN POIGNANT TERMS ABOUT THE "NORMAL" LIFE THAT THEY FEEL IS ALWAYS JUST BEYOND THEIR GRASP.

There are so many novels about a character who rebels against his family and leaves home to find himself. It's a great story, but what if you don't have a family that's stable enough to rebel against? How can you run away from a home that you don't have? Both Leeann and Patty are people on the margins of society, and their dream of stability is very understandable, though I think they also find that their experiences help redefine what normal means. They do achieve an oddly stable "family," even if it isn't the traditional kind.

WHO DO YOU SEE AS YOUR AUDIENCE? DO YOU IMAGINE A READER AS YOU'RE WRITING? DO YOU SHOW ANYONE YOUR EARLY DRAFTS?

This may sound odd, but the only people I consider while I'm writing are the characters. I almost feel as if they are reading over my shoulder, making sure I tell their story honestly, keeping me from any tricks or gimmicks or "writerly" moments that would be about me and not them. When I begin the editing process, I do think about the audience—not a particular audience, because I hope my books can be read by women and men, teens and older people, anybody and everybody—but the general notion of someone outside of the story who has to be brought in and convinced to stay in this world until the last sentence.

CAN YOU TELL US WHAT YOU'RE WORKING ON NOW?

I've just finished a short story for an anthology of original stories inspired by songs called *Lit Riffs*. Each writer had to pick a song; I picked a piece from Pearl Jam's first album, "Why Go." I love jazz, but I also like rock and classical and even a lot of pop music. (Unlike Jonathan, I believe something can be popular and still be good.) I'm also writing another novel that will be published by Pocket Books, probably in 2005. The working title is *What a Difference a Day Made*. It's about the way a heart can be broken by the tragic events of a single day, yet a single day can also bring a new chance at love and the possibility of redemption. It's been very interesting to write because it has a larger cast of characters, three locations (New Mexico, California, and Missouri), and two distinct time periods: the late seventies and the present. There is a subplot about what music means to one of the characters. I can't imagine writing a book without *something* about music.

Don't miss Lisa Tucker's critically acclaimed debut novel, *The Song Reader.*

My sister Mary Beth was a song reader. Song reading was her term for it and she invented the art as far as I know. It was kind of like palm reading, she said, but instead of using hands, she used music to read people's lives. . . .

Her customers adored her. They took her advice—to marry, to break it off with the low-life jerk, to take the new job, to confront their supervisor with how unfair he was—and raved about how much better off they were. They said she was gifted. They swore she could see right into their hearts.

Sometimes I thought Mary Beth's gift would bring us everything.

Available from Downtown Press

do**W**n t**O**wn press

0-7434-6445-1
$12.00 U.S. • $19.00 Canada